Byron was interested in what she was saying. But her lips—plump, slightly parted, and bearing t⬚⬚⬚⬚⬚⬚⬚⬚⬚⬚⬚⬚⬚⬚⬚⬚⬚—were ma⬚⬚⬚⬚⬚⬚⬚⬚⬚⬚⬚⬚⬚⬚ concer⬚⬚⬚

"I enjoy you," ⬚⬚⬚⬚⬚⬚⬚⬚⬚⬚⬚⬚⬚⬚⬚⬚⬚red to align with hers. "Thanks for your company."

Their lips met, and it felt like clouds bumping into each other in a rainbow sky. His tongue slipped into her parted lips, even as he took a step closer, pinning her between his body and the side of the car. Somewhere in Cynthia's mind there was a caution sign blinking. But she couldn't slow down. His touch was more like a promise, an introduction, an invitation of what might be in store.

Everything about her turned him on: soft hair, fragrant skin, the way she fit him perfectly. If they got together, the lovemaking would have to go nonstop, for at least a week, before he'd have enough. His desire for her was so strong it was scary.

Also by Zuri Day

Lies Lovers Tell

Body by Night

Lessons from a Younger Lover

What Love Tastes Like

Lovin' Blue

Love in Play

Heat Wave (with Donna Hill and Niobia Bryant)

The One That I Want (with Donna Hill and
Cheris Hodges)

The Morgan Men Series

Love on the Run

A Good Dose of Pleasure

Bad Boy Seduction

The Blue-Collar Lover Series

Driving Heat

Published by Kensington Publishing Corp.

Driving
HEAT

A Blue-Collar Lover Novel

ZURI DAY

Dafina
BOOKS

Kensington Publishing Corp.

http://www.kensingtonbooks.com

DAFINA BOOKS are published by

Kensington Publishing Corp.
119 West 40th Street
New York, NY 10018

All Kensington titles, imprints, and distributed lines are available at special quantity discounts for bulk purchases for sales promotions, premiums, fund-raising, and educational or institutional use. Special book excerpts or customized printings can also be created to fit specific needs. For details, write or phone the office of the Kensington Special Sales Manager: Kensington Publishing Corp., 119 West 40th Street, New York, NY 10018, Attn: Special Sales Department, Phone: 1-800-221-2647.

Dafina and the Dafina logo Reg. U.S. Pat. & TM Off.

ISBN-13: 978-1-61773-425-0
ISBN-10: 1-61773-425-X
First Kensington Mass Market Edition: April 2015

eISBN-13: 978-1-61773-426-7
eISBN-10: 1-61773-426-8
First Kensington Electronic Edition: April 2015

10 9 8 7 6 5 4 3 2 1

Printed in the United States of America

For you, Freddie "Lightfoot" Woodley . . . enjoy the read!

Acknowledgments

I am so excited about this series, inspired by an online book club chat in which the readers were asked what they wanted in romance novels that they didn't currently see. A few members said, "Regular guys." Instantly, my mind went to the wonderful men I know who may live ordinary (whatever that is) lives, but who have extraordinary character, faith, integrity, skill, and personalities. From Papa Nash, the farmer, who as a childless single man in his forties married my grandmother, who came with five grown kids, and who was kind and funny and hardworking, and the best grandfather ever! To my dad, Rev. Willie Hinton, Jr., who when not in the pulpit worked construction before starting his own lawn business; my brother, Johnny, and the many men all over this country who've provided such great examples to pull from in writing this series.

When thinking about occupations for the five Carter brothers, bus driver was the first one that came to mind. For no special reason, I thought, except that it sounded blue collar. Then a couple months into the writing I got the news that a twenty-five-year-long friend, who was more like a brother to me, had earned his angel wings. "Foot," to whom this book is dedicated, was a father, son, brother, uncle, musician, singer, song-writer, radio announcer, and life of the party wherever he was. It was another month or so before it hit me. His first job? The one he had when I met him? Bus driver for the Kansas City metro. Felt rather like a full-circle moment that made me smile. Interesting how life works out.

A huge thank you to my sister, Dee, the certi-fied peer specialist whose information and in-sight helped Cynthia's character come alive, and also prevented her from breaking American Counseling Association rules. ☺ Love you, sis! As always, to Team Zuri including Selena, Natasha, and Janice for the spot-on cover, smooches. To the Lovely Day VIPs, members of A Lovely Day Experience, supporters, and friends who sent love, light, and prayers to assist this book's com-pletion, amen! To all ordinary brothers who are extraordinary men . . . thank you.

Prologue

"Byron . . . this feels so good."

A cocksure smile appeared on his face as Byron Carter enjoyed one of his favorite pastimes, pleasing his woman. He led this timeless dance of love with precision, establishing a rhythmic beat with his hips, and melody with his lips. Without warning, he stopped. She opened her eyes to find him staring at her.

"You're beautiful." Raining kisses on her face— eyes, nose, cheeks—he began to grind again. Slowly. Reverently. As if she were priceless china, or handblown glass.

"I love you." He kissed her then, so tenderly and lovingly that the act almost brought tears to her eyes.

This is what my BFFs don't understand about why I'm with you. This is the feeling of being loved that Dynah and Gayle can't grasp because, sadly, it's a depth I'm sure they've never experienced. If they had, they'd accept you without question, and be happy for me.

"Is this enough for you, huh?" No answer, just

eyes back, mouth slack. His hips stopped mid-motion. "I didn't hear you."

"Yes," she eked out between pants. She moved her hips feverishly, the spot he'd branded missing its iron. "Please . . ."

He chuckled, happy to be in bed with this woman, the love of his life.

For long minutes this continued, until her panting became more labored. Though not a singer, as this first orgasm began in her core and spiraled to her cranial, her voice went from a guttural low tenor moan to a respectable High C squeak. Some men would consider themselves finished after such a performance. But for Byron Carter, if there weren't multiple moments of ecstasy for his woman, then he felt he wasn't doing his job.

Listening to her breathy mewling as her body twitched and muscles gripped his still-hard rod, he felt his own imminent climax begin to build. Using discipline honed in the sixteen years he'd been sexually active, he stopped, held himself against her as she relaxed beneath him. They'd just begun. On such a special morning, it wouldn't do for him to come too soon.

When he felt her lips touch his neck in the lightest of kisses, he began to stir again. This woman was everything, and not just because of the body beneath him that so turned him on. Cynthia, the one some had thought was above his pay grade, and others believed he could never have. Whether it could happen or not had never been a question in his mind. He was a

Carter, and can't wasn't in his family's vocabulary. Now whether or not it *would* happen had been a point up for grabs.

Not anymore.

Suddenly and without warning, before she could catch her breath, Byron adjusted his body so he could say good morning to the berry-colored nipple now aligned with his lips. He flicked his tongue. Goose bumps appeared, a seeming contradiction to the hot breath coming from his mouth, or the way Cynthia's body arched when he laved his tongue across the now-pebbled protrusion before gently sucking it into his oral entrance. Her body was his breakfast and he ate his fill, turned her over, and filled her up. Moans, grunts, and heavy breaths replaced the bird's good morning. Sweet release was the dew that moistened their skin. Again she began to tremble, her voice repeating its earlier song, eyes shut, toes curled. This time Byron joined her, ground himself into her velvety softness as liquid love flowed from his soul to hers. But instead of allowing the moment to slowly subside into a cozy cuddle, he encouraged her to lie on her back, pressed his lips against hers, and rolled out of bed.

"Hey, where are you going?"

"To take a shower."

"What if I'm not ready for it to be over?"

Byron stopped, turned around. "That's how I always want to leave you, baby . . . wanting more."

She huffed with annoyance but joined him in the shower. He understood her hunger. For these single parents these were treasured moments alone, when his daughter spent the weekend with her mother and her son enjoyed a play date with friends. Still, after refusing to give in to her greedy demands for yet another round with his six-inch supersexer—his word—Byron slipped on a pair of boxers and headed for the bright and airy kitchen of Cynthia's bi-level condo.

"Are you fixing breakfast?"

Byron laughed. "It's either that or starve, since you're not cooking."

He walked to the refrigerator, opened the door, and felt a sting as Cynthia popped his butt with a dish towel. Slowly turning around, his eyes narrowed. Cynthia's grew large. "You shouldn't have done that, girl." His look was purposely predatory as he took a step toward her.

"I'm sorry!" Spoken through laughter, the apology hardly sounded sincere. She took two steps back. After a couple more steps he made a quick move around the island and reached out to grab her.

Cynthia yelped, ran into the living room, and quickly put the couch between them. "Really, Byron, cut it out. Let's make breakfast together. I'm hungry."

"No, girl. You started something. I'm going to finish it."

He captured her and soon they were tousling on the couch. Cynthia hated to be tickled, so, of course, that's what he did. Wearing just a spaghetti top and panties, her entire body was fair game.

"Stop! Byron! Stop it!"

She begged. He laughed. The teasing turned into a tantalizing kiss. His tongue began a journey from her stomach to her freshly showered treasure. Cynthia shifted to give access. Both froze when the doorbell rang.

Byron spoke first. "Who's that?"

"I don't know!" was Cynthia's panicked whisper. "Jayden isn't due back until tomorrow!" They both looked toward the door for answers. "Let's just stay quiet so whoever it is will go away."

The doorbell rang twice more before an incessant knocking started. "Cynthia, we know you're in there. Open the door!"

Byron arched a brow. "Whoever that is sounds determined to see you."

"Shit!" She pushed Byron off of her and scurried off the couch. "It's Gayle, a friend from Chicago." The whisper had lessened to near pantomime. "What's she doing here?"

Byron thought of their situation, the big secret, and shrugged. *This is going to be good.*

"Um, just a minute."

She ushered him up the stairs and was right on his heels. After grabbing and throwing on a robe, she scurried back downstairs. She hoped her look wasn't one of just-been-screwed and WTH, but felt that chance was most unlikely.

She opened the door. "Gayle!" Seeing another woman, she added, "And you, too?"

"What took you so long to answer?" This from Dynah, another BFF, who was straining her neck to see what lie behind the door numbered 215.

"I'm the one who should be asking the questions." Cynthia crossed her arms, still blocking their entry. "What on earth are you two doing here?"

"Being your best friends," Gayle replied, pushing her way into Cynthia's home without being invited. "We're here to talk some sense into you."

"Before you make the biggest mistake of your life!" Dynah's eyes never stopped moving, visually inspecting the room like she was CSI.

Thank God he's in the bedroom. Cynthia hoped Ms. Snoop couldn't smell sex in the air. *Jesus be an air freshener!* Inside she was cringing, but relaxed her stance. "And what mistake would that be?"

"Probably me." Three pairs of eyes watched a jeans and tee-clad Byron walk calmly down the stairs. He came up next to Cynthia, put a casual arm around her waist, and split a challenging yet slightly amused look between her two unexpected guests. "Ladies . . . am I right?"

1

A few months earlier

"Good morning!"

"Is it?" Cynthia side-eyed Ivy, her eternally effer-vescent assistant.

"Absolutely! I'm reading a self-help book that says what you think about you bring about. So I'm thinking that this is going to be an excellent day!"

"We'll see." *That girl is entirely too cheery for a Monday morning.* Cynthia decided to wait until after downing her supersized mocha latte to form an opinion.

She unlocked the door and walked into her office, determined to change her dark, Monday morning mood. Any number of reasons could be blamed for it: LA traffic, the oncoming monthly, a feud with her mother, a love life so bleak that her coochie had cobwebs. But all of those took a back seat to today's mandatory meeting. The

H.E.L.P. Agency, a social service organization funded through grants and private donation, was reorganizing. The director of the agency was taking an unexpected early retirement. The position she'd set her sights on two years ago was suddenly coming available and at least one other applicant wanted it as much as she did. Considering her background, that of a privileged, upper-middle-class debutante who didn't have to work, one might wonder why her career meant so much. But those who knew her understood her passion to help young people, particularly young girls. This news, delivered on the previous Friday, could have been assuaged with a bottle of wine and a clearing of cobwebs. Instead, she'd gone home to an eight-year-old, his good friend Bobby, and video game mayhem. Not a good formula for a great weekend. It had gone downhill from there.

What you think about you bring about!

With hopes that some of Ivy's positive energy would waft into her office, Cynthia fired up her laptop and waded into the day's agenda. An hour later, she pushed the intercom button. "Ivy, has my nine o'clock appointment called?"

"Not since I arrived at eight-fifteen. There were no messages either."

"Okay. Give her a call and make sure she's on her way."

"Will do."

A few seconds later, Ivy walked into Cynthia's office. "The call went to voice mail. I left a message for her to call you ASAP."

Cynthia's brow creased. "This client is truly

irritating. She's two seconds away from a jail sentence and is still acting irresponsibly. We'll give her another thirty minutes and if she's not here by then, I'll need you to go over and deliver the warning letter."

"My daughter has a doctor's appointment. I'd planned to leave for that in thirty minutes."

"Right, I saw that on the schedule and forgot that quickly." Cynthia drummed her fingers against the desk, searching for a solution and finding none.

"Too bad we can no longer use messenger services."

"The agency dodged a bullet with that Anderson case. I doubt anyone other than staff will be able to handle these formal notice deliveries for the next ninety days. There's no way I can miss today's meeting."

Ivy stole a quick glance behind her and lowered her voice. "Speaking of, she came by this morning?"

So much for Ivy and positive energy in the room. "Margo?" Ivy nodded. "What did she want?"

"Snooping, I'm sure. Asked if you were here, looked at her watch when I said you weren't."

"I so don't have time for her right now, or to wait for Ms. Thompson. The last thing I need this week is a client getting probation revoked on a technicality. Print out a final notice form. Get it notarized. I'll take it over. If I leave right now, I'll be fine."

Fifteen minutes later, Cynthia left downtown Los Angeles and headed for Compton Boulevard on the city's south side. Even with a stack of cases needing attention and traffic still fairly heavy, she welcomed getting away from the office. The mere thought of Margo and her underhanded tactics could make her blood boil. For today's meeting, she needed a cool, clear head.

Cynthia's thoughts were interrupted when an eighteen-wheeler drifted into her lane, almost sideswiping her car.

An expletive accompanied the blast from her horn. She quickly switched lanes and accelerated. As it lurched forward, her car made a loud, knocking noise.

"Oh!" *What the heck is that?* She checked the instruments on the dashboard. They all looked fine to her, which, given that she barely knew the brake from the gas pedal, didn't mean much. A few miles down the highway and she heard the sound again. Just as she began to worry that something serious might be wrong, the noise stopped and the car settled back into its normal smooth ride. The scare was quickly forgotten. She exited the freeway with the missing client on her mind.

Though it was her first time in this area, GPS made finding the address easy. Cynthia pulled to the curb of a small, yet well-kept home on what appeared to be a quiet, established block of similarly designed residences. She was embarrassed at her surprise. All she'd heard of Compton was what had been made popular by rap artists and news reports. She'd half expected to find gang members walking down the street smoking blunts and blaring rap music. After a quick look around (after all, they could be hiding), she exited the car and walked to the door.

She wasn't sure the doorbell worked. So after pushing the button several times, she knocked and then pounded on the front door, with no response. Cynthia pulled out her cell phone.

After reaching the mother and learning that she had no clue as to her daughter's whereabouts, Cynthia continued. "Ava, for legal reasons I am required to tape this portion of our conversation. Do I have your permission? Okay, thank you." She tapped the Record icon. "Ms. Thompson, I, Cynthia Hall, am attaching the final warning notice for your daughter to appear in our offices near the bottom of your inside door, the part hidden by solid metal. Is that okay? Good. I will also send a copy to the e-mail address listed in our files." She confirmed the e-mail address. "She needs to contact our office ASAP and get this meeting rescheduled. It has to happen this week, per the conditions of her probation. If she does not comply, a warrant will be issued for her arrest. Do you understand?"

Mission accomplished, Cynthia headed back to her car. "I understand, Ava. This isn't something I want to do, but unfortunately it isn't up to just me. These actions have been mandated by the court. If she makes it to my office, I'll do whatever I can to keep her out of jail." She opened her car door and stepped inside. "You're welcome. Have a good day."

Cynthia placed her key into the ignition and turned. A whining, grinding noise accompanied the car's attempt to start. *This is different.*

Undaunted, she tried again. This had been a pre-owned purchase, but this regularly washed, regularly serviced vehicle had not given her an ounce of trouble since its purchase two years ago.

Whine. Grind. No start-up.

"Really? When the meeting starts at one? Come on. Please start."

Following Ivy's suggestion and as best she could, Cynthia thought about turning the key and hearing the car engine rev, imagined pulling away from the curb and heading downtown. But after a third attempt with continued silence, she admitted the obvious—the car wasn't going to start.

Stay calm, Cynthia. Just call Triple A. She pulled out her phone, dialed the 800 number, and received the disheartening news that because of an unusually high number of calls and where she was located, her wait time would be anywhere from ninety minutes to two hours.

She called a taxi company and scheduled a pickup. The operator said it would be fifteen minutes. Thirty minutes later, she called another company. They said she'd be picked up in ten. Ten minutes after this lie had been told, Cynthia's calm threatened to join positive attitude, which had already disappeared. It was almost noon. Time was running out!

She banged the steering wheel. "Dammit!" *This cannot be happening right now!*

A slight tap on her window almost caused a heart attack. She turned to see a kindly older man with a pleasant smile.

She eased down her window. "Yes?"

"Good morning, miss. Having car trouble?"

She nodded. "Cab trouble, too."

The older man scratched his scruffy black and gray beard, smiling to show even, white teeth. "Hard to get a cab on this block."

"Why? This seems to be a nice, quiet neighborhood."

"Looks can be deceiving," the old man responded. "A driver who was resisting a robbery got killed a month or so ago. Haven't seen one on this block ever since. One young fool makes it hard for everybody."

With head in hand, she muttered, "How am I going to get back to work?"

"Where do you work?"

"Downtown."

"That shouldn't be too hard. The number 53 runs about every thirty minutes and will take you straight there."

Cynthia looked at herself in the rearview mirror. *Did he just suggest that I walk down a street where a man got killed . . . and then catch a bus?*

2

"Did you say take a bus?"

"Yes, ma'am."

"Like . . . a city bus?" Even though she'd never ridden one, Cynthia hadn't meant for the question to sound snobbish. This unexpected delay on a most important day had thrown her for a loop.

"You could catch the blue line, the train, but you'd have to walk farther."

What he'd said about robbers and murderers made a long walk in these parts about as attractive as getting a root canal without Novocain. "Where do I catch the bus?"

"Right on the corner there, just two short blocks up. There's a bench and a sign on the light post. You can't miss it."

The old man found humor in Cynthia's horrified expression. "It's clear you're not the type to take one much, having this fine car and all. But short of walking, that's the best option."

With every other option exhausted, Cynthia

reached for her purse. She exited the car and locked it. "You say the stop is at the corner?"

The friendly neighbor nodded as he pointed. "Not this corner, the next one. That main intersection where you see the traffic lights."

"Thank you so much."

"You're very much welcome, pretty lady." He winked. "What about your car?"

"I'll have it picked up later."

"Don't worry, it'll be fine until somebody comes and gets it. I'll make sure of that."

Cynthia headed for the bus stop. Her four-inch heels quickly helped her forget that Grandpa had tried to flirt. Had she been planning a stroll today, she would have worn sensible shoes.

Just before chucking all decorum and walking a public street in bare feet, she reached the corner and an empty bench beneath the bus stop sign. Here the area's blight was more noticeable: empty fast-food bags, broken bottles, smashed cans, and cigarette butts littered the street. Pulling her purse closer, she prayed for the bus, a bit embarrassed at the fearfulness among her own. A homeless man pushed his worldly possessions in a red cart bearing a Target logo. She gave him a dollar when he passed. She continued to watch this area's meager every day unfold amid liquor stores, pawn shops, nail salons, and check-cashing establishments, and realized she often took her comfortable salary, spacious Culver City condo, and pristine neighborhood for granted.

The relief she felt as the express bus pulled up was palpable.

"Are you headed downtown?"

The bus driver gave her the once-over. "Even if I wasn't, I'd give you a ride."

Resisting the urge to roll her eyes, she got on, almost falling when the bus pulled away from the curb. The quick reflexes of the bus driver kept her upright. "Careful now."

She leaned against the meter to steady herself and pulled out her wallet. "How much does this cost?"

The driver glanced her way again. "Metro card only. No cash."

"Will a debit card work?"

"I said *Metro* card, not debit card."

At the end of her patience, Cynthia snapped. "I don't have a Metro card!"

He reached the end of the next block where more passengers waited, and pulled to the curb. "Guess you'll have to get out here, then."

"You can't be serious. What business doesn't take a debit card these days?"

Cynthia stepped aside so that Metro card–carrying passengers could place what she didn't possess into the metal machine. Once they'd all entered, the driver looked at her.

"I have got to get downtown," she said softly. "It's important, for work."

"You'd better be glad you're fine and I'm in a good mood," he said, looking into his rearview mirror and pulling away from the curb. "Sit down, gorgeous. You're a pleasant distraction that could become a liability if you trip and fall in those nice-looking pumps."

First gramps and now the bus driver. She ignored the comment, but was totally aware of how his sexy eyes framed by curly lashes had caused her core to clench. And how the scent of whatever cologne he wore teased her nose. *A shame,* she admitted, as she slyly eyed the short, thick fingers that had gripped her arm so tightly. *That's the first time I've been manhandled in about nine months.* She was tempted to fake a fall again, just so he could catch her.

"Why are you still standing here? It's not safe."

"Oh, um, I need to be sure I'm on the correct bus. Do you go to Seventh and Wilshire downtown?"

The bus driver slid his eyes down her body once more, with a crooked, confident smile. "You're on the right bus."

Cynthia looked to her right and took the first available seat. She covertly eyed the cocky driver, wondering why he was smiling and even more why did she care? She knew guys who were way better looking, passed them in her office building every day, and her body didn't react this way. He couldn't be a DHOP—degreed, home-owning professional—and after where breaking the rules and "dating down" had gotten her the last time, she had no desire to go there again.

So opening an app where notes were stored, she tried to focus on the talking points for her department that she planned to present at the meeting. But unless they included big brown eyes, juicy lips, thick fingers, and a smile, her attempt was not at all successful. Something this important coming up and yet her attention was on a man she wouldn't see again? The dictation drought was worse than she'd realized. Dictation, the code word her friends used for sex, which combined a word describing what she craved with the word situation, had never consumed her. But getting moist at the touch of a stranger was proof that something must be done. Her friend Lisa was a regular Adam & Eve patron. Cynthia felt it was about time for her to visit the garden. Especially when her thoughts kept returning to him. Sexy eyes. Musky scent. Juicy lips. Thick fingers. She looked. He winked. Her body had the nerve to react with pitter-patter heartbeats and squiggles down south. *Traitorous flesh!*

Cynthia turned her body away from the driver, determined to occupy her mind with something important, something that mattered. Something like making sure that a certain Margo-come-lately didn't undermine two years of hard work and get the job that Cynthia felt *she* deserved.

3

"What's your name?"

Cynthia heard him. Felt his gaze. But she'd been riding in the bus for ten minutes and had regained hormonal control. *He could be talking to someone else.* He wasn't. She knew this, but played it off anyway. Working to look preoccupied, she found a name and began tapping the keyboard.

You won't believe where I'm at and what I'm doing! I'm—

"Okay, you're a newbie, so I'll give you a pass and explain how this particular Metro operates. This is Byron Carter's bus, and there are rules. Number one: Never ignore the person who is responsible for your safety, has travel information you just might need, and because of the unfortunate events of 9/11, can put you out at any stop no questions asked and police for backup."

The chance that she might miss the meeting immediately improved her hearing. She raised her head, glanced around, and then looked at him. "Oh, are you talking to me?"

"He sure isn't talking to me!" The gray-haired, pleasant-faced lady sitting next to the door, an obvious regular, had been chatting nonstop since Cynthia boarded. "I've been riding this route for going on fifteen years. Remember this boy from when he first got the job, but he was over on Slauson then." She leaned over and whispered, so loudly that she needn't have bothered. "Got so close to cars you couldn't push a toothpick between them. I never prayed so much in my life."

Byron laughed. "That wasn't a mistake. That was skills, Ms. Davis. Have I ever hit anything?"

"Other than football players or your girlfriend? I don't think so."

The other regulars joined Ms. Davis in laughter. Byron side-eyed her. "You know you're wrong for that." He shook his head, chuckled low and deep.

The sound—smoky, beguiling—stirred something in Cynthia's heat as the thought of that voice whispering commands in the dark popped up unbidden. A subtle headshake dispelled the thought. *The garden. This weekend. Definitely.*

"I'm just kidding, baby. That's a good man."

"Thank you, Ms. Davis." At the next stop light, he again looked over at the side seats. "What is it?"

"Cynthia."

"So you did hear me."

"I heard the question. I didn't know it was aimed at me."

"Only because I can't prove otherwise, you can

stay on for a few more stops. But"—he paused to focus while he navigated a turn—"you've got to comply with rule number two."

"Which is?"

"Smile. Can't have anyone too serious riding my bus."

Curt smile and then Cynthia returned her eyes to the cell phone screen.

"What brought you over to the south side?"

A soft sigh helped quell her premenstrual/car broke down/important meeting irritation. A good thing, because "shut the eff up" might get her literally kicked to the curb. "Why do you assume I don't live there?"

That chuckle, more of a snicker this time, trickled from his mouth and tickled Cynthia's earlobe. And why'd he have to offer just a glimpse of his tongue as his teeth briefly pulled on his lower lip, right side, in that sexy way only certain brothers could do.

After what seemed like an eternity—during which time she could have finished her text but was distracted by thoughts of tongues down low and sexy done right—he answered her question. "You don't live there."

"You're right." Delivered in a clipped, professional voice that meant "please leave me alone I don't want to be bothered."

"So why were you there, if you don't mind my asking? And how did you end up on my bus."

A great bus driver, maybe, but his translation skills needed work.

"I was visiting a client. My car broke down. I

have an appointment for which I'm preparing, so while I don't want to be rude—"

"You want me to shut the hell up." A few riders who'd been watching the exchange reacted: laughter, head shakes, and a he-told-you-snort from the woman in the first forward seat, the one who'd eyed her coldly since she'd boarded the bus.

"I wouldn't have worded it that way, but basically, yes."

Byron laughed, gave her a wink in his rearview mirror.

Cynthia didn't catch it, but first forward did. "Why didn't you say so instead of acting ignorant? For people to know what you want, you have to speak your mind."

"Tanya, stop harassing my riders."

"Okay, baby."

The answer to a question I hadn't even considered. And how cute, the girlfriend keeps him company while he works. Cynthia's e-mail indicator pinged. It was Ivy with perfect timing. The answers to the assistant's questions thankfully kept Cynthia occupied until they reached downtown and she got off the bus.

Byron lay stretched out on the couch. It had been a long day, yet he couldn't relax. The ex-high school and college football standout before a knee injury ended his promising career had his eyes on the TV screen, but his mind was on the sexy woman who'd brightened his bus. He liked them chocolate, but something about all that butterscotch beauty had him ready to change flavors.

His cell phone screen flashed in the darkness. He picked it up and checked the ID. "Hey, sis."

"Hey."

"You don't sound good. What happened?"

"It's your niece, again."

Byron sighed as he returned his head to the comfy couch pillow. Unlike the ex who tried to beg, borrow, and steal her way through life, his sister, Ava, was an excellent mother: hardworking and involved. After her marriage ended, she'd sacrificed her own dreams and desires to give her two children everything they'd need for a successful future. The bullet that reached her twenty-year-old son didn't know this, took the life of a promising college freshman during a fun-loving weekend out with friends. Ava had been devastated, but the real emotional carnage was endured by Leah, the younger sister by four years, who'd not been the same since his death.

"What'd she do this time?"

"Disappeared again; hasn't called since Friday. She missed a court-appointed meeting with the counselor today."

"Aw, man, Ava. She knows better. That girl acts like she wants to go to jail."

"All she wants is to run behind Redman."

Byron sat up. "Redman? Are you serious?"

"Yes, that's who she was seen with yesterday.

She swears nothing has happened between them, but forgets that I was once seventeen."

"He was what, two or three years older than Lance? And messing with a minor? I'm getting ready to go have a talk with him."

"Don't, Byron. That'll just make it worse. He's filling the void left by Lance's death."

"You know Redman's a dog, Ava. His brother taught him everything he knows, and you know Gavin is rotten to the core."

"I tried to tell her. But he's not my biggest worry right now. Leah's appointment has been rescheduled for tomorrow. She can't miss it. If she does, they might revoke her parole. She could be placed in juvenile detention or, since she's seventeen, county jail. I'm trying to keep my baby out of the system."

"Isn't she already in there?"

"Technically, yes, but her counselor says if she completes these sessions, gets on the right track, and doesn't have any more legal problems, her juvenile record can be expunged so she can still be eligible for scholarships to get into college, and not have that on her record when she looks for a job."

"So do you need me to go look for her?"

"I hope it doesn't come to that. Maybe, for now, a call will do. She looks up to you. When seeing your number, she might answer her phone. Maybe you can talk sense into her, get her to understand that she can't miss this appointment. She doesn't listen to me anymore, but you know she loves her Uncle Byron."

"Hold on. I'll do it right now."

He placed Ava on hold and tapped Leah's name. The call immediately went to voice mail. "Leah, this is Uncle Byron. Unless you want the brothers out looking for you, and you know how we do, you need to call me as soon as you get this. And then you need to call Ava. I know why you're acting out. We're all still hurting. But worrying your mother isn't cool. So call me. No matter the time. You've got an appointment that I'm going to make sure you don't miss, even if I have to find you and take you myself."

4

Cynthia sat in her office with the door closed, venting to the friend she couldn't reach last night.

"You should have seen her at the meeting yesterday, Dynah, giving me a fake smile while listing all the reasons she'd make the perfect director. Well, back in Boston," Cynthia mimicked, nailing her accent to a tee. "I did similar work for the Hughes Foundation."

"How did you respond?"

"By just as sweetly reminding the board that what she'd done in Boston is what I've done here for two years, with less money and more cases. And then I casually mentioned my recent appointment to the board of a major donor's foundation."

"Ha!"

"Oh, Miss Margo thinks her friendship with Tracy, the current director, has all but sealed the director deal. I'll admit that Tracy's opinion matters. But so do facts and money."

Cynthia's intercom buzzed. "Hang on, please."
She clicked over. "Yes, Ivy?"

"Your ten o'clock is here."

"Give me five minutes. Thanks." Back over to
Dynah. "Duty calls, girl. Thanks for listening.
We'll finish up on Sunday."

"Okay. Keep calm, and act like a director."

"Thanks, girl."

Cynthia closed her eyes and took a slow, deep
breath. She hoped that her client would be cordial and cooperative. Still bothered by Margo's
antics, this was not the day for attitude. Cynthia's
singular goal with each of these kids was to put
them on the right track for a viable future. This
meant keeping their names out of the criminal
system, and their person out of jail. But given
Cynthia's tense disposition, if little miss came in
sulking and pouting, giving shrugged shoulders
instead of answers or the teenaged universal "I
don't know," this young adult might be headed
for lockup.

After checking her makeup and replacing the
compact, Cynthia pushed the intercom button.
"All right, Ivy, send her and Ms. Thompson in."

She cut off the intercom, belatedly realizing
Ivy was saying something else. Instead of buzzing
her, Cynthia decided to just go out there. She
stood. The door opened. A greeting was swallowed with a quick intake of air, expertly covering
surprise with a soft cough.

The bus driver.

The one whose image had kept sleep at bay.

The man she thought she'd never again see
in life.

Oh. My. Goodness. With one quick sweep of her lashes she'd taken him in: about five-foot-nine or ten she guessed, freshly shaved, wearing black slacks with a tan and black striped shirt—tail out—that complemented his complexion and hid the slightly flabby tummy so clearly visible yesterday. He'd cleaned up nicely. Too nicely, considering the work Cynthia had to put in to look nonchalant. *It's that cologne, darn it! And those eyes . . . and lips.*

A slight smirk graced said luscious lips, and though he undoubtedly was just as surprised as she, it didn't show on his face.

Hers either, and she silently thanked her mother who drummed poise at all times into her head. Composure firmly in place, Cynthia held out her hand. "Hello, Leah."

"Hi."

Shifting her attention to Leah's chaperone, she smiled with hand outstretched. "Hello, I'm—"

"Cynthia." He grasped her hand. "I remember."

Leah looked from her uncle to Cynthia. "Y'all know each other?"

Cynthia was thankful for Leah's unbridled response of surprise. It gave her a chance to recover from the feel of Byron's rough, meaty hand caressing her skin. Rough, unlike the hands of the men in her circle who'd not done hard labor. *The way this man affects me makes no sense whatsoever. He's nowhere near my type!* If only she could get this message through to her pulsating pearl.

Subtly pulling back her hand, instead of snatching it as if away from a hot stovetop like she wanted to do, Cynthia turned to respond to Leah.

But he answered first. "Cynthia rode my bus yesterday."

Leah's face showed even more surprise. "You rode a bus to the hood? Why?"

Byron smiled at Cynthia, his eyes twinkling. She knew what he was thinking. *Yesterday's question gets answered after all.*

"When I drove over to deliver the notice, my car stopped. But that's all handled and as of five o'clock today, my car will be fine." Her attention returned to Byron. A slightly raised eyebrow and the merest of smiles were the only signs that Cynthia had guessed Byron's message and formed a reply. *Not so fast, Mr. Bus Driver. This is my office, so we'll go by my rules.*

"We didn't meet formally. I am Cynthia Hall."

"Byron Carter."

They shook hands. Cynthia braced herself before looking into the seductive eyes that were boring into hers.

"Nice to meet you, Mr. Carter. Are you related to my client?"

Leah answered the question directed to Byron. "He's my uncle."

"I see. Is Ms. Thompson all right?"

"She's okay, but asked for my assistance in bringing in Leah."

"I wish this had been communicated when she and I spoke yesterday."

"Why, is there a problem?"

"Not exactly, but along with discussing a general strategy, this session is where the procedures for those who come here by way of the legal system are explained to the parent so that they, along with the client, can be fully aware of what's required to fulfill the diversion program. For that reason, I'd prefer that Ms. Thompson were present. However, you can sit in for her and I'll make sure she gets a copy of all that's discussed. Please"—Cynthia motioned toward the two chairs in front of her desk as she walked behind it— "have a seat."

Once they were settled, Cynthia got right to the heart of the matter. "Leah, why were you a no-show for yesterday's meeting?"

Eyes fixed on fingernails. Silence. Shrug.

Uh-oh.

Her face was once again a mask of professional composure, but behind it, Cynthia was steaming. The people around her obviously cared more about her future than did Leah herself. That she was with young men who were stopped by police, men who had known criminal records was a bad thing. That one of them had given her a gun and a sizable amount of drugs to hide in her purse, which was subsequently searched by the police, was worse. At seventeen, she could be convicted as an adult for drug possession or the charge the officer preferred, possession with intent to sell. She could get five years for spending time with these friends. Instead, with the diversion program, she'd get probation and hopefully no lasting record.

And she answers my question with a shrug?

Thoughts that were processed in seconds as Cynthia casually tapped her pen on the desk's edge a couple times before turning to her computer. *I have no patience for this dogged insolence. Maybe jail time will teach her the lessons she needs to learn. End this session. Call the court. Law enforcement can take it from here.*

The words were on the tip of her tongue, about to spew out. And then . . .

"Leah." One word; spoken with such authority, conviction, and implied intent that it changed the room's atmosphere.

Leah's posture changed. "Yes, Uncle Byron?"

Cynthia sat back. *Well, now.*

"You were asked a question." He looked at Cynthia. "I'm sorry for interfering with your meeting, but—"

Cynthia held up her hands as if to say, "Go right ahead."

Byron cut his eyes back at Leah. "Remember our discussion, and my promise."

Leah cleared her throat. "I'm sorry for not showing up yesterday. There is"—quick glance at her uncle—"no excuse."

"Apology accepted, Leah. Now"—Cynthia reached for two stapled documents, handing one each to Byron and Leah—"let's discuss your future."

During the next thirty minutes, Cynthia went over the legal requirements of the program, and briefly explained the plan she'd designed to facilitate Leah's successful transition into life as a responsible adult. The plan included Leah's taking summer courses to successfully graduate high school on schedule and, since it was too late for the universities, hopefully getting into a community college. By the time the meeting ended, the disinterested countenance on Leah's face had been replaced by one showing cautious optimism. Cynthia's impression of Byron-the-bus-driver had changed as well.

The three stood near Cynthia's now-open office door. "Leah, would you mind waiting in the reception area while I have a word with your uncle?"

5

Closing the door, Cynthia turned to Byron. With her client gone, the atmosphere shifted. *Maybe closing the door wasn't the best idea.*

"About yesterday, I'm sorry if I appeared rude. There was a lot on my mind. Still, had I known you were related to one of my clients . . ."

"What? You wouldn't have dissed me, treated me like a low-level public servant instead of a gainfully employed man who simply paid you a compliment?"

Quickly crossed arms made her defensiveness clear. "That's not fair."

"Oh, really? How would you describe your funky attitude?"

"That of someone unimpressed with game you probably use on every female rider when"— Cynthia tapped each finger for emphasis—"one, my car had broken down for the very first time; two, Triple A had a waiting time of at least ninety minutes; three, I was in an unfamiliar neighborhood that looked pleasant enough to reside in, but where a murder had occurred, so no taxi would come to pick me up." Cynthia took a breath. "While on your bus, being threatened with eviction if your rules weren't obeyed, I was trying to prepare for a very important meeting that I came precariously close to missing. So if I was not as cordial, chatty, or flirtatious as you'd like, you now know why."

Cynthia watched as Byron's direct gaze left her face and gave her body a quick perusal. When their gazes locked again his expression was neutral, but not his eyes. Curiosity, appraisal, and appreciation were all conveyed as he digested what she'd said.

"Thanks for the explanation. That indeed sounds like a bad day. Though I have a feeling that had we met under more, say, comfortable circumstances, I still don't think you'd have given a brother like me the time of day."

"It's obvious you have another woman doing that."

"Who?"

"Your girlfriend, the one with the charming personality sitting in the first seat."

"Tanya? She's not my girlfriend. And she's not the one who won't give me her time."

His gaze pierced Cynthia's soul and dared her to lie. An energy of chemistry—indefinable, undeniable—wafted around them, an invisible cocoon of possibilities that neither expected.

"I'm trying to take time right now and thank you for helping Leah. It's obvious she respects you and that you or someone has had a talk with her in a way that after your slight encouragement produced results. I've also apologized for behavior justifiable considering the circumstances. But it seems you've already formed an opinion about people like me, who we do or don't see, even where we reside so . . . there's not much more to be said." Cynthia stepped around him and walked toward the door.

"Have I been wrong about anything?"

Silence as she turned around.

"Do you live on the south side, over by where you caught the bus?"

"No, I don't."

"Will you go out with me?"

"Mr. Carter—"

"Byron is fine, since I'd prefer calling you Cynthia and not Ms. Hall."

"Byron, in light of the fact that I'm counseling your niece, I—"

Byron's genuine laugh interrupted her. "Oh, the job's the reason. All right, that'll work. I appreciate what you're doing with Leah. I'm sure you know all about why she's having a hard time. Her brother was her world and when he died, she changed. From what my sister told me, it's gotten worse. So I'm going to do what I can to help Ava and make sure Leah gets it together. I believe my contact information is already in her file." He held out his hand. "Hopefully today is going better than the one that landed you on my bus. You take care."

This time it was Cynthia watching Byron's back as his long strides quickly ate up the distance to the door.

"What about coffee?" *What are you doing?* She didn't know. But she kept doing it. "Something quick, early in the day on Saturday maybe, to make amends?"

He turned around. The look in his eyes warmed her heart, and other places. She told herself the feeling was because a professional cordiality was important for Leah. *Liar.*

"I'd prefer dinner, but coffee's all right. Can I have your number, or would you prefer mine?"

"We can do both."

She reached for her phone. They exchanged numbers and decided on where to meet. Byron held out his hand. Cynthia braced herself, and shook it. "I'll see you on Saturday, Cynthia. Looking forward to it."

They joined Leah in the general area just outside Cynthia's office. Byron stared unabashed as she gave Leah a parting encouragement and a light hug. When she glanced his way, he winked. There was no explanation or excuse for what that single eye action did to her insides. She'd tried and failed to figure it out, but something about his fire did something to her ice. Once again, she was left melting, inside of the mask. "Thanks for your time, Mr. Carter." Professionalism oozed from every pore. "Good-bye."

"Ivy, hold my calls for a half hour or so. I need to . . . take care of something."

"Sure thing, Cynthia."

Cynthia walked into her office, closed and locked the door, and relieved the pent-up energy due to lack of dictation, the Margo frustration, and this Byron situation by twenty minutes of meditation with Deepak and Oprah.

6

Later that evening, Byron parked in front of an older, yet well-tended apartment building less than ten minutes from his home. He bounced up the outer stairs to the second level and was barely in the door before conversation began.

"Man, you're not going to believe the day I've had."

"Uh, and what's up to you, too, Byron."

Byron plopped down on the couch and placed his shoed feet on his brother's coffee table.

Exasperation showed in the eyes that witnessed the blunder. "Are you drunk?"

Byron and his next youngest brother, Douglas, had always been close. Douglas was younger by a year and two months and taller by two inches. When it came to standing up for himself and voicing an opinion, Douglas didn't hesitate . . . not even with big brother.

Byron slowly removed his feet. "You and your bougie nonsense. I don't know where you got that, but it wasn't from Mom and Dad."

"There's nothing wrong with owning nice things." Douglas picked up a bottle of water off the dining room table and joined his brother in the living room.

"But better to put nice things in a home you own, at least that's how I see it."

"If anybody gave two cents about your vision, it would matter. Since I don't, well . . ." He took a long swig of water. "So what happened that brings you over at nine o'clock on a weeknight?"

"I met this chick on the bus yesterday."

"Breaking news so far."

"Not just any woman, Douglas. The woman of my dreams! I don't get many of her type on my bus. Come to think of it, she acted like she'd never been on one before."

"Man, if you think this is exciting, you need to get out more."

"Will you just let me tell the story?"

"Do I have a choice?"

"No, so I'm talking to her, joking around as usual, and she ignored me."

Douglas placed his hands on his chest. "Fool, you're killing me."

"It gets better. I promise. Her uppity attitude pissed me off, so I gave her the space she wanted. But damn, her body was everything! Plus, she was well put together, had that corporate look going with the suit and the pumps, talking all professional, all proper. Damn that stuff was sexy . . ."

"Sounds like she's way above your pay grade, bro."

"You're probably right. Women like her want to date actors, professional athletes, men with six-figure bank accounts." Byron rested his head against the back of the couch and locked his hands behind it. "But I still pulled a date."

"Quit bullshitting."

"I told you the story would get better."

"You asked her out, while driving the bus."

"Turns out she's Leah's counselor."

"Whoa! Real talk?"

"I couldn't believe it when I stepped into the office and saw her standing there. She was more stunned than me, but I have to give it to her. She kept up that stiff professional veneer. I'd like to . . . relax her a little bit."

"Ha! From what you're telling me about her, almost any man would." Douglas drained the bottle. "I thought you were seeing someone. What's that girl's name, the one who went to school with Nelson?"

Nelson was the middle brother out of five, younger than Douglas by 364 days.

"Turns out that behind those designer shades and that luxury car that she probably can't afford was a thirsty female out for what she could get."

"Sounds like Tanya."

"Man, don't even mention Tanya. That girl's a trip."

"What else is new?"

"She's back to claiming that Ricky is my son."

Douglas made a sound of disgust. "Again?"

"Yep."

"Her and big Rick's on and off relationship must be in the off season."

"You're probably right. She was even on my route the other day, just happened to be over there, she said. I asked where her car was. She said a friend was using it. Can you imagine Tanya letting someone use her car while she took the bus?"

"Heck, no."

"Me neither. She's up to something."

"Bottom line, dude? She knows she messed up and wants you back."

"More like she wants back my paycheck."

"Yes, that would mean more child support." Byron shook his head. "Me and Ava tried to tell you how to stop that madness."

"I know. But when she and Ricky moved in together and they had another baby, I thought that lie was finally put to rest."

"A woman like Tanya will say anything, and do anything, to get a man. I had a similar conversation earlier with your baby bro."

"Barry?"

"Who else, fool?"

Byron laughed. "What's that fool into now?"

"Too many pussies, without protection. I told him his time would be better spent looking for a J-O-B."

"He still talking that personal trainer nonsense?"

"It wouldn't be nonsense if he'd get serious and put some real work into getting steady clients who actually needed his services, instead of these size-two sistahs who only want him to practice pushups while they do leg lifts."

"Ha!"

The two brothers were silent a moment. Out of the five Carter boys, Barry, the youngest, was by

far the most spoiled, the only one still at home
and the only one who didn't work full-time.

Douglas stifled a yawn. "When is this date with
your fantasy woman?"

"Saturday morning, ten o'clock."

"Not a lot of time to smooth out the rough
edges but enough for you to learn a couple tips
from a pro."

Byron made a big deal of looking around.
"Where's he at?"

The brothers laughed. Douglas teased him
about being on a "Carter come up" by going
after a woman outside the realm of those he normally dated. Byron headed home feeling a little
less nervous about his meeting with Cynthia. But
not much.

Cynthia resisted the urge to squirm and
worked to look interested in the speaker's impas-
sioned endorsement of the national health care
system. Not that she disagreed with anything said,
but that other matters were vying for attention.
And winning.

After another torturous hour, Cynthia made
her escape. Halfway home, her cell phone rang.
"Lisa?" Cynthia quickly answered the call. It
was almost midnight in Chicago. She hoped her
friend was all right. "Hello?"

Whispered words, frantic, garbled, played
through the car's speakers. "Lisa?"

". . . in five minutes." Cynthia made out through
irritating static.

"Do what in five minutes? Lisa, what's the matter?"

"Call me! In five! I'll explain later."

"Where are—"

The line went dead.

What in the world is going on? She considered calling Gayle or Dynah, the other women in their four-person posse, but decided to wait the five minutes Lisa requested. If Lisa didn't answer, the cavalry would be called.

"Is Mercury retrograde?" Ironically it was Lisa who'd told Cynthia about this planetary phenomenon, when the planet appeared to travel backward and communication went crazy. While remaining somewhat skeptical of the planet's effect on human experiences, in this moment she felt cosmic insanity would explain the odd occurrences of the last two days. Four minutes and fifty-nine seconds later, she tapped the redial button.

"Okay, what's going on?"

"Excuse me, who is this?"

"Lisa, I am not in the mood for foolishness. Are you all right?"

"Yes, this is Lisa. Oh, hi, I'm sorry, wasn't expecting to hear from you this late at night. Is the paperwork in order?"

"So . . . I'm supposed to figure this out on my end."

"Yes, I have that information, but it's at my house and I'm not there right now."

The lightbulb flashed.

"Seriously? This is a rescue call from another one of your illicit adventures?"

"Hold on a minute." Cynthia heard muffled mumbling. *SMH*. "I'm leaving right now. No, no, it's okay. This is important. I'll get over there as soon as I can."

"You do that, heifah," Cynthia managed between laughing. "Because I have a newsflash, too."

7

Byron arrived at the coffee shop early, as he'd planned. Nerves had been replaced with a curious attraction. He wondered if she lived here, Marina Del Rey, where she'd suggested they meet. It was an expensive area. If this was her neighborhood, she was either independently wealthy or her job paid very well.

Douglas had been right about one thing. Cynthia wasn't the type of woman he usually dated. Byron wasn't fazed. As an LA native, and a ten-year bus driver, there weren't many parts of the metropolitan area that he'd not at least driven through or any echelon of individual whom he hadn't met. Whether five-star or two for five dollars, the surroundings didn't matter. The kids who'd been raised by retired Sergeant Willie Carter were nothing if not comfortable in their own skin.

"The early bird catches the worm. The smart one eats half and saves some for later." That mantra from Willie, that Byron had heard from the time he was five, is why he sat scrolling the Internet on his cell phone, sipping a bottle of water, and thinking about his fantasy woman.

Had she been able to read what was on his mind when she entered, there wouldn't have been the need for coffee to heat her up.

"Good morning, Byron."

"Hello, pretty lady." Byron stood to greet her.

Cynthia held out her hand. Byron took it and pulled her close, giving a chaste kiss on the cheek.

They sat. Byron watched as she positioned her purse strap on the chair. If he hadn't known better, he would have sworn she was a little flustered. *By that little kiss? Naw . . .*

"It's Saturday and you look like you're headed to work. Do you ever let your guard down, lose the professional look?"

"Slacks and a top hardly qualify as that. But if that was a compliment, thank you."

"Oh, you look good. There's no mistaking that. What are we drinking?"

"I'll take a small mocha, decaf."

"That's all?" She nodded. "No roll, croissant, breakfast sandwich?"

"No, I'm fine, thanks."

An unreadable smile touched his lips and met his eyes. "All right, then. Be right back."

Within minutes he returned with her drink selection and then went back for his order, a large fruit smoothie and gooey cinnamon bun. He took a large bite and chewed it with appreciative abandon.

"So . . . you're one of those, huh?" he said while licking his fingers before another bite.

"What?" She'd heard him, but her mother's voice had been louder. If Anna Marie Hall ever saw Cynthia lick her fingers *anywhere*, she would have gotten popped.

"Bird nibbler."

"Meaning . . ."

"You know how y'all do. Go on a date and eat like a bird. Be so hungry by the time you get home that you clean out the fridge and empty the cabinets."

Cynthia laughed out loud. Another Anna Marie public no-no. But she'd been that bird a time or two. "No acting here. I'm an early riser and have already had breakfast. But don't mind me. Enjoy your food."

"I intend to." He finished another bite, wiped his hands, and took a drink. "Do you live around here?"

"Close by, Culver City."

"Do you like it?"

"It has its pluses and minuses, but overall it's a nice place to live."

"I have a few friends in the area. It can get congested down here on the evenings and weekends."

"It can get congested just about anywhere in Los Angeles."

"True."

Silence descended as Byron enjoyed his roll.

"Byron, as I said at the office, I am very pleased Leah has you as a positive male role model. I understand she's endured hardships and—"

"Whoa, wait a minute." Byron hurriedly finished his bite and wiped his mouth with a napkin. "I've loved my niece since she took her first breath and will do whatever I can to make her life better. But I did not leave my warm bed and risk missing the March Madness game that comes on in an hour to talk about Leah."

"Okay. What do you want to talk about?"

"You." He lowered his voice in a way that Cynthia imagined had separated many a woman from the clothes she wore. "What's your story?"

"I never give a specific answer to a general question. What would you like to know?"

"I want to know it *all*," he said with exaggeration as he made a face. His goofy antics reminded her of Cedric the Entertainer. She laughed again and realized this type of easy joy hadn't been felt in a while. "For starters, where are you from?"

"I grew up near Minneapolis."

"Minnesota, huh. Do you know Prince?"

"Oh, sure. We went to school together."

"That's what I get when visitors find out I was born in Compton. Do you know Ice Cube or Dr. Dre?"

Cynthia remembered her thoughts as she drove to Ava's house. She kept them to herself. "I don't meet many LA natives."

"We're here. Never been to Minnesota, though."

"You should visit. It's a beautiful state."

"I know you're not married, but do you have kids?"

"What is it with you assuming so much about me? Just because I'm not wearing a ring, doesn't mean I'm not married. As a man, you should know that's not true."

"Are you married?"

"No, but—"

"But what? I just said you're not married. You've agreed that's true. What's the problem?"

Cynthia became very interested in the taste of her coffee.

"Look, when you're interested in people and you have an occupation that has you surrounded by them for over ten years, you develop keen observation skills. It's not personal."

"Let's talk about you."

"All right. You know my name, Byron Carter. I'm the oldest of five hardheaded boys."

"What about Ava?"

"She's the big sis of all of us."

"You come from a large family."

"It's all relative. There are families on the block who had ten, twelve kids. We were raised by two parents married thirty-five years and still together. I'm a single father. My daughter, Tyra, is almost ten years old. And I'm looking for a mama to raise her and give me at least five sons. I'm trying to outdo my parents." As Cynthia tried to rearrange the look of near-horror his comment brought out, it was Byron's turn to chuckle. "I'm just kidding with you, girl. Don't run away."

"Okay, because I was about to grab my purse and hit the exit!"

They both laughed; the first moment of true camaraderie between them since Cynthia boarded the bus.

"By that statement, I take it you have only one child?"

"Yes, and she's a handful."

"You share custody with her mom?"

"I have primary custody. Contrary to popular belief, there are black men who take care of our children."

"I'm thankful for those who do. More men like you mean fewer children like Leah coming into my office."

"By the way, that girl hating on you the other day? That's Tyra's mother."

"Oh, I see."

"No, you don't. Tanya and I basically grew up together. We never really dated, just messed around. When she got pregnant we tried to make it work but broke up three years later. That was almost seven years ago."

"Why was she on your bus?"

"The same reason you were on it, to hear her tell it."

"Sounds like you don't believe her."

Byron shrugged.

"It's really none of my business. I wanted us to meet today to prove I have nothing against you personally. As Leah's counselor, it can also be beneficial to know a little about her extended family."

"Leah wasn't always the person you see. She was a bright, funny kid, full of sunshine. She doted on her big brother and when he died, I think a part of her did, too. But we're not going to talk about work, remember?"

"We're not. We're talking about Leah's extended family."

"What about your family? Do you have siblings, kids?"

"I have a younger brother attending law school at NYU—"

"Nice . . ."

"And a son, who just turned eight."

"Does he like California?"

"Are you kidding? Wonderful theme parks, the beach, neighbors his age, and basketball court and skate board weather all year-round . . . he'll probably never leave."

"Where did you live before?"

"Chicago."

"Ah, that makes sense. I spent a whole winter in Chicago one night."

Cynthia responded with a tinkling chuckle. Byron immediately decided it was a sound he'd like to hear more often.

"My plane was grounded due to a mechanical problem. The airline put us up for the night and I had the bright idea to check out the city. Stepped outside and oh, man! I'd never experienced wind that could cut through cloth."

"That's why it's called the Windy City."

"Windy is the air that sways palm leaves or helps a kite float in the air. What I felt that night went way beyond windy."

"It can get pretty intense."

"Sounds like your son is a smart young man."

"I think so."

"I never appreciated all my parents did until Tyra came to live with me. Raising kids is hard work when two people are doing it. By yourself it's even more difficult. Add to it the fact that I'm raising a daughter and the responsibility seems overwhelming at times."

"I have similar feelings when it comes to raising a son."

"My hats are off to all the single mothers out there who've held it down. It's a labor of love, though. I'd do it all over again, except I'd choose a different mother. Not that I chose this one to tell you the truth."

"Baby mama drama?"

"You don't know the half."

"Actually, I do, except with me it's less about drama and more about . . . well, it's about the pitfalls of having a parent missing from a child's life."

"Sounds like there's a story there."

"Yes."

"Sounds like one you don't care to share."

"Correct."

Byron slowly nodded, eyeing her with interest as his curiosity grew. "I can respect that. What is one of your biggest challenges dealing with him? With my daughter, it's clothes and the styles she wants to wear! Why do they make outfits for ten-year-olds as if they're eighteen?"

"Unfortunately, fashion is largely driven by a pop culture that pays little attention to the term *age appropriate*. Look at the people singing the music she loves or the shows she enjoys watching on TV. They're probably the ones she's emulating, and they're probably not much older than her." Cynthia took a sip of coffee. "Jock straps."

The roll on its way to Byron's mouth was stopped halfway there. "Excuse me?"

"One of the challenges in being a single mother raising a son. I have no personal knowledge of that particular apparatus."

Byron's look was that of a confident man. "It just so happens I'm an apparatus expert. What would you like to know?"

The two continued chatting and getting to know each other. One topic flowed into another without effort and before either of them knew it, two hours had gone by. Cynthia left for her hair appointment. Byron headed over to his parents' house to watch what remained of the game. Both left having experienced the unexpected. For Byron, it was that Cynthia wasn't as uppity as he thought she was, and even more beautiful when relaxed and smiling. For Cynthia, it was that they had so much in common, and since he wasn't her client's immediate family . . . that she'd agreed to join him for dinner tomorrow night.

8

Anyone listening to the cacophony that greeted Byron as he stepped into the Carter household would have thought there were thirty people in the Carter living room. Instead, it was just his dad (the loudest), three brothers, Tyra, and a cousin who was around Tyra's age. As he entered, they ran out of the room in search of more age-appropriate, girly entertainment. Byron greeted them and then entered the living room and immediately made his presence known.

"How can y'all hear the TV with all this hollering?" he yelled loud enough to be heard over the din. "Stop all this yakkity-yak. I'm here to watch the game!"

"Shut up, fool. You're louder than anybody!"

"Nobody cares why you're here."

"You bad, come over and shut me up!"

"Hey, big brother, we learned from the best."

"Byron, go sit down."

Barry, the youngest son, delivered this command and got bopped upside the head for his trouble. Byron sat down beside him. "Shut the hell up."

"Hey!" Elizabeth "Mom Liz" Carter walked into the room wearing a scowl. "Cut out all this ruckus! And stop all that got damn cussing in my house!"

The room erupted into an even louder cacophony as all but one of Byron's brothers—Douglas, Nelson, and Barry—verbally reacted to her comment. The girls, Tyra and her cousin, ran back into the living room, looked at their grandmother with wide-eyed glee, and plopped down on an oversized floor cushion in a way that suggested the best entertainment was in this room. Liz was a walking, talking tornado who made no apologies for who she was. At five-foot-eight, she was just two inches shorter than her husband, and outweighed him by about fifty pounds. Both bark and bite, with a heart of gold. Would curse you out one minute and feed you the next. Her family loved her to death.

Byron jumped up to give her a hug. "What's up, Mama Lizzie?"

"My blood pressure. What's up with you?"

"The price of gas. You want to sit here, on the couch?"

"Since it's my house I'll sit where I please. You'll know where that is when my ass hits the cushion." She sat in the place Byron had vacated. "Now move out the way. The game's back on." Liz reached for the remote and turned up the volume.

"Gram, when's the pizza getting here?"

"When the doorbell rings, Tyra, now stop asking. You and your cousin go play."

Byron looked around as the room quieted. "Where's Marvin?"

"Out sniffing after some feline." Willie grew up in the south, Mississippi, and brought his slow speech and pronounced accent to LA. It never left and neither did he.

"What's a feline?" the young cousin asked.

Liz's brow furrowed. "Your kitty cat."

Now Tyra was confused. "Uncle Marvin is smelling her cat?"

"Not an animal, girl. Your vagina, coochie, beaver . . ."

"Beaver!" This description sent the young cousin into fits of laughter.

"Dang, Mom!" Byron shook his head, eyes glued to the screen.

"What? She asked? Would you have preferred I said p—"

"Come on now, Liz . . ." Willie's speech sped up a notch or two.

"I can't say pocketbook?" Her eyes twinkled as she gave Byron a wink. "That's what they called it back home. Told us to keep it closed and put a lock on it." She looked at the girls. "Did you hear that? Closed, and locked."

Tyra frowned. "But, Gram, how do you—"

"Tyra. If you want a slice of pizza, I suggest you go play like Mama told you until it arrives." Once they'd gone, Byron fixed Liz with a look of exasperation. "Really, Mama?"

"Humph. It's a good thing I'm talking, from the looks of things. She needs to know about her

body and she needs to know early. Before some
cute little boy with a wink and a smile comes
shopping for a purse."

His brothers chuckled. Byron sighed. "Never
mind."

"I never do. And you're welcome."

"Ha!" Knowing few people won an argument
when Liz was the opponent, he left the living
room in search of a beer, thinking about Cynthia, and wondering what she'd think of his
crazy family.

On the other side of the city, Cynthia was
trying to convince the girls that she wasn't the
crazy one. It was their Sunday afternoon tele-
phone powwow, a staple event in these best
friend's lives since Cynthia had left Chicago for
Los Angeles two and a half years ago. Only a job
like the one at H.E.L.P. could have pulled her
away from these BFFs who all still lived there.

"I don't see anything wrong with it." Lisa had
cut off an appalled Gayle to make her point. "If
she was talking love and a future, then, yes, concern would be appropriate. But this is just dinner,
no big deal."

"We don't do dinner with bus drivers," Gayle,
a truly snooty sister, retorted.

"We don't marry bus drivers," Lisa corrected.
"But hey, why turn down a free meal?"

"Where is he taking you, Cynthia . . . Pizza Hut,
Subway?"

Even though she knew they couldn't see it,
Cynthia rolled her eyes. "I love you, Gayle, but I

swear sometimes your uppity ass gets on my last nerves."

"Don't pay attention to her nonsense." Dynah sounded equally annoyed, before her tone changed. "Cynthia, I do have a concern."

Coming from the mother hen of the group, Cynthia wasn't surprised.

"Is it okay for you to go out with this guy since he's part of your client's family?" Dynah asked.

"Before this year, the answer would have been an unequivocal yes. But this year, for the very first time, the American Counselor Association has added a section to the code of ethics expressly prohibiting personal relationships with a client, of course, or their family, which the H.E.L.P. Agency defines as immediate family members."

Having similar restraints in the field of education, Dynah pressed the issue. "How can the definition be left up to interpretation?"

"A lot of counselors are asking the same thing and so far there is no one, right answer. But again, this is dinner, not a date."

"At least you're going out," Dynah finished, obviously placated for the moment. "Besides Gayle, did anyone else have a date this weekend?"

"I did."

"Not a booty call, Lisa, and not a club pickup. A date, when the man comes to your house, opens the car door, pays the bill, and kisses you good night."

"He came to my house and kissed me, in a few places. Does that count as a half date?"

The women laughed.

"Why are y'all trying to make so much out of

this? I'm going to a casual dinner with someone whose conversation I enjoy. End of story."

"Tell us more about him." Mother Dynah, always the voice of reason. "He isn't a professional, but does he have the other required qualifications?"

"He went to college."

"Did he graduate?"

"Not everyone can be summa cum laude, Gayle."

"Or even praise de Lawd," Lisa mumbled.

Dynah snickered.

"Lisa?"

"Yes, Cynthia?"

"Stop drinking." Even Gayle laughed at this. "He went to school on a partial football scholarship, but got injured in his junior year. Without the scholarship money, he couldn't finish. So he took a job with LA's Metro system. He's worked there ten years and is a homeowner."

"That's good," Dynah said.

"You have to have good credit to get a home loan," Lisa added.

"In a desirable neighborhood?"

"Gayle, calm down." Lisa was one of the few who could get Gayle to actually do this.

"Okay, fine. He's got a mortgage. But he's not a college graduate or business professional. Are you willing to settle for one out of three?" Gayle asked.

Cynthia bristled at the overall tone of the conversation. When hearing these required standards used against Byron, they didn't sound good. *And if I tell them he's a single father* . . . There was no need to get into that. It wasn't like their sharing a meal would become a regular event. "Listen, I have touted the notion of DHOP or die single as fervently as any of you. A degreed, home-owning professional is still my ideal. You guys are reacting as if he and I are shopping for rings."

"Cynthia Eileen Hall, don't even try it." Lisa's use of her full name showed she was serious. "If it was one of us, you'd be talking the same way."

"Maybe so, but the point is I'm not dating Byron. We're meeting for dinner, as friends, nothing more. I enjoyed his company yesterday, more than I thought I would. The hours I put in at work and caring for Jayden have left very little time for making friends here or developing a social network. The company felt nice. Yes, he is a blue-collar brother. But one who's intelligent, funny, interesting, considerate—"

"Are you attracted to him?" Asked in a way that showed Gayle was not only incredulous, but clearly not on board.

"He is totally not my type."

"That's not what she asked," Lisa said. "Are you going to give him some? That's what we really want to know." No immediate answer. "I would. He could be shorter than Kevin Hart and look like Flavor Flav. But if my dictation drought had lasted as long as yours, I'd let his pool cue sink an eight ball!"

The conversation turned silly then, with each woman talking about how they'd sex someone after a lengthy celibacy. Lisa's foolishness made them forget about the question, but even after the call ended, it stayed on Cynthia's mind.

Byron wasn't her type. His niece was her client, a potential conflict of interest. He was not a DHOP, her standard for potential liaisons. So if given the chance, would Cynthia have sex with Byron?

Absolutely not! The idea in and of itself is ridiculous! Or was it? Time would tell.

9

Cynthia had never gone to the restaurant that Byron suggested and had given herself plenty of time to get there. She arrived early. Byron had as well. He stood as the hostess brought her to the table, and helped her with the chair.

"Oh, thanks. You didn't have to do that."

"Men like me don't do what we have to do. We do what we want to do." He returned to his seat. "It's how I was raised."

"Well, compliments to your father."

"This is for you." He handed her a medium-sized black box wrapped with a purple ribbon.

"What's this for?"

"Really? Okay, since you feel most comfortable wearing your professional veneer, let's say it's a token of my appreciation for your working with Leah and keeping her out of the system. How's that sound?"

"I'm just doing my job, Byron, the same as I do for every case file that lands on my desk. I'm not sure accepting this would be appropriate."

"Then would you please be inappropriate and open the gift? Otherwise, you're being rude to a client's relative, which probably isn't appropriate either."

Cynthia shook her head as she pulled on the satin ribbon to undo the bow. "You're something else."

"I know."

The box was lined with purple satin that held two crystal flutes filled with silver-wrapped kisses.

"These are gorgeous. Wow. Thank you."

"You're welcome."

"You really shouldn't have, and not"—her hand came up quickly, silencing the protest on his lip—"because of our professional relationship. You're acting as if we're on a date, and that's not what this is."

"Oh? What is it?"

"Two people meeting for dinner."

"And what's a date?"

"You know what I mean!" she said with more attitude than intended. His cool, confident demeanor was getting on her nerves. It was so sexy!

His gaze was thoughtful as he looked at her and said nothing at all.

Several more seconds went by, during which time the waiter came and took their drink orders. She felt best when their conversation centered on subjects held in common: kids, exes, home-owning, travel, less personal topics such as those they'd shared yesterday. She picked up the menu.

"I've never spent time here, in Silverlake. The area is a bit unkempt, but the atmosphere here is nice. How'd you find this place?"

"I basically grew up in LA, remember?"

"That doesn't necessarily mean one knows the city. When I first arrived I was shocked to meet young clients, native Angelenos, who'd never gone ten miles outside their neighborhood. Who'd never been to any of the landmark tourist attractions such as Hollywood, Disneyland, Universal Studios . . . even the beach! Visitors pay thousands of dollars to visit what is in their own backyard."

"One of my college buddies grew up in this area. His parents still live here. I used to come and hang out with him and his family. But you're right. I know people who've lived most of their lives within twenty or so square blocks, maybe less. When your focus is on avoiding drug dealers and gang bangers, not getting pulled over by the police, or worse, trying to find food because your mom is an addict and your dad is in jail, there's no time for Mickey Mouse."

Without thought, Cynthia shifted to counselor mode. "Is that how it was for you?"

"No, not at all, thanks to my mom. While Dad was deployed, she had to hold down the fort with six rowdy kids. Books, videos, games, TV . . . not the stuff kids want to watch, but the PBS, History, or Biography channels, documentaries . . . that was our entertainment. She'd quiz us, too, to make sure we watched. We had a white Volvo station wagon and on the weekends, we'd pile in and head off to places unknown. The beach, museums, different parts of LA . . . it was always an adventure. I didn't like it then, wanted to run the streets with my friends. But those trips are what made me curious, and well-rounded. So I appreciate it now."

"Hmm. That reminds me of the family trips we used to take, my brother and I, and our parents. Every summer we took a road trip to a different place. We'd laugh, play CDs and car games. Good times for sure."

"How old is your brother?"

"Twenty-six."

"Four years younger than me. How old are you?"

"How old do you think?"

"Here we go, a woman who doesn't want to tell her age. Well, are you older or younger than your brother?"

"All of these appetizers sound delicious. What do you recommend?"

"See, that's what I was thinking about earlier and you just did it again. When I tell you something that's accurate, you say I'm being presumptive. But when I ask a question, you don't always answer."

"Which I admit is a perfectly legitimate, if somewhat annoying choice." Once again, she perused the menu. "Anything in particular you'd suggest?"

Byron picked up his menu. "Everything I've eaten has been good, but they're known for their pasta. If you like veal, that dish is an excellent choice."

"I don't recall ever eating veal."

"Then try it. Let go of that rigid, controlled persona you hold on to and live life on the edge."

"I. Am not. Rigid." Of course, when she said this her back was as stiff as a board.

"No?" He chuckled, that low, slow sound that started deep in his chest before rolling up and out into the atmosphere.

Cynthia refused to acknowledge its effect. "No," she dared say again, thankful for the loose-fitting top she wore that hid her pebbling nipples.

His eyes swept over that very area, almost as if he not only knew what he was doing, but knew he'd succeeded. His words further unnerved her. "I guess we'll see."

They placed their appetizer and entrée orders. As the food arrived, the conversation moved to the safe zone that Cynthia wanted. They talked, laughed, and learned more generalities about each other's lives. But something was different. Both of them felt it. Neither brought it up. Attraction. Desire. Hot. Pulsating. Weaving itself around them, and not letting go.

The waiter came for their entrée dishes and suggested dessert.

Byron deferred to Cynthia, who reached for her purse even as she was speaking. "I have absolutely no room left. But everything was delicious. Thank you."

"Why are you reaching for your wallet?"

"Why not? You treated me to coffee yesterday."

"Yeah, and that buck fifty almost broke me."

Put that way, Cynthia's statement sounded stupid to her own ears.

"This isn't a date, I get it. We're just eating. But I'm paying for it. If it means that much, you can pick it up next time."

Cynthia wasn't touching that one. "It's not nice to eat and run, but I have a few things to do before work tomorrow."

"No worries. Give me a minute. I'll walk you out."

She waited, but barely. Byron caught up with her as she walked out the door. "Where are you parked?"

"Around the corner."

"Okay."

They reached her car. She turned to him. "Thanks for inviting me to dinner, Byron, and introducing me to this place. I'll definitely come back here." She held out her hand. "And thanks again for the crystal glasses."

Byron ignored her outstretched hand. Closing the distance between them, he wordlessly pulled her to his chest and wrapped his arms around her. "Handshakes are for the office. Hugs are for two people who've enjoyed each other's company."

He released her. "Look, just so you know, I don't want to date you either." An arched brow confirmed her surprise at this news. "But I do like to eat. So . . . can we go on another . . . dinner?"

Cynthia tried to hold it in, but the twinkle in Byron's eye was impossible to resist. "You are so silly," she said, while laughing.

"This time you can choose the place."

"How are you so sure my answer will be yes?"

"Are you turning me down?"

Cynthia spoke through gritted teeth. "You drive me crazy doing that!"

"If asking a question drives you crazy, wait until you see what else I can do." He opened her door and held it as she slipped inside. "Call and let me know where I'm going on Friday."

"Good night, Byron."

"Good night."

Cynthia couldn't pull away from the curb fast enough. "*Arrogant Negro!* I am not going to go out with him again." At the light, she programmed her GPS to guide her home. True, she was unfamiliar with the area, but she could have been a block away from home and would have still needed help to get there.

He's got nerve to be so sure of himself. Merging onto the highway, she pressed on the gas pedal and quickly reached seventy miles per hour. *And to think he knows all about me when we just met? Pure arrogance.* Changing lanes to pass a vehicle, she quickly resumed a high rate of speed. *You're not even a DHOP.* A cop on the side of the highway was motivation to reduce her speed. Would that she could rid her thoughts as easily. *Gayle is right. Dating him is out of the question.* Cynthia could just about imagine her parents' reaction at bringing someone like Byron home. A bus driver with no degree? No matter how good his character, Anna Marie the socialite would never accept him as family. And with Cynthia having already been responsible for one stain of disgrace on the Hall family name, she dare not risk seriously dating a commoner as another. Taking the Olympic Boulevard exit, she shut down her mind until she got home. But once in bed, she could no longer deny how she'd felt in Byron's arms.

Monday was busy, passed before she knew it. The constant activity kept thoughts of Byron at bay. She worked out and then went to a play with a coworker.

Tuesday was tougher, a day filled with meetings. That night she had a glass of wine to help her sleep.

Wednesday was the day she stopped fighting the feeling. A long shower followed her workout; then she reached for the phone.

She got voice mail. "Byron, it's Cynthia. Do you like Indian food? If so, I have a great place in mind to go on Friday night. Let me know."

10

Thursday morning, Cynthia bopped into the office with Pharrell's happy tune looping inside her head. There were many reasons. She'd awakened to a message from Byron agreeing to "go on a dinner" Friday night, hit the gym for some much-needed cardio, and then walked out into a perfect seventy-five-degree California morning. There was just one more day before the weekend arrived. She expected a smooth day at work. The only potential hiccup would be if Leah failed to show up for their counseling session. Last night, it had crossed her mind to call Byron and ask for his assistance to make sure she showed up. But she quickly abandoned that idea. To do so, she decided, could definitely open the door for a conflict of interest. Part of her job with Leah was to teach independence and self-reliance, and she needed to see how well her client handled the mandated responsibility of showing up when required. As long as Leah walked into her office for their three o'clock appointment, Cynthia thought nothing else could go wrong with this day. Then she reached her office.

"Good morning, Cynthia. I have a message for you."

Ivy's somber mood was evident. *Where is Miss Sunshine?* "What's going on?"

"Tracy came looking for you. She wants you to stop by her office as soon as you arrive."

The cloud over Ivy's desk wafted into her office. She pushed the intercom button. "Ivy, I need to see you."

"Sure."

Ivy hurried into Cynthia's office, closed the door, and didn't wait for a question. She talked fast, her Mexican accent becoming more pronounced in her excitement. "I arrived at eight-thirty and Margo was here."

"Where?"

"At my desk, going through the folders sitting there."

"You're kidding me, right?" More clouds and now, the rumble of thunder.

"No."

"She is so devious; wasn't expecting you to get here early. What did she do when you arrived?"

"Oh, there you are, Ivy." Said in such a perfect Bostonian/Latina accent that as peeved as Cynthia was right now, she still laughed. "'I was looking for a client file. You delivered it on Monday and—wait! I remember . . .' Then she rushed off, but not before I saw the red creeping up her neck. She knew she'd gotten busted."

"What about Tracy? When did she get here?"

"I'm not sure what time she arrived."

"Okay, Ivy. Thanks."

"I'll keep my eyes out for anything sneaky."

"I appreciate it."

After taking a moment to gather her thoughts, Cynthia reached for her coffee and left her office for the conference room. Outside, the sun blazed, its light streaming through the blinds. In the office, a storm was brewing.

Byron excused himself from being a bus passenger's psychiatrist so he could answer his phone. Much like barber and beauty shops, one could hear some of everything while moving the masses from one place to the next. He was a good listener and had his father's common sense, so Byron was told more than most.

After glancing at the cell phone screen attached to the dashboard, he tapped the answer button on his Bluetooth. "It's about time you called."

"Sorry, Uncle Byron, I just got your message."

"Where've you been?"

"School!"

"Where else, and don't lie."

"Nowhere. I had to come home and get ready for my meeting with Cynthia."

"Good. I'm glad you remembered."

"Are you going to remember what you promised me when I graduate?"

"That's not all you need to do to get a car."

"And get into college, I know."

"Don't worry about that. My memory is fine. Look, I'm working. I need to jump off."

"All right. Talk to you later."

"Leah."

"Uh-huh?"

"I'm proud of you."

"Thank you."

"Leah."

"What?"

"I love you. Leah?"

She chuckled. "What, Uncle Byron?"

"Good-bye."

A smile touched his lips as he ended the call. Memories of Leah, three or four years old, running and jumping in his arms. Dancing to Usher or Nelly's "Hot in Here." *Full of life, that girl.* Nothing but legs, hair, and a great big smile. And then her brother died. Changed everything.

"Should I take him back?"

"Huh?" Byron had pulled over to pick up passengers and now looked back at the woman who'd bared her soul. "Oh, I'm sorry, forgot what we were talking about for a minute." He paused as several passengers got on. "I can't tell you how to live your life. But I will say this. If a man can't visit you in the daytime, you shouldn't let him visit at night."

His phone vibrated. At the next light, he looked down to see who'd called. *Cynthia?* No, the person who made him feel the exact opposite of how Cynthia did. The woman who could send his mood from fine to foul in less time than it took a streetlight to change. Byron had called her last night after being asked by a mutual friend if he was little Ricky's father. Had she answered, he'd planned to demand that she stop spreading lies. Left alone with his own thoughts, he went back to yesteryear and that pregnancy's timing. As much as he felt that Tanya was being untruthful, he had to admit the possibility of the worst possible outcome: that the child almost three years younger than Tyra could be his.

Later that evening, at exactly 8:15 p.m., Byron arrived at the restaurant Cynthia had suggested. Had he thought one might put a public, customer-driven establishment behind a black fence, he would have arrived sooner. The gate was locked, but after noticing a buzzer near the handle and hearing a click as the gate unlocked, he walked through a nice-sized patio area with holiday lights stringed between the trees. Tables were scattered throughout the area, many of them filled.

What in the world?

Inside, the place looked just as interesting. Small, quaint, colorful, and crowded. He'd often heard that if an establishment was busy, you could just about bet that the food was good. Just as the hostess greeted him, he spotted Cynthia smiling broadly from a corner booth.

"How in the world did you find this place?" Byron slid into the empty seat across from her.

"A colleague highly recommended it."

"Took me awhile to find it and once I got here, realized I'd passed it twice."

"I almost did the same thing. The place looked closed."

Byron casually looked around. "It's different."

"It's nice to introduce you to someplace different."

"Is that why you're smiling so broadly? Or will you admit it's because you're happy to see me."

"I love Indian food and am excited to try this southern India variety, but I must admit there's another reason."

A slow smile spread across Byron's face. "Oh, yeah? What's that?"

"I arrived first."

A scowl chased the smile away. "Seriously? That's why you searched for the most obscure, out-of-the-way place in all of LA, so you could beat me here?"

"And you're not happy about it." Byron's scowl fueled her laughter. "My friend said the food here is really good! I'm just such a stickler for promptness that it's rare when I'm not the first to arrive. I wasn't trying to throw you off."

"But you don't feel bad that you did." A sexy smile started pushing the scowl away.

From the grin on Cynthia's face, it must have been contagious. "No, I don't."

"Glad I could make you happy."

The waiter brought over menus and glasses of water. Byron picked his up and began to read.

Cynthia picked up hers, too. "Honestly, I'm always the early one. My friends used to tease me because of how much time I'd give myself to get somewhere. You're the first person I've met who has the same idiosyncrasy."

"Whatever you just said? I don't have that! My dad taught all of us that it was always better to be early rather than late."

"Smart dad."

"Very." His eyes narrowed as he scanned the menu. "How am I supposed to know what to order?"

She pointed to the column that provided English translations for the Indian dishes. "My friend recommended the Samosas or *bondas,* potato balls, for appetizers"—she scanned the menu—"and—I'm not even going to attempt the Indian pronunciations—the vegetable curry with basmati rice or the stuffed Indian bread for a main dish."

They continued perusing the menu. Finally, Byron asked, "Where's the meat?"

"Oh, that's the thing. This is a vegetarian restaurant."

Byron gave her a look. "A meal isn't complete if it doesn't have meat!"

"I was assured that the food is amazing and that we would leave full and satisfied. Come on. Aren't you up for an adventure?"

Byron's eyes narrowed as his look turned sultry. "Oh, yes. I'm definitely up for an adventure, and it involves tasting things, too. But this no-meat-can't-pronounce-Indian whatever isn't exactly what I have in mind."

11

"Byron, we've already discussed this."

"You gave your opinion, but there was no discussion. Look, I don't need to tell you what you already know. You're intelligent, sexy . . . but that's not why I'm feeling you, and, yes, I'm as attracted to you as I've ever been to any woman in my life. I'm not going to lie. But the most beautiful part about you is your heart. You're kind of seddity—"

"I beg your pardon?"

"You can beg all you want to because I can see past that. Not enough to know the real you, but just enough to know that I want to. That's why I asked you out. I don't talk in circles or play games. I'm trying to get with you, see if there's a connection. I would like to move past the cordial but guarded interactions and see where this can go. If you're not interested, I'm a big boy. I can handle that, no problem. I can have dinner with family, go out with Tyra on father/daughter dates.

I've got a pocketful of friends I can call to grab a bite any day of the week. That is not why I'm here with you."

"I don't know what to say."

"You don't have to say anything."

An awkward silence joined them at the table, pushed away by the waiter coming to take their order.

Byron gave the menus to the waiter. "There's a first time for everything. I don't think I've ever had a meal without meat."

"I'm not a vegetarian, but on occasion I will go two or three days without it, give my intestines a break and clean out a bit. If you're open to new experiences, I think you'll enjoy this food. It's the spices and the way they use them . . . just amazing."

"What shut you down to new experiences?"

"What do you mean?"

"Why aren't you dating?"

"For any number of reasons, no time, no prospects . . . LA is an interesting place to be single."

"We can definitely agree on that. If you're looking for a serious relationship, LA can be a trip! I'm a native and can tell you that firsthand. Kids may have never visited Hollywood, but that whole flash/baller/gangster mentality definitely infiltrated most areas in this city. Women are looking for the man who has it all—money, status, looks, house, car, everything—even if they don't possess these qualities. These days, men are pretty much looking for that, too. What happened to just looking for someone compatible, a person you could talk to, dream with, plan a future, like my parents did? Those days are gone, replaced by a whole hell of a lot of single people looking for love."

He watched as a myriad of emotions played across her face.

"But I have a feeling that's not your story. A woman who looks like you, with the background to match, could get just about any man she wants. So are you one of those independent, don't-need-a-man, never-get-married types?"

Cynthia took a sip of her drink. "I'm very open to having someone in my life and was in a relationship when I moved here two years ago to work for H.E.L.P. The position was a great opportunity for career growth, and one hard to refuse. It is a great addition to my résumé. We stuck it out for about nine months before admitting that neither of us was cut out for the long-distance relationship scenario. The breakup was mutual and we're still friendly, a better ending than some."

"And since then?"

"I've dated, but only one turned fairly serious. We were compatible, and both wanted the same things . . ."

Byron leaned back. "But . . ."

"I don't know. There was just something about the situation that didn't feel comfortable to me, like there was a part of his life kept separate from our life, and things about him I didn't know. Rumor has it that there was a long-time girlfriend somewhere but . . . I never knew for sure."

"What about your son's father?"

"There's a story there, too." Cynthia eyed him for a second, as if trying to figure him out. "How is it that we always end up talking about me?"

"Probably comes from my years on the job," Byron said with another of those delicious smiles. "Sitting in that seat day in, day out, people tell me all sorts of stories. Sometimes, more than I want to know. They talk. I listen. Plus, I'm curious. I like to know about people."

"Well, I want to know about you."

"I'm an open book, so that's no problem. I've got women coming at me all day long, could have been some of everybody's husband right now." When she huffed, he hurriedly added, "I'm not saying that to be arrogant. I'm just keeping it real. Women are lonely, looking for love, attention, protection, security, fathers . . . and some are willing to do just about anything you ask to make that happen. I got caught up in that madness once and lost a lot. Not more than I gained, though, which is my daughter. So instead of multitasking several different women, I have a friend with benefits."

"You actually shared that without embarrassment or guilt." Cynthia couldn't believe what he'd said.

"Why would I be either?" Byron couldn't understand the problem.

"Does she know that's her status?"

"Absolutely, otherwise it wouldn't work. She and I used to work together, and became good friends. One time when we were both in between relationships . . . we added benefits. Lately, there hasn't been anything physical going on. I think both of us are ready for something more meaningful."

From the way he looked at her, Cynthia was definitely that.

The meal arrived and the topic shifted to the distinctive spices that made the food so tasty. Byron learned more of Cynthia's journey from Minneapolis to LA by way of Chicago and a couple other places. Cynthia was impressed with Byron's knowledge of LA. Still, a part of her mind stayed on the comments he made before their food arrived, about being ready for a more meaningful relationship. Her, too.

Cynthia was only able to eat half of her food. When Byron pushed back his plate, it was almost clean.

"You'll have to thank your friend who recommended this place. Can't believe it, but I really enjoyed a meal without meat."

Cynthia nodded toward his plate. "I can tell."

The waitress removed their plates and laid down a dessert menu. "Any recommendations for dessert?"

Cynthia set down her menu. "No, and for me it doesn't matter."

"Are you doing that bird act again? You didn't eat dessert last time either."

"No bird act this time. I don't care much for sweets."

"I probably should pass as well." Byron patted

his stomach. "Watching my figure and all, you know how that goes."

After a bit of wrangling over who would pay for dinner, Cynthia pocketed the receipt and met Byron outside.

"Where are you parked?"

"Just down the street."

She began walking toward her car. He fell in step beside her, switching their positions so that she was on the inside, away from the street. Once again, conversation stilled, as unspoken thoughts consumed their attention.

Her car was parked close by. "You drive a nice car," he said, as he opened her door. "I meant to ask you last time how you liked it."

"This is the type of car both my father and brother drive. They suggested it. I bought it." She shrugged. "Haven't much thought about it more than that."

Byron heard her, and was actually interested in what she was saying. But her lips—plump, slightly parted, and bearing traces of dark red lipstick—were making it hard for him to concentrate on mere words.

"I enjoy you," he whispered, as his head lowered to align with hers. "Thanks for your company."

Their lips met, and it felt like clouds bumping into each other in a rainbow sky. His tongue slipped into her parted lips, even as he took a step closer, pinning her between his body and the side of the car he'd just admired. Their bodies touched. Somewhere in Cynthia's mind there was a caution sign blinking. But she couldn't slow down. His touch was more like a promise, an introduction, an invitation of what might be in store.

He felt himself harden and put space between them. In his mind, he ended the kiss. But his tongue had other plans. It obviously wanted to make acquaintance with her tongue, then stick around for a slow and thorough get-to-know. Her tongue must have had a similar goal the way it swirled against his, tentative at first and then, as he pulled back to hide his excitement, with more confidence, boldly making sure his tongue knew that hers was exactly where it wanted to be.

Everything about her turned him on: soft hair, fragrant skin, the way she fit him perfectly. If they got together, the lovemaking would have to go nonstop, for at least a week, before he'd have enough. His desire for her was so strong it was scary. If this kiss lasted too much longer, his burgeoning manhood would tap Cynthia's thigh and deliver this news.

Reluctantly, he lifted his head and ended the kiss. "I'm sorry about that. Should have asked first."

"I enjoyed it."

Their faces were mere inches apart; lips so close that one slight move and they'd reconnect.

"Would you like another one?"

"I would, but—"

"I'll get that."

Cynthia had turned toward her car and made

a move for the door handle. Byron opened it for her. "I probably shouldn't."

Byron's eyes quickly swept over her and landed on two tell-tale protrusions from the front of her top. "You're probably right." She stepped into the car. He held the door. "What I just tasted was delicious, like I got dessert after all. But it only served to whet my appetite. Is there any chance I can . . . get another helping?"

Cynthia was glad to see that the moment had affected him as it had her. "Right now, there's a very good chance."

"So who follows whom?"

"Oh, no, it can't be tonight. I promised the sitter I'd be home at a certain time. And it won't be at my house. I don't bring dates around my son."

"What about tomorrow? Tyra is spending the weekend with her mother."

"Let me think about it, give myself time to come to my senses."

Byron leaned in for a last quick kiss. "Drive safely. Shoot me a text so I'll know you made it home."

He closed the door. She started her car and with a quick wave pulled away from the curb and into the busy Friday night traffic on Sunset Boulevard. Byron walked to his car and soon merged into traffic without a particular destination in mind. The only thing he knew was that it wouldn't be home. With his daughter away and his body revved up, he needed a distraction. After mentally running through the family and friends list, and what he knew of their weekend plans, he decided to call his brother, Nelson, who'd soon be off from his job at LAX.

As Byron and Cynthia headed in different directions, their thoughts were the same. Both were questioning the rightness of their decision and both could not wait for tomorrow night.

12

"Mom, why do I have to go over to Bobby's house?"

Cynthia sighed inwardly as she placed cinnamon raisin bagels into the toaster. Even before she'd announced the plan, she knew an inquisition would follow. It was a shame that her schedule was so routine and going out on a Saturday night was so rare it was a cause for twenty questions.

"Do you not want to go, Jayden? I thought you and Bobby were good friends."

"We are, but . . ."

"But what?"

"I don't know. It's just different, that's all."

"These are almost ready, Jay. Get the butter and jelly out of the refrigerator and put it on the table."

Cynthia wouldn't pass herself off as a cook for any reason and was almost shamed by what a huge role dining out played in what Jayden ate. Since she passed up fast-food drive-through opportunities in favor of healthier eat-in choices, a car note could be paid with her monthly restaurant bill.

But on Saturday mornings, she pulled out her limited breakfast recipe repertoire and made breakfast for her son. So after pouring them both a glass of apple juice, she divided the egg, turkey sausage, and cheese omelet that had been kept warm in the oven, placed it and a scoop of fresh fruit mix onto their plates, and joined him at the dining room table.

Jayden clumsily added a generous amount of grape jelly to the butter he'd already spread on his bagel and took a large bite. "Mom," he began around the mouthful of food.

"No, we do not talk with our mouths full of food. How many times do I have to remind you of that?"

Jayden kicked his legs and bounced around as he finished the bite, softly humming some unknown melody.

Cynthia began eating, deciding to chill out on the etiquette tips, and refrained from demanding he not only chew with his mouth closed but be still as well. When her brother, Jeff, was Jayden's age, he did the very same thing. When she was Jayden's age, her mother did the same thing to her—critique and instruct every gesture and movement. She'd hated it and even now was self-conscious as a result. She watched as he reached for a grape with his fingers, and remembered her aversion to Byron licking his in public. *We are not in public, baby. Enjoy your food.*

The last of the bite was probably still traveling

down his throat when Jayden began speaking. "Why am I going over to Bobby's?"

"Because I'm meeting a friend for dinner."

"You just did that last night."

"That is correct."

"And you're going to do the same thing again? Sounds boring."

"For you, it probably would be."

"If you're just going out to eat, then why can't Tanishia just come over again? She's fun. We play video games and sometimes she beats me, even though she's a girl!"

Cynthia frowned. "What makes you think being a girl has anything to do with winning and losing?"

"Come on, Mom. You guys are weak."

"Oh, really, according to whom?"

Jayden shrugged. "Everybody."

"While sometimes physically stronger, women are just as capable as men in getting jobs done. Don't I do a good job taking care of you?"

"Yeah." He offered a slight smile and speared another chunk of omelet.

But she'd seen it. The look of hurt that flashed in his eyes before pulling out a grin to cover it. When he first started school, the question came often. "Why doesn't my dad live in the house?" These days, he rarely mentioned it. But clearly the pain was there.

"Are you thinking about your dad?"

"I try not to. He obviously doesn't think about me."

"You don't know that."

"Uh-huh. 'Cause if he did, he'd come see me. I have my own cell phone and he doesn't even call."

There was no pretty answer to this ugly truth and no discussing the equally regretful reason why Jayden had never met his father. On the other hand, Cynthia's world revolved around this little boy. Even single, raising him was a joy. But she'd give anything to go back in time and change the sperm donor. Amazing how one short month could so irrevocably change one's life and affect many others. Her parents, brother, godmother, and one of her mother's good friends had all felt scandalized when she announced her pregnancy. When the identity of the father was revealed, leaving no doubt that marriage was off the table, her cloak of heady accomplishments was replaced by a tattered shawl of shame. Mortified, and banished to upstate New York to have her child in secret, she'd danced with the idea of ending it all. The only reason she didn't was sitting at the table, picking up pieces of fruit with his fingers.

"While I'm clearing the table and cleaning things up, why don't you call your uncle Jeff? I forgot to pass on that he'd asked about you. It might have something to do with just the two of you hanging out . . ."

The light she so loved returned to his eyes. "Yes! I'll go get my phone!"

"Don't run up the stairs!"

Smiling, Cynthia sent Jeff a text to give him a heads-up on this little white lie. *My brother is great, but Jay needs a male role model who lives close by.* When Byron's face instantly appeared in her mind, she was not as much surprised as she was doubtful if that could ever happen.

Thanks to running errands, doing laundry, and a spontaneous movie date with her son, the day passed quickly. While dropping him off for his play date, Byron had called with a plan for their evening, the beginning of which he said was a surprise. That's why instead of meeting him at the venue, she was now on her way to his house so they could ride together. "Once I've got you trapped in my car," he said after she'd agreed to the arrangement, "we'll no longer be going on a dinner, baby. We'll be on a date."

He's silly. And so was the smile on her face if she'd looked in the mirror. The thought of being with him made her happy and scared, too. *Why can't somebody like him be in the body of a man that my parents would like and approve?* "Don't get crazy, Cyn," she warned herself. *A week or two, maybe a month at the most, and this secret tryst to scratch your itch will be behind you.*

13

"What a wonderful idea, Byron. This was awesome."

"You enjoyed the music?"

"The music, the food, the ambiance . . . everything."

"You left out one of the most important components of what made it special."

"What?"

"The man who was sitting beside you, baby, the *company*."

She gave him a look. "Yes, the company, too." She looked around at the throng of people chatting and enjoying the perfect California night as they strolled from the venue. "I can't believe this is my first time at the Hollywood Bowl. The sound is amazing. I've been missing out."

"That exceptional sound is because Janelle Monáe was performing, not to mention Earth, Wind & Fire. They could play in a barn and sound like that."

"That's probably true. Very smart how convenient they make it to dine there, too. Now I know why you were quizzing me on meal choices earlier, so that our dinner could be preordered. Nice touch."

"Well, you know . . ." Byron began an exaggerated pimp strut.

"Oh, no. Please stop." Cynthia's face warmed in embarrassment, but she couldn't help laughing at his funny ways. The guys she'd dated had all been so concerned with decorum and perception. She couldn't imagine one of them acting silly behind closed doors, let alone on a public street.

"To continue the positive impression you're forming about me—"

"And here I thought we might get through the evening without assumptions."

Byron stopped. "Are you not impressed?"

"If I weren't, that's not information I'd share with you. That would sound ungrateful, and be impolite."

They reached a stoplight. A couple stood beside them as all waited for the walk signal. Byron tapped the man on his shoulder. Both the man and his petite brunette companion turned Byron's way.

"I'm sorry to bother you, sir, but could I ask your lady a question? I need a second opinion, preferably from a woman."

Looking at the woman, he said, "That's up to my wife, not me!"

"You can ask, doesn't mean you'll get an answer." The woman, who looked around the

same age as Byron's mom, also seemed the type
to say exactly what she meant.

He placed an arm across Cynthia's shoulders.
"Take a look at this lovely woman here. Look at
her face. Do you think she's impressed with me?"

Said face was being partially hidden by a hand.
"I can't believe this," she mumbled.

"Well, let me see you, honey."

Cynthia looked up. "We're sorry to bother you."

"No bother at all. Oh, my, yes." The lady looked
from Cynthia to Byron and back again. "She's
very impressed." Wink. "And with good reason."

"Thank you, ma'am."

The light changed and once across the street
the stranger couple waved as they turned right
while Byron and Cynthia kept straight.

"You are truly mental, one of a kind."

"What?"

"Stopping complete strangers and asking
advice, hello! Is there anything that you
wouldn't do?"

"Not much."

They continued conversing, easily shifting
from one topic to another. They arrived at the
car and got in. As Byron reached to start it up,
Cynthia touched his arm. "The concert was your
surprise for me. Now, I have one for you."

"What's that?"

"A reservation at the Luxe, on Sunset Boulevard."

"A hotel?"

"Uh-huh."

"Why'd you do that? I told you Tyra would be
gone for the weekend."

"I know but . . . I've been wanting to stay there for a while. This gave me the perfect opportunity."

Byron eyed her for a second or two and shrugged as he started the car and merged into traffic. "I guess it's fine if you want to spend your money to sleep in a bed when you could do the same thing for free. Where on Sunset?"

Cynthia gave him the address. He turned on the car stereo. Neo soul music replaced the sounds of silence. Byron wondered about the real reason she didn't want to stay at his house and Cynthia hoped he wouldn't guess. Halfway to the hotel, Byron reached over and grasped Cynthia's hand. She looked at him and smiled. It appeared they'd both decided to let it be what it was, relax and enjoy the moment. It was the first time they'd ridden together, the first time he'd reached over to hold her hand. Yet for both of them it felt like a move that had been made endless times, the most natural thing in the world.

They reached the hotel, left the car with the valet, and went inside. Cynthia walked confidently toward the front desk as if she belonged there. Byron followed at a slightly slower pace, checking out the surroundings. The understated, soothing shades of tan, brown, and ivory beneath subtle lighting blended effortlessly, creating an ambiance that was simple yet elegant.

This damn sure ain't Motel 6 or Super 8.

Not that Byron had stayed at either of these motels lately. In fact, as he joined Cynthia at the counter, he was trying to remember the last time he rented a room, or taken a vacation for that matter.

"Here are your room keys, Ms. Hall. Enjoy your stay at the Luxe."

"We will, thank you."

She turned toward the elevator, Byron at her side. "For someone who hasn't been here, you seem to know your way around."

"Why do you say that?"

"You headed straight for these elevators, didn't look around at all."

Cynthia mentally chastised herself for the slipup. Byron was super observant. She'd have to be careful or be forced to admit that one look at the dirty socks on the floor and food-stained dishes on the coffee table of his messy living room had made her flinch at what she assumed was the state of the sheets on his bed. While not a walking ad for OCD, Cynthia came close enough for jazz.

They reached the room, where Byron continued to admire the swanky décor. "Check this out . . . sitting area, workspace, four-poster bed . . ." He walked to the window.

"They must have given me a complimentary upgrade. I didn't reserve a suite."

"This room is sweet all right, so I thank whoever hooked us up." He turned from the window and walked to where Cynthia sat on the bed, removing her heels. "And thank you." He took her hand and kissed it. "You didn't have to do it, and I'm definitely not used to anything this fancy. But it's nice."

She kissed him on the lips. "You're welcome."

"So . . . are we officially on a date?"

"Ha! Yes, Byron." He smiled big. "We're not dating! But this is a date."

"That's good enough for now." He hugged her, and in doing so noticed a mini-fridge. "They've got a mini-fridge in here. I should have stopped and got some wine for us."

"There's probably some already in there."

Byron went over to investigate. "What's anybody going to do with these little bottles?" He held one up, a dubious expression on his face.

Cynthia laughed. "When you see the price of it, you'll really frown."

"What, the stuff in here doesn't come with the price of the room?"

"Please, you know better than that."

Byron picked up the refreshment menu. He whistled. "Dang!" Then he pulled out a second bottle and reached over for the two wineglasses on the table above the fridge. "Who cares about money? It's time to live large!" Raising a brow, he quickly added, "You are paying for this, right?"

Cynthia burst out laughing, his desired response.

He opened the bottles and poured their drinks. "Okay, since this is a special night, we need to toast. What should it be to?"

Cynthia thought for a moment. "I don't know. You go first."

"Shoot, that's easy for me and I'm going to keep it real." He held up his glass. "Here's to me getting some of that good stuff!" Her mouth dropped open. "Hey, it's been a minute for a brother. It's not just the state of California that's been in a drought. It's some of its citizens, too, you feel me? Because I've been needing rain for a while . . ."

Having longed for dictation, Cynthia couldn't help but agree. "Officials have called it a state of emergency."

". . . bring a thunderstorm, hell, a damn tsunami up in this muh-fuh!"

"Muffuh? What's that?"

"Really? You don't know?" She shook her head. "I guess not, the way you mispronounced it. Muh. Fuh." Her confused expression didn't change. "It's a polite way to say Em Eff. Dang, girl, you need to hang with me, ride my bus, and spend some time in the hood!"

They sipped their wine. "Maybe I'll do that."

"Good." He stood, set his glass on the night-stand, and began unbuttoning his shirt. "Now, can I spend a little time where I want to?"

"Where's that?"

"I'll show you. But you can't go with me until you take off your clothes. All of them," he said over his shoulder, walking to the bathroom in nothing but his boxers. "When I come back in here . . . I want you in the bed buck naked."

14

Muhfuh? No. Muh. Fuh. Cynthia stood, shaking her head as she walked to the window. *He's so different from any of the other guys I've dated. From everyone around me really . . . except Lisa. Dynah would probably come around once she got to know him. But Gayle?* Cynthia giggled at the very thought of those two in the same room. Undoubtedly, Gayle would act uppity and Byron would probably call her on it using his colorfully creative language. The more she imagined the encounter, the greater was her desire to see it played out.

"What are you doing?"

She quickly turned around. Byron stood before her in all his naked glory, hands on hips, legs spread, face fixed in a scowl. She gave his body a millisecond perusal. "Oh."

"Oh? That's all you've got to say?"

"You scared me and I . . ." Another quick look before she averted her gaze and headed toward the bathroom.

Byron caught her arm as she passed him. "What's wrong?"

"Nothing. I just need to use the restroom."

"You're lying. And since we're planning to get all personal in here tonight, the least we can do is be truthful with each other."

"It's nothing." When she tried jerking her arm away, she found out Byron's grip was tighter than it felt. "Byron, let go of my arm."

His look told her that he wasn't happy, but he released her anyway.

Cynthia closed the bathroom door behind her and sat on the toilet. She made eighty thousand dollars a year. Right now she'd pay half that to have brought in her cell phone to make a call.

It's thick but so . . . short!

What she'd seen was totally not what she'd expected. One of the reasons she'd decided to sleep with a non-DHOP (but would never admit to anyone other than herself) is because of what Lisa had told her about "men from the hood." According to her, they all had ten-inch dicks, tongues like a serpent, and were freakier than a one-legged dog riding a bicycle at the circus! Since becoming sexually active, only one of the four men with whom she'd been intimate had come close to Lisa's description, Jayden's father. It's part of the reason that to get over him, she had to leave the state. Her college sweetheart and first love had been okay, the one after that was slightly above mediocre (but he was a DHOP, a doctoral graduate at twenty-six, and her parents adored him), and her most recent guy who couldn't handle the distance could rarely go the distance. Premature ejaculation was the worst. Thank God for oral or an orgasm would never have been achieved. But not only was he a DHOP who fit into her circle perfectly, his parents were noted members of Tennessee's Black Bourgeois (or "bur-ghees" as Lisa called them), and he was a member of the coveted Sigma Pi Phi. Her mother was furious when they'd split. There had been a horrible fight about it, one of many this mother/daughter duo had endured. Cynthia had come precariously close to being disrespectful and telling her mother to go eff him herself, and had run out of the room to prevent it from happening.

That day on the bus, when she locked eyes with Byron and her body reacted, she attributed part of the reason to what she imagined existed between his big legs. When she turned and found him naked, she'd expected to see a chocolate ruler swinging like a pendulum, or a mushroom-tipped python that could almost be thrown over his shoulder. Instead, she gets a weenie?

"Great," she muttered, as she sneered at herself in the mirror. *Well, let's go girl. You can't hide in here forever.* So she took a deep breath, practiced a smile, and left her sanctuary.

"There you are." A totally naked Byron watched a still fully dressed, somewhat wary-looking Cynthia come out of the bathroom. He'd set a mood by turning off all but a light in the corner of the room, turning its beam toward the wall, creating an amber glow. The silky sounds of Trey Songz added to the atmosphere. *Yeah, here comes my cake right now. And I'm about to have a slice.*

Cynthia sat on the bed. "Sorry that I took so long."

"No worries. We've got all night." Her smile was tentative. He placed a hand on her arm, slowly, lightly moving his fingers up and down. For several seconds he lay there, perched up on pillows, watching the shadow of his fingers play across her velvety skin. His eyes went from her arm to her breasts, then her neck to her mouth, until finally their eyes connected. "Look, I only want to do what you want to do. If you've changed your mind and want to just talk, we can do that. If you want to lay here and cuddle, that's cool, too. If you want to go home even, or want me to leave . . . I'll understand and won't be mad."

"This is rather new for me."

"What, sex?" Byron pulled back his hand, entwined his fingers behind his head. "With an eight-year-old son, you're not a virgin. Not unless he's adopted or came by way of the Immaculate Conception."

"I'm not a virgin." Cynthia placed her hand on his arm, felt the fine hair that wasn't so noticeable against his copper-toned skin. "But this is . . . you're . . . different than the men I've dated."

"How so?"

"People see me and often imagine a confident, worldly, educated woman. I am those things, but at the same time, my life has been sheltered. My parents, especially my mom, are very society conscious, and very concerned with how others perceive her and her domain, which growing up, and somewhat even now, includes her children. There weren't many people of color where I lived and those who were there, at least the ones I encountered pretty much until I went to college, were like me: upper middle class, cultured, educated—not to say that you're not!" Her hand left his arm and went to her mouth as she realized her faux pas.

"Baby, I'm a hood rat, and not at all ashamed of where I come from." He reached for her hand. "Come here. I'm lonely in this big, soft bed all by myself. What kind of mattress is this anyway? I thought every bed was the same, but this muh-fuh makes me feel like I'm floating on a cloud!"

Cynthia climbed on the bed. "It's probably a pillow top." She tucked her legs beneath her and leaned into Byron's waiting embrace.

He felt her body, rigid, and simply held her, breathing evenly and, for a few seconds, allowing Trey to serenade them both. She relaxed. A little. "You were saying?"

"Who knows. I'm just rambling . . ."

"No, you're not. You were telling me about where and how you grew up. I find it interesting, and want to know these things."

"The bottom line is the men I've dated have been reserved, some with a hint or more of arrogance." She turned to him. "You just say what's on your mind, and act crazy in public without caring who sees you, and I don't know . . . seem to not live by any rules."

"I have rules." Once again he stroked her arm, circular movements this time, and watched as a line of goose bumps trailed his thick middle finger. She relaxed a little more. "But only the ones that either myself or my parents created. Oh, and the law. I have a problem with tight, locked spaces, so I try and follow those, too."

"Obviously the rules set down by your mom and mine were very different."

He placed his face in the crook of her neck and nuzzled. "Probably."

"I like it, though, that you're free to . . . just be yourself."

He inhaled her scent, moved a little closer, and placed his free hand on her leg, introducing his fingers to her thigh. "If you're not being yourself, who are you?"

A long, quiet pause and then, "The daughter my mother envisioned."

At this comment Byron sat up and looked at her, looked past the flawless skin, long eyelashes, perfectly puckered lips, and nice, naturally long hair. He looked into her eyes and saw a wounded soul, struggling to find itself. He knew the look, had seen it in the eyes of teen mothers getting on the bus with two, three kids, a group of loud, high, rowdy boys with fake swagger.

He relaxed against the pillows, holding her close. "Tell you what. Tonight, you can be yourself. If you don't know who that is, then just be. And the real you will show up."

She turned her body toward him, cuddled deeper into his embrace. Lifting her face up to see his eyes, she whispered, "Thank you."

He lowered his head. "You're welcome."

The kiss began as a tender touch, a wispy brush of cushiony softness moving back and forth over hers, lightly, languidly, as though they had all the time in the world. His fingers moved up her arm, across her collarbone, along her cheek and neck, and down to the outline of the nipple protruding against her blouse. He cupped her breast and circled it with his thumb. She moved her body forward, body language that said it was all right to touch it. He knew that. But not yet. He was helping her be herself.

Her breathing increased and so did the pressure of her lips on his. She relaxed fully against his body, pressed her breasts against his chest, her flat stomach against his dough-boy middle. He moaned, pressed his tongue inside her mouth. His feathery fingers danced across her butt. It wasn't the big, bubble booties he was used to and preferred, but it was hers. His fingers slid under the silky fabric of her blouse to her spine and into her hair where he gently massaged her scalp. And deepened the kiss, slowly circled her tongue with his, pressing her closer and shifting his body to make them both more comfortable. He put his whole head into the kiss, circling it as he circled his tongue. The rest of his body joined in, his hips slowly grinding against the sheet that touched her pants that hid the body he longed for. But not yet.

Trailing kisses across her cheek, he moved to her ear, flicked his tongue against the lobe, nibbled down her neck, shifted his tantalizing tease from her right breast to the left one. Her body strained against him, nipples begged to get some of what the areola was feeling. He kissed and licked the exposed flesh down to the first button of her blouse, and under her chin and back to her mouth. Softness was replaced by hard, fervent desire, his tongue demanding entry, their lips smashed together. The kiss lasted for seconds. It lasted forever. It blocked out everything else in the room and took all the air.

Gasp!

Cynthia sat up. Her breathing was labored, her eyes half-mast.

Byron stopped all movement, immediately concerned. "Are you all right?"

"No."

"What's the matter?"

"I have on too many clothes." As she reached for the top button on her blouse, a sexy smile slid into place.

15

He'd dated a skinny woman here and there, but for the most part Byron liked his women thick and juicy. The woman on top of him was quickly changing this preference. Cynthia removed her pink lacy bra to reveal pert, B-cup charlies with berry-dusted nips. He imagined taking one whole into his mouth, swirling his lips around the nipple, and holding her breast captive with the strength of his lips.

He did that now. Leaned forward, teeth bared, and nipped the protrusion begging attention, holding it between his teeth as he flicked it once, twice, a third time with his tongue. She hissed, gasped, tossed her hair from this simple pleasure. Byron licked a path to the other breast, all the while making light, stroking moves with the fingers wrapped around her small, taut waist. His soldier began to salute. After not having sex for the past two months and being so turned on by who sat astride his thighs, he knew tonight would call for the ultimate discipline. Because his plan, his goal was simple—to leave this girl turned out and thoroughly whipped.

"Get up for a minute, baby." Though whispered, it was clearly a command.

Cynthia pulled her leg from the other side of him and prepared to get out of the bed.

Byron stopped her. "Where do you think you're going?"

"I'm just going to take off my—"

"No, I am. Lay down."

She did, her eyes never leaving his as she did so. He leaned over, caught the zipper clasp of her slacks between his teeth and pulled, revealing bare skin and a pink thong that matched the bra removed moments ago. Gently pulling aside the material, his head dipped once more, and his tongue traveled across the band of her thong, lightly, almost reverently over and again, until finally it stiffened and slid just inside the elastic to meet skin as smooth and bare as a baby. *No hair. Damn, I'm going to tear this up.*

After a few more excruciating moments with his tongue traveling to the top of her lips, gently nudging but going no farther, he gripped the waistband of her slacks and pulled down. Cynthia raised her body off the bed, anxious for his tongue to be back on her skin, his average-size penis to be inside her.

She was the only one in a hurry. Once again Byron lowered his head to her pelvic area, placed kisses across her stomach and along the elastic of the thong she wanted to rip away from her body and fling across the room. Who knew a mere wisp of material could prove such a distraction? Her hips gyrated, body language for "enough fore-play, let's get to it!" Instead of getting with the program, Byron proved he was directing the show. He gripped her hips to still them and used his thumbs to communicate what would happen next. Placing them near her inner thighs, he pulled slightly. She got the message and spread her legs.

Very good.

He shifted until his tongue was aligned with her treasure and then swabbed the crease of these lips through the flimsy thong. The friction of his tongue and the material was maddening, increasing Cynthia's desire to the point of no control. He sensed this, and after ever . . . so . . . slowly pulling the thong down her long legs and off of her foot, he spread her legs wider, exposed her quivering pearl, placed his mouth over her whole heat, and devoured the flower. His tongue went everywhere, inside places she never dreamed, and it wasn't long before her body began shaking as never before. Unintelligible noises slipped from her mouth as an orgasm rolled like a wave through her body, as Byron held on for every drop of the ride.

Before she had a moment, a second it seemed, to contemplate what kind of hurricane just swept through the room, he was inside her. He raised her legs in a way that allowed him to go—*ah! Oh, my!* Cynthia couldn't believe what she was feeling. Barely over one orgasm and felt another one coming? Byron had discovered a part of her body that had obviously gone untouched before. He twirled his hips in a unique, jerky fashion and every time he did, the tip of his penis—the short one she'd discounted, weenie she'd called it—connected with whatever piece of anatomy that made women come.

"Oh . . . oh . . . ooh!" she panted, her eyes wide with amazement that she was having another orgasm. When they focused, it was to discover Byron's hooded orbs boring into her, a knowing look on his face.

"Uh-huh." He twirled and pumped and grinded, and thrust, the right side of his lips drawing into a snarl. "Wasn't expecting this, were you?"

Cynthia opened her mouth but at the time seemed virtually ignorant of the English language.

He turned them over until she was on her knees and he was behind her. Quickly reentering her void, he somehow pumped upward, hitting her "come button" over and again.

Cynthia shrieked. Byron laughed.

"It's not what you've got, baby. It's how you use this muh-fuh."

The words formed a rhyme, delivered to the beat of his thrusts. He spent a good part of the night making sure that Cynthia got the message.

16

She was startled awake by the sound of her son's ringtone. Cynthia sat up while trying to free herself from the heavy thigh thrown over her hips and the sheet that entangled her foot. Sliding her leg from under Byron's was easy enough, but because his heavy weight held the sheet taut around her ankle, it wouldn't untangle. In trying to free her left foot or the sheet, her right foot slammed into a deeply sleeping Byron's shin.

"Good morning to you, too," he mumbled, still on his stomach.

"Move your leg, Byron! I'm trying to answer my phone!"

He moved. She raced to the purse that was across the room, retrieving the phone just as it stopped ringing. "Darn it!" Clearing the missed call, she noticed the time. "Oh my goodness. It's nine o'clock?"

"Is that a problem?" Byron yawned and scratched, still trying to wake up as he sat against the headboard.

Clearly the two of them woke up in different gears.

"Yes, it's a problem. That was my son."

"It's not like you can't call him—"

"Shh! It's ringing." Walking to the closet, she retrieved a guest robe and slid it on. "Good morning, sweetheart." Byron got out of bed. "Yes, I know. The phone was in my purse."

Cynthia eyed him wearily as if any minute he was going to bellow a greeting and reveal she was not alone. "I'm not at home right now. How are you? Did you and Bobby have fun last night?"

Once Byron had closed the bedroom door, Cynthia relaxed. She walked over to the room's sitting area and perched on an armrest. "Oh, really? Well, let me talk to her."

In her calmed state, images from the past eight hours filled her mind. The memories alone made her hot and bothered, sure that how well she'd been sexed was stamped on her forehead. *Diamonds aren't the only good things that can come in small packages . . . who knew?*

"Hey, girl, how are you? Did you invite Jay to go with you guys, or did he invite himself?" She spotted where her thong had landed after being flung to the floor, and walked over to retrieve it. "But I only packed enough for one night." She nodded her silent agreement that their boys were the same size. "Well, thank you for including him. He'll have a wonderful time."

Byron walked out of the bathroom and hugged her from behind. She turned to face him with eyes conveying both excitement and a warning. "I only gave him twenty dollars. When you guys

get back, let me know what I owe you." He hugged
her. She smelled clean skin and toothpaste, evi-
dence of a quick wash-up.

*But no shower? Hmm . . . he must have something
besides checking out in mind.*

"That will be great. You can call if you'd like,
but I'll be at home. Okay, thanks again. Bye."

He watched her end the call. "May I speak
now?"

She hugged him. "Yes, but I shouldn't con-
verse in person with anyone until I brush my
teeth. Be right back."

He tightened his embrace. "Not so quick, Ms.
Hall. Let me at least get a good squeeze or two in
before you run away." He ran his hands along her
waist to her butt, pressing her against his quickly
hardening tool. "Just so you know it's getting ready
for you," he whispered, before letting her go.

All kinds of sultry comebacks bounced around
in her head, quips that Lisa would have already
spouted. But this blatant sexuality and bold,
tawdry proclamations were new for her. So simply
smiling, she turned and walked away.

After a quick shower, Cynthia returned to the
living area in nothing but a towel, and was surprised to see Byron wearing T-shirt and boxers,
reading the room service menu.

"Oh." She stopped, a bit embarrassed.

He looked up. "What?" His eyes took in her
damp hair, bare feet, and the slender body he'd
gotten up close and personal with last night, and
he smiled.

"Nothing, I just thought . . ."

"And you thought correctly, babe. I'm nowhere near done with all that sweet, fresh goodness hidden behind that towel. I wanted to take care of one appetite before I took care of another one. But looking at the prices of breakfast on this menu, I think I'd need a second job. This shit is ridiculous!"

"Don't worry about that. Get what you want." He looked ready to object. She went on before he could. "You showed me such a great time last night—"

"And was the concert good, too?"

"Ha-ha, Mr. Carter. Everything was wonderful. So this morning's breakfast is my treat."

After placing their room service order, Byron took Cynthia's hand and walked them to the sitting area.

"What are you doing?"

He tightened his grip. "Bringing you to sit next to me so we can get to know each other."

"Isn't that what we did last night?"

They sat down, with Byron keeping Cynthia close to his side. "It was a good introduction, there's no doubting that. A lot of men are only interested with the physical aspect of a woman, but you're much more than that sweet pot of honey you let me taste last night. While I intend to give that a good deal of attention, I'm genuinely interested in all of you."

Cynthia took a deep breath.

Byron noticed. "Does that make you uncomfortable?"

"Frankly, yes. There are aspects of my life that

have been buried, hidden, things that have caused me to be . . . reticent about opening up."

"Re-ti-who?"

"I'm sorry."

"No, don't be. I like hearing you talk all Wikipedia and shit. I'm like, damn! Y'all hear that? My woman is intelligent."

He overenunciated each syllable and bobbed his head for extra emphasis. His actions made her laugh, calmed her paranoia, and helped her relax. "What do you want to know?"

"About your son, for starters. You were pretty nervous that you missed his call."

"He worries when he can't reach me."

"Looks like you were pretty worried, too."

"I try not to be overprotective, but I'm all he's got."

"Where's his father?"

"Out of the picture."

Spoken in a tone meant to dissuade more questions along this road. Unless you were from the Carter clan, who didn't run from controversy and treated discomfort like a friend.

"Right, I remember you not wanting to talk about the sperm donor. Your son doesn't see him at all?"

"No." Clearly, he was someone she still didn't want to discuss. Straightened back and clenched lips were the exclamation on this one word: Don't go there.

Byron rolled right through the caution light. "Why not?"

"Because he doesn't! The reason why is nothing I want to talk about."

"Given how upset you get, you probably should." She crossed her arms, silent. Curious to know more, he still shifted gears. "Tell me more about your family. Are you close?"

"We love each other but are not as close as the relationships I see in other families. My dad is on the quiet side, lets my mom rule the roost, which she does with a meticulous hand."

"What does that mean?"

"Meticulous?"

"Yeah, you keep using fifty-dollar language on a five-dollar man. But I don't mind. I can learn some new words and I might be able to teach you a thing or two."

Her expression as she looked at him was hard to read. "It means finicky, critical, sometimes hard to please."

"Well, why didn't you just say that?"

"I didn't know that—"

"Girl, I'm just messing with you." He reached an arm around her neck and began massaging her shoulder. "Trying to get you to chill. You're so uptight."

"Certain topics will do that to me."

"What about you and your brother?"

"Jeff is who I'm closest to, for sure, though even with him there's still distance. Not so much because of either of our personalities, but more so because of the five years between us and the fact that I went off to college before he turned thirteen. We bonded when I had Jayden. He's a great uncle, and my son adores him."

"That's good. A boy needs male role models in his life."

"Just yesterday, I thought that very same thing and am hoping that Jeff's schedule will allow Jayden a short summer visit." Placing her hand on top of Byron's, she rolled her neck to one side and the other. "That feels much better. Thank you."

"You're welcome."

"So tell me about your daughter and how it is that you have full custody." The focus effectively shifted, Cynthia relaxed and pulled her feet beneath her.

"Tanya and her son's father live together, a man I don't particularly care for. When my daughter began feeling uncomfortable around some of the company they were keeping, and Tanya refused to stop associating with that company, I took care of it."

"You were worried your daughter would be abused?"

"I was worried about a lot of things. Tanya is and always has been a party girl. Her and Rick keep it too turned up for my taste, especially with children around. My life is boring. I work. Go home. Hang out with my brothers. Nelson, the middle brother, has a daughter a year younger than Tyra. They're like sisters, and love to play together. It works out." He reached over, gently stroked her chin as he gazed at her with lust-filled eyes. "I'm an open book, baby. I'll tell you anything you want to know. But it'll cost you."

"Oh, really? What?"

A knock at the door announced that room service had arrived.

"As soon as we knock out this breakfast and build up my stamina, I'll be more than happy to show you the price."

17

By the time Byron finished showing her the cost of learning about him, Cynthia wanted to pay him again. Once she'd informed him of her unexpected free Sunday, and the desire to spend another night at the hotel, they'd divided their time between talking, eating, and making all kinds of love. The things this brother did with his mouth was enough to make her forget all about her standards of a degreed, home-owning professional as the only choice for a mate. The melody his fingers played in her music box made concern for what her high-society friends might say a very low priority. The magic spot his slightly curved penis had discovered—which for her was equal in importance to Madame C. J. Walker discovering a straightener for kinky hair and Ford inventing an alternative to horse-powered transportation—gave her the kind of orgasms that produced thoughts of standing up to her formidable mother, something that Cynthia hadn't done a day in her life.

Following a particularly mind-blowing, award-winning performance, Cynthia surprised herself by suggesting she perform oral sex, something she'd previously found undesirable but now felt necessary. "Do you want me to . . . you know . . . return the favor?"

"Hell, yeah!" Byron adjusted pillows behind his head, looking at her with such anticipatory delight and appreciation that it left her emboldened. She kissed him hungrily as he smoothed his hands down her back until they reached and squeezed her cheeks. His purposeful fingering brought her to wanton abandon and sent her on a journey from his mouth to his chest, and farther to the slightly flabby stomach that not long ago would have been a total turnoff. The guttural sounds heard when her tongue touched his tool made her feel powerful. She wanted to treat his body as reverently as he had hers, and wanted to make him feel just as good. Because it was something she'd suggested, something she wanted to do instead of what in other instances had been demanded or expected, she lost herself in the enjoyment of his pleasure, so much so that when his fountain erupted, she imbibed with fervent, if previously unexperienced, delight. By the time Monday morning rolled around and they checked out of the hotel, Byron had gone from being a convenient reliever of sexual tension to someone who'd seeped into her very soul. The thing was, Cynthia didn't know it yet.

Which was probably why as the passing scenery went from uber-chic to urban blight and stages in between, a heavy dose of reality punctured the bubble that the past forty-eight hours of bliss had created. There was no plausible way Cynthia could see any type of lasting relationship happening between her and Byron. Simultaneously, however, she could not imagine any possible way of living without the sheer happiness she felt when around him.

"You okay?"

They'd reached Byron's block before she realized it, and she'd been quiet most of the way. "I couldn't be better." She placed a hand on his arm as he pulled into his driveway and shut off the engine. "Thank you for a wonderful weekend."

"It doesn't have to be over yet, you know. You're welcome to come inside."

"No, I have some things to do before Jayden returns home."

"All right, then."

After retrieving her bag from the back of his SUV, he walked her to her car and waited until she'd gotten inside and started it up. "Holler at me later," he said, before slowly walking backward up the sidewalk to his door. He stopped and didn't go inside until she pulled away.

She'd only gotten a few houses away before remembering that she hadn't set her GPS. Pulling over, she quickly tapped the button for her preset address, then reached into her purse to get her sunglasses.

Shoot, they're in my overnight bag.

She popped the trunk, jumped out of the car, and quickly retrieved the designer case from the bag's side pocket.

"Can I go with you?"

The close proximity of this strange male voice so startled Cynthia that she bumped her head against the trunk before whirling around to face the man who'd crept up on her without making a sound.

"Damn, baby, I didn't mean to make you hit your head." The man, dressed in jeans, T-shirt, backward ball cap, and dark glasses, took a step toward her and reached out his hand to touch the scratch on her forehead. "Let me help you feel better."

"Get away from me." What was intended to sound authoritative came out in a breathy tremor as she tried to push past him.

He blocked her progress. "I'm not going to hurt you, baby. Just trying to talk to you. Why are you acting all scared, like I'm getting ready to carjack you or something?" He glanced at the car, then back at her. "Although this is a nice ride."

Again, Cynthia made a move toward her open car door. This time, the man turned and grabbed her arm as she passed.

"Let go of my arm!" She yanked her arm away and raced to get inside the car and lock the door.

"You scratched my arm you stuck-up bit—"

"Don't. Touch. Her. Again."

Cynthia had one foot inside the car but at the sound of that familiar, authoritative voice she removed it, turned, and stood straight. *Byron!*

He ignored her, focused on the stranger who

after seeing that Cynthia was watching once again found his voice. And a gun. *Click.*

Byron's focus went from the man's face to the gun and back again. His expression didn't change.

"Who are you?" he asked Byron in a taunting voice, ending the question in a harshness of language that gave Cynthia new appreciation for Byron's use of muh-fuh.

"The brother who's not going to let you mistreat the woman behind you."

"How are you going to stop me? Or this bullet I'm getting ready to put in your chest."

"I'm not afraid of you or that weapon, son."

"Guess you're not afraid of death either."

"Not trying to get shot, but if I lose my life protecting her, I'll die a noble man. Besides, death is something that can happen anytime. You might shoot me and then get hit by a bus as you try and get away. More than likely it will be one of my coworkers that I nudge on my way out."

The stranger aimed the gun at Byron's head. "Where you from?"

Byron had the nerve to laugh. Cynthia was amazed but too frozen with fear to show it. "You know where I'm from, *Clarence.* And I know where you're from, too. I knew your father before he got locked up. And more than that, I know your grandmother."

The stranger's scowl remained, but the gun slowly lowered. "The bus driver."

"That's right. I've been driving Ms. Davis around for the past ten years. She sacrificed too much in raising you for this to be how you represent her. That's what you're doing, right? Representing?" No answer. "Why don't you represent a proper way to exit by leaving me and my woman alone?"

The stranger glanced at Cynthia, then pointed the gun at Byron as he began walking. "You better be glad my boys aren't with me."

"You're damned lucky my brothers aren't around."

The stranger spit out several expletives and threats as he continued down the street. Once he'd turned the corner, Byron rushed to Cynthia who fell into his arms.

"Oh, my God! I was so frightened."

"I'm sorry, baby." He hugged her tightly, even as he continued to scan the street. "Park the car. Come into the house with me."

Seeing how she was shaking, Byron quickly backed the car to his house and hurried them inside. He embraced her, until the shaking subsided.

She stepped away from him. "He had a gun."

"So did I." She pulled back to look at him. He removed a weapon from under his T-shirt. Her mouth opened, but nothing came out. "A necessity, not a choice. I could have shot that young blood a dozen times while we were talking, but would only have done so if absolutely necessary."

"You would have killed him?"

"No, but I would have trimmed his dreads."

"This isn't funny, Byron. *You* could have been killed."

"Would you rather I had stood back and let him attack you?"

"No, but—"

"No buts, no need to answer. That would never happen. I'm not a violent man. I don't like to fight. I don't go looking for trouble, but won't run from it if it finds me. And I will never stand by while someone hurts you, you got that?"

18

Cynthia's mind hadn't stopped whirling since this morning's incident. Even when Jayden was dropped off by the neighbor, and she'd feigned interest in his excited chatter about their night of camping, thoughts of Byron and his actions consumed her. Before being accosted, the time spent with him had been nothing like she would have imagined. It had been . . . in one word . . . amazing. After he became her real-life, if errant, knight, and following their one-hour heart-to-heart afterward, Ms. Wikipedia couldn't think of one word to adequately describe how she felt about him. Enamored? It was more than that. Love? Not quite. Intrigued? Totally, but not just captivated. With Byron, and even before the morning's events, she not only felt protected but secure and special. She'd dated men with more money, education, and power. But none of them had ever made her feel as Byron did. And how was that? The words to describe this feeling had come quickly. Cherished. Adored. Valued. The type of recognition that had been missing for most of her life. The type of validation she wasn't truly aware she needed until Byron gave it to her.

When the clock chimed seven o'clock, she thought about missing the weekly call with her BFFs. Normally it was held on Saturday, but since the other three had attended a wedding, they'd moved it to tonight. She'd mentioned no conflict when the day and time were changed, so a no-show would only increase their suspicions and with them their questions. As if to underscore her thoughts, the phone rang.

Instead of answering the call, she walked into Jayden's room. As usual, he was playing video games. "I'm going to be in my room for a while. Do you need anything?"

His eyes stayed affixed to the screen as he answered. "No, I'm okay. Why didn't you answer the phone?"

"Because I knew it was my friends and that I'd be on the phone for a while. I wanted to check on you first."

"Are these the friends you were with this weekend?"

"Good try at being nosy, but you know where Gayle, Lisa, and Dynah live."

He paused the game. Obviously this comment had gained his full attention. "You know I was with Bobby. Why can't I know who you were with?"

"Because it's not important, you don't know them, and while children may not always be informed, mothers are required to know the whereabouts of their children."

"That's not fair!"

"Life often isn't; a fact best learned early. I was out with a friend, okay?" She glanced at her watch. "If you want snacks, there are veggie sticks and dip in the fridge." She left the room, her head shaking at the overly curious gene she'd passed on to her son. *I'd rather he'd gotten the one that liked a clean room.*

Once in her room, phone in hand, she again vacillated on whether or not to join the conversation. She wasn't up for the weekly BFF chat, wasn't ready to reveal this new and unexpected development to her friends. He wasn't a DHOP. He wasn't rich. He wasn't a bunch of things she'd thought were important. And she didn't care.

Her cell phone rang again. "Hey, girls," she said once Dynah had added her to the conference call.

"We almost thought you weren't going to make it."

"Why, because I wasn't on the line at exactly seven o'clock?"

"No," Lisa interjected. "Because all weekend, you've been MIA."

Inwardly, Cynthia cringed. *I meant to return her missed call from yesterday.* "Sorry about that, Lisa. I meant to call you back, but . . . Jayden wanted to go to Knotts Berry Farm."

That statement was technically true. He had wanted to go with Bobby and his family, and he did, before they went camping.

"I thought maybe dinner had been so good last weekend that you went back for seconds."

Lisa . . . please shut up.

"That's right. You went out with the bus boy last weekend." Gayle's tone left no doubt that she thought this uncouth. "And didn't say a word about it during last week's call."

"That's because there's not much to tell. Lisa's three-way play-by-play was a lot more interesting."

Dynah was all ears. "We still want to hear it. How did it go?"

"Dinner was fine, the conversation okay, and the night ended early. That's about it."

"Thank goodness for that. What about the work front? Any updates?"

She could have kissed Gayle for the change in subject. "Margo is Tracy's watchdog, snooping around my department and reporting back what she thinks she knows."

"Are you documenting all of this?" Dynah inquired.

"Absolutely."

"Girl, what are you going to do if that heifah gets promoted and becomes your boss?"

"Lisa, the day Margo becomes director is the day I resign."

"And move back to Chicago?" Out of the three, Dynah had been most opposed to her leaving. "Both the NAR and the ABWA meet this week. While I don't encounter many professionals from the mental health field, I'll keep my eyes and ears open for opportunities. In Chicago, of course."

"Of course."

An hour later, during which time Byron had called twice, the call ended. After spending time with Jayden and ordering his dinner from their favorite Italian eatery, Cynthia walked out on her patio to return his call. As her finger hovered over the phone's face to redial, it rang in her hand.

"Yes, Lisa?"

"Yes, Lisa," she mimicked. "Don't act all innocent like you don't know what this call is about."

"I'm not acting."

Lisa laughed. "You'd get away with that if I didn't know you so well."

"Get away with what?"

"And if I hadn't called you not once, but three times this weekend."

"What?"

"Uh-huh. You saw my number, but you didn't check the history, and thought I'd only called once. I called you Friday night, around eight or nine your time, Saturday night, at, like, ten o'clock, and then Sunday morning at two a.m., while driving home after breakfast with a booty call."

Crickets.

"My thoughts exactly, so either spill the secrets or be exposed."

"You fight dirty."

"Don't hate the boxer, hate the gloves." They laughed. "So, what happened?"

"Okay, I'll tell you. But first, you have to swear to me on all you hold dear that you won't share this with Dynah and Gayle."

"Ooh, this must be good because all of us share everything."

"They'll know eventually. But I have my reasons for why that won't be right now."

"Why, other than the fact they'll be totally opposed to the situation, which, since we're all grown, shouldn't be a problem?"

"You'll just have to believe it's in my best interests."

"Okay, I won't tell them."

Cynthia sighed, positioned her chair so she'd see if Jayden approached, and got comfortable. "I'm actually glad to talk to somebody about this because I am just . . . so . . . confused right now."

"About what? Never mind that, start from the beginning."

She did, from the strange attraction she'd felt on the bus to the concert at the Hollywood Bowl. "I kept thinking the physical reaction was due to my drought." Lisa laughed at the use of her lingo. "But the more we talked, the more I started liking him as a person, even as I gave myself a hundred reasons why that was not only crazy but impractical. We could have sex and I'd feel better for a couple days. But then what? You know me. I've never been able to do the casual thing, never viewed sex as just a means to an orgasmic end."

"Don't knock it till you try it, kid, especially with somebody like Big Dick Danny. And speaking of dictation, is his big and have you tried it?"

"Yes, I've tried it and, no, it isn't really that big."

"Oh, I'm so sorry."

"Don't be. It's the best sex I've ever had."

"For real?"

"I can't believe I'm telling you this, but then again, you're about the only person I would." She looked at the patio door. No Jayden. Still her voice dropped to just above a whisper. "So . . . after the concert, we went to a hotel."

"I thought he owned a house."

"He does, but you know how anal I can be."

"Yes, not comfortable unless where you are looks like a magazine ad."

"I'm not that bad. Am I?"

"You are your mother's daughter. Look, you can't help how you grew up. I'm not ashamed of growing up in broke-down Gary, Indiana. You shouldn't feel bad that you're privileged."

"Thanks for that, Lisa. Sometimes I do."

"Well, that's more than I can say for Gayle."

"True! Anyway, we started kissing and fooling around and when it was time for the clothes to come off, I was disappointed. From your stories, I was looking for—"

"Big Dick Danny?"

"Yes, he isn't that. But it's curved, and he did something . . . moved his hips and I came immediately. It was crazy! Then, not even ten minutes later, it happened again. It's always been hard for me to have an orgasm. But his thing is like magic."

"When a man hits that G-spot it does feel pretty magical."

"Is that what happened?"

"Girl, please don't tell me this is the first time that happened. You've already had a baby and are how many years old?"

"Except with Jayden's father, I've rarely had orgasms, and never more than one in a night. I thought it was me."

"Sounds like things are going to get interesting,

because this doesn't sound like someone you're going to give up, at least no time soon. And as close as we are, you're not going to be able to keep this secret forever."

"I know. In hedging the truth earlier, I already feel bad."

"Why, you didn't really go to Knotts Berry Farm?"

"Jayden went with one of his friends while I experienced a different kind of thrill."

Cynthia shared a few more highlights from her and Byron's impromptu yet memorable weekend together. She left out the life-saving dramatic ending that had given Byron Carter an even more special place in her heart, figuring there was only so much a friend—even a BFF—could keep to herself.

19

"How'd it go today with Leah?"

It was Tuesday evening. Cynthia had just showered and climbed into bed when Byron rang her phone.

"Aren't you the one who didn't want us to talk about her?"

His deep, throaty chuckle sent vibrations through her heat. "You're right. It's just that Ava stays so worried about her. She's a good kid who's made a couple bad choices. We all want so much for her life to get back on track. This isn't who she is."

"I believe you. I want that, too."

"So, how's she doing?"

"Our sessions are confidential."

"How can you say that when she's a minor?"

"Technically maybe, yes. But in the system, she is being viewed as an adult. This case comes through that system. And even if it didn't, counselor/client confidentiality would still prevent discussion."

"Okay, but it's not like a stranger is asking you."

"Which is why this feels uncomfortable, and undoubtedly why the association's stipulation on family was just put in place. Though not a part of her immediate family, you seem to be very much involved in her life. I know your concern is genuine, and so are my constraints regarding this conversation."

"If something bad was going on with her, if she were having real problems, would you tell me?"

"When a client is facing life-threatening difficulties, we notify the appropriate parties. In this case, one would be your sister."

An awkward silence followed. Cynthia wanted to break it with a sexy-sounding come-on. But she'd never been good with that kind of flirty stuff. *Where is Lisa or Dynah when I need them?*

"You didn't have to go all professional on me," Byron finally said. "But I hear you. It's cool. As long as that doesn't mean you're going to decline my invitation to our family Memorial Day barbeque. And before you tell me all the reasons why you can't chill with me on the holiday, hear me out. This isn't an intimate gathering with just my family. It's a tradition that started with a couple of neighboring families, and has grown to an event where on average a hundred people show up."

"That you assume to know my thoughts is very annoying."

"Are you going to tell me that Ms. I'm-so-professional-I-wear-a-suit-to-bed wasn't going to play that card?"

"I do not wear a suit to bed." It was a struggle not to laugh, but she managed.

"You did the other night. Your birthday suit. And I liked it."

"You're incorrigible."

"Damn, I don't know what that means, but the way you said it sounds so sexy that I'll try to make sure and stay that way."

"It means that your mother probably tried her best but realized there just was no changing you."

"Are you talking about my mama?"

"Excuse me?"

"Never mind, girl. Just try and act like you weren't going to turn me down flat and use work-related nonsense as an excuse."

"I'm not even going to dignify that statement with an answer."

"Because you'd have to admit that I'm right, again. Although if you're planning to hang with me, and I hope you are, you should probably get used to that."

"Were you always so full of yourself?"

"Me? Never that. I'm very much my mother's son, and say what I know when I know it." No response, so he continued. "Just like right now I know you'd like me to hit that spot again, the one that had you bucking and squirming this past weekend. My bad, there I go knowing what I know, which is probably going to get me in trouble again."

Arrogant men normally made her angry. But hearing this "ordinary" guy toss around confidence with such unpretentious nonchalance made her smile. Fifteen minutes after ending the call, turning off the light, and snuggling against her pillow, here she was still thinking about him.

The phone rang. *What does he want now?* Thinking of their conversation's steamy ending, she could just about imagine.

"Let me guess. More expertise on the G-spot?"

Silence.

"Hello?"

"What a crass greeting."

Cynthia sat up straight. "Mother?"

"Unfortunately, yes."

"I apologize for answering that way. I thought you were . . . never mind. It's almost one o'clock there. Is something wrong? Dad, Jeffrey, are they . . . ?"

"Everyone is fine, Cynthia, at least until I was jolted with that offensive greeting. I can't imagine anyone with whom you associate allowing such talk."

Cynthia bit back an explanation. Sometimes there was no need to waste one's air. No matter the topic, Anna Marie Hall's irritation at her daughter came not from present conversation, but from the shame brought on the family almost nine years ago. Cynthia rested her head against the headboard and slowly counted to ten. One peek, two seconds to check the caller ID, and she'd be on her way to sleep right now.

"I hope you haven't once again lowered your standards to the degree necessary for a gentleman to be comfortable with that type of conversation."

"Mother, you've made your displeasure abundantly clear, and I've apologized. May we move on to the reason for this call?"

"I need a reason to call my daughter?"

"It's been a long day," Cynthia replied, through a sigh. "I have an early-morning meeting tomorrow, and should be asleep. This—*for starters*—is why I asked."

"You're the one who chose to be a modern woman and join the workforce. Hal Lindsey was more than ready to make you a very comfortably maintained society wife."

A headache threatened to join Cynthia's nervous stomach. As hard as she tried and as long as she'd been gone from home, her mother still knew which pushed buttons would get her riled. Knowing that there was no right response, Cynthia turned off the lamp, settled into bed, and after turning down the volume, placed the phone next to her ear so that if her mother asked a question worth answering, she'd know.

After a few seconds of silence, her mom got the message. "I called regarding the upcoming holiday. Because of his impending birthday celebration, your dad and I are planning a low-key holiday, a casual luncheon on the boat. I understand from one of the couples who will be joining us that their son will be home for the holidays. He's a dentist on the leading edge of technology who's invented a specialized laser treatment. Even more amazing, he's still single! I thought this weekend's casual atmosphere would be a perfect place for the two of you to meet. What time are you arriving?"

"I won't be coming home for Memorial Day weekend."

"Why not?"

"I've made other plans, and they can't be changed."

"With whom, may I ask?"

"With someone you don't know, Mother, a friend here in Los Angeles."

"A male friend, I presume?"

Tricky territory. Proceed with caution. "Yes."

"What does he do?"

"Nothing that tops a dentist with inventions." Cynthia knew this call had to end, and quickly.

"I'm glad to hear you're making new friends. I trust you've checked his pedigree, as I've instructed."

Pedigree? What's that mean? Imagining Byron's likely response made Cynthia almost laugh out loud. "I'm sorry I'll miss the party, and will phone you this weekend when there's more time to chat."

She ended the call. Sleep remained elusive as she pondered the spontaneous decision her mom's question had prompted. Her head had not planned to accept Byron's invitation to attend the block party where his family lived. She guessed that tomorrow would be soon enough to tell him what her heart had decided.

20

This was his first since joining the LA Metro Bus Company almost ten years ago, which should have made Byron feel better. But as he sat at the curb in a slightly damaged Metro bus, following a freak accident caused by a texting teen, all he felt was irritated. In fact, he'd been troubled for the past few weeks, ever since Tanya revived the story that he had two children instead of one. He'd kept himself busy, doing just about anything to not think about that loathsome possibility. With time on his hands as he waited for the transportation supervisor, his mind went straight back to that conversation. Even though it wasn't her first time for doing so, the jeering way she'd told it this time made mentally recalling the conversation almost as traumatic as when it had actually occurred.

"Really, Tanya? This money is for Tyra?" Byron shook his head, still cursing the blasted broken condom and overzealous tadpole that tied him to this woman for at least eight more years. A former classmate and all-around go-to girl in between the would-be wifeys, she'd flipped the personality script as soon as the pregnancy test showed two lines—demanding marriage, money, and most of his time—not necessarily in that order. After almost three years of trying, he'd firmly closed the door on marriage, which only left her to threaten and complain about what she loved most.

"Why are you still on this child-support trip, even though I've got primary custody and don't owe you a dime?"

"Eff that stupid judge and what he said. I still need money for when she's at my house!"

"Aren't you working?"

"Yes. So what? I have other mouths to feed."

"And another man to feed them; their daddy, the man who lives in your house."

"And handles his business, something you couldn't do."

"Then why are you on the phone sweating me about his children?"

"Look, Byron, can I get the three hundred or not? I promise I'll give it back as soon as I get my income tax check."

Byron knew the truth. If Tanya gave him all the money she owed people, he could retire. He almost said this, but didn't want to fight. "Tanya, I have said and the court agrees that because I have primary custody, you are not owed additional child support. Alimony either, because— *thank God*—we were never married."

"Yeah, and that's probably your biggest regret, huh?"

No, my biggest regret is buying a generic box of gloves. Trying to save five dollars is going to cost me fifty stacks in college tuition. "Tanya, I've got stuff to do. I'm getting off the phone."

"You're not going to give me the money, for real? It's for little Ricky. We're enrolling him in a baseball league. He needs a uniform and gloves and stuff. All you do is work, so I know you've got it."

"Get it from the man who handles his business." He'd promised otherwise but couldn't resist the sarcasm. When they were together, Byron took care of everything. He loved Tanya and Tyra, and manned up to his responsibilities. But he caught her in a lie and soon the whole web of fabrications unraveled to reveal that she'd cheated on him with Ricky the whole time. "Since according to you he's so much the man, have him take care of his son, like I take care of my daughter."

"You mean take care of your son?" she asked, her tone as light and airy as carbon dioxide, and just as deadly.

Byron sighed. "You already know that lie won't work."

"Who says I'm lying?"

"If that boy were really mine, you wouldn't be waiting until now to let me know."

"I didn't. You knew when I was pregnant that he was yours."

"I knew what you told me, which isn't always the truth. You told Rick the same thing."

"I told Rick what he wanted to hear."

"Your greedy behind wouldn't have cared about that. Not if you could get my money. Now say I'm wrong."

"I'll say you're stupid, that's what I'll say. Most men are . . . can't even do simple math. And what happens? Their children end up calling another man daddy. Bye, Byron."

"No, Tanya, wait—"

But she'd hung up the phone.

Since then she'd either dodged his calls or his questions regarding the boy, which bothered him as much as her trying to get him to believe that little Ricky was his child. Why had she begun this again after all this time? Was it like his brother Douglas believed, that her and Ricky's father were on the outs? He tried to convince himself that either this was it or she was lying. But what if she wasn't? Byron hated the mere thought that he may have a son seven years old whom he didn't know.

He chased away these thoughts with those of last night's conversation with Cynthia, which made him remember what Douglas had said when told she'd been invited. "You sure that should be the first meeting? If our family or crazy neighbors don't frighten her away, the smell of Mama cooking chitterlings surely will."

Just as Byron pulled out his phone to put in a request to his mom for what not to cook this coming holiday, it rang in his hand.

He put the call on speakerphone. "What's going on, Ava?"

"What's up, Byron? You okay?"

"I've been better."

"From what I hear, life's better than it's ever been."

"According to who?"

"According to the person you told about dating Cynthia Hall, when the one who should have heard first is me!"

Byron grimaced as his sister delivered the justifiable verbal punch, glad he knew she was teasing. And glad he hadn't told his loose-lip brother about the past weekend. "Man, Doug never could keep his mouth shut."

"Is it a secret?"

"No, and we're not dating either . . . just went out a couple times."

"Byron, you are something else."

"What?"

"How are you going to hook up with my daughter's counselor?"

"See, it's not even like that." He gave the short version of their initial meeting. "I was actually joking when I dared her to go out with me and was surprised when she agreed."

"I am, too. Actually, shocked is more like it."

"Wow, sis. Thanks for the vote of confidence."

"I'm being honest. She's so polished and intelligent. I mean, she looks like a friggin' model! There's no way I'd ever imagine a woman like her dating someone . . . like . . ."

"Uh-huh, keep digging. That hole will be big enough for you to jump in pretty soon." They laughed. "The supervisor is finally pulling up. Let me get through this report stuff so I can head home."

"You're still at work?"

"Yes, I was involved in an accident. Not my fault and no one hurt, but it blemished a record that lasted ten years."

"Sorry to hear that, and I'm even sorrier for your supervisor's timing. I'll pause this Cynthia tape for us to continue playing later because I definitely want to hear more about you two going out."

"I'm sure you do, big sis. But you know how Cynthia can't tell you what's discussed between her and Leah? I'm under that same, uh, confidentiality situation when it comes to her and me."

21

An hour after arriving home, plowing through a plate of chicken and rice his neighbor brought him, and helping Leah with homework, Byron took a nice, long shower. All the while he thought of Cynthia. As soon as he'd dried off and donned his favorite big boxers, he plopped down on his unmade bed and called her phone.

"Can you cook?"

"Hello?"

"Yeah, it's me. Can you cook?"

"Byron?"

Pause. "No, Harry."

"Oh, hi, babe!"

Longer pause. "Who the hell is Harry?"

The sound of her laughter erased the frown that had instantly popped up on his face. "He's obviously someone who thinks that after two, three dates he and I are exclusive."

"We're not?"

"Are you going to try and tell me you're not seeing anyone else?"

"I don't have to try and do that. It's easy. I'm not."

"I'm not either. But that doesn't mean I won't, or that you shouldn't. It's not like we're in a relationship."

"True, but I thought we both felt something a little deeper than friendship this past weekend."

"Oh, I felt something all right. You're a really good lover. Before Saturday night I'd only heard about multiple orgasms but doubted whether or not that was even possible." Her voice lowered. "I am now thoroughly contented proof of that claim."

The compliment stroked his ego better than he'd stroked her pearl. "Can I ask you something?"

"Sure."

"Are you looking for a relationship?"

"I wouldn't say looking, but eventually I'd like to be married."

"What kind of man do you consider husband material? Oh, and the answer can be simple. 'Somebody like you,' for instance."

She laughed again, bringing back the frown that her earlier glee had chased away. *What's so funny about that?*

"Husband material . . . let's see. Someone who complements me and my lifestyle, spends his days in the office and his weekends on the golf course."

"You play golf?"

"Not much lately, but, yes, I enjoy the game. Do you play?"

"Not at all. Football is my game."

"I attended a Super Bowl once. So brutish! How can being tackled or hit by a bulldozer be fun?"

"It's not, unless you're the bulldozer."

"Perhaps, but that game's not for me. Basketball I can handle. Baseball is fine, though overall I'm not a huge sports fan. That doesn't mean my husband won't be. It's just not a prerequisite."

"So, your dude has to be a professional, a golf lover . . . what else?"

"Comfortable financially, educated, health conscious, and most of all, he has to pass the Jayden test."

"Your son, right?"

"Yes."

"Kids are a pretty good judge of character."

"Yes, they are."

"So if Jayden likes me, can you forget about the fact that I'm a poor, bus-driving college dropout with a gut hanging over my belt?"

"Ha! You're too funny."

"What if I'm serious?"

"It's too early for us to be serious, and I don't introduce dates to my son."

"I guess that puts a hitch in my plan to come over there tonight and pet your kitty cat."

"Unfortunately, yes."

"And you're not coming over on Memorial Day."

"Actually, Jayden is spending that weekend

and the following week with his uncle. So I'd like to join you."

"Really? All right, then. Cool."

"Now, may I ask you something?"

"Sure."

"The other day, when faced with that wretched man holding that gun, you said you'd die for me. Why?"

"Because it's true. I'd take a bullet before letting any woman I knew get jacked up by some dude."

"Oh."

"You sound disappointed."

"No, I just . . ."

"Thought you were special? Never doubt that, baby love. I'd take two bullets for you."

"You wouldn't."

"Damn, you got me. I'd take three. But only one to the head."

"Seriously, I'd never been so frightened in my life. Yet you sat there conversing as if it were about the stock market or baseball scores. He had a gun trained on you, and you weren't even scared!"

"Did you forget that I wasn't wearing a bullet-proof vest and my bullet-stopping Superman cape was at the cleaners?"

"What does that mean?"

"It means that while my face looked as calm as a muh-fuh . . . my ass was scared as hell."

Cynthia laughed. "At least you're human." And then more softly, "You still make a pretty convincing Superman, even without the cape."

They made plans to meet on Friday and shortly

after that ended the call. Byron wasn't happy about some of what Cynthia had shared. But they were going to spend the weekend together. This was enough to send him to sleep with a smile on his face.

22

"Oh, no! It's raining!"

It was eleven o'clock on a Friday night. Byron and Cynthia had just left the movie theater after seeing what had been touted as the year's best movie. Earlier, parking the car a block away in crowded Culver City hadn't been a problem. But now . . .

Cynthia peered out of the double doors and back at Byron as she subconsciously brought a hand to her freshly flat-ironed, bone-straight hair.

With a brief shake of his head, Byron held up a hand. "You don't even have to say anything. The hair, I already know. Be right back."

Minutes later, a dry and impressed Cynthia was seated in Byron's SUV. "Thank you for being such a gentleman," she said, once she'd directed him toward her house and they were on the way. "And with an umbrella, even. While living in Minnesota and Chicago, I always stored a variety of weather gear in my trunk. The weather here stays so much the same, I never thought about it."

"I should just keep my mouth shut and let you think I'm that thoughtful and prepared. Which I am," he firmly added. "But my mom left that umbrella the last time she rode with me. When we go over there on Monday, remind me to give it back to her."

"What's your mom's name?"

"Elizabeth. Everybody calls her Liz. My dad's name is Willie."

"Short for William?"

He shook his head. "Just Willie."

"You'll want to get in your left lane before that second light." He switched lanes. "Have your parents met many of your girlfriends?"

"Mama's met just about all of them! Growing up, our house was like Grand Central Station. Kids love Mama because she doesn't pull any punches, and keeps it real. Topics that many parents shy away from Mama takes head-on—sex, drugs, crime—you name it. She can make me blush to this very day!" He followed her next direction. "What about your parents?"

She hesitated, her voice soft when she answered. "Of the few men I've dated, they've met two."

Byron glanced over, noting Cynthia's pinched features. Obviously she was not going to say more on the matter, and just as clearly a story was being left untold. His mind drifted back to the hotel and the time he'd asked about her son's father. She'd clamped down then, too. *What happened to*

*you, Cynthia? And what did your baby's daddy have to
do with it?*

Thinking of her child's father brought to mind
unpleasant thoughts that Tanya's latest accusations had created. This made him view Cynthia's
unwillingness to talk in a different light. Sure,
he'd opened up about family, the job, and some
past relationships. But he hadn't shared everything.

They turned onto a quiet street anchored by
condominiums on the corner and single-family
houses lining the rest of the street. It was dark so
he couldn't see much, but from what he could
make out it looked a little less congested than
where his friend who'd moved to Culver City
lived. The houses appeared to be a bit larger
than Byron's, by a couple hundred square feet,
he guessed, but cost a couple hundred thousand
more dollars.

"You're moving less than ten miles from your
current home," Byron had told his friend.

His friend had shrugged, and kept loading
furniture. "Different area code, different life."

As Byron stepped into Cynthia's vaulted ceiling
living room, he'd have to agree. The place looked
as though it had been torn from the pages of an
upscale interior design magazine: dark hardwood
floors, walls of the palest blue, large windows letting in the flickering lights against a darkened sky
seen from her fifth-floor view. Her light-colored
furniture looked unused and gave him pause.
*Does she really have a son younger than Tyra? If so, this
living room must be out of bounds.* Byron knew that

within five minutes of being moved to his house there would be jelly on one cushion, a magic marker mark on the second, and a big splat of mustard after Sunday sports.

Wow.

"Byron?"

Only when his name was called did he vaguely remember hearing verbal chatter. "Uh, yeah, what did you say?"

"Are you okay?"

"Sure. Why wouldn't I be?"

"Because you haven't moved since entering my living room and didn't hear one word I said."

He walked toward the kitchen, where she was headed. "I was just taking in your place. It's very nice."

"Thank you."

Man, stop acting like you've never been inside a nice home. Except he hadn't. He'd been in fancy homes, but not one like this. It wasn't so much the architecture or materials used, although Byron believed it all to be designer and top grade. It was the way everything was put together, with purpose and precision. As he followed her from the living area to the combined dining/kitchen space, he didn't see a speck of dust or piece of anything out of place.

"What would you like to drink?"

"Some of you." He quickly closed the distance between them and pulled her in for a smoldering kiss. This scene of seduction was right in Byron's comfort zone, right in his element.

After a couple minutes, Cynthia gently pulled

back, her hand to her chest. "Wait, Byron, you're taking my breath away."

"Baby, that's what I'm supposed to do."

She smiled and walked over to the fridge. "I feel like a glass of wine. What about you?"

"Since I doubt you have either beer or Hennessy, I guess I'll join you with a sissy drink."

She gave him a look but made no further comment while she poured a glass of wine from the pricey case she'd purchased during a trip to Napa Valley and saved for special occasions. In her mind, a man staying overnight at her place, in her bed, for the first time since her breakup, was definitely such an event.

"Here you go."

Byron looked dubious. "Is it sweet?"

"Not too."

She took a delicate sip. Byron took one as well. It was quickly followed by another. And then he drained the wineglass.

"That was pretty good," he admitted, after wiping his mouth and enjoying a healthy burp.

Cynthia was now the one shocked speechless. *Did he just guzzle a glass of sixty-dollar-a-bottle wine as though it were water for ninety-nine cents?*

How gauche.

His action and her unconscious reaction brought back a memory as clearly as if it had happened yesterday. She and her mom at the dinner table with then-best friend Natalie, who'd made the egregious error of slurping a spoonful of tomato bisque.

"When eating or drinking, there should be

no sound. Only from the uncultured do noises abound."

First-time guest Natalie, having not understood the jab nor known it was directed at her, had happily gone on slurping the soup before telling Mrs. Hall how much she'd enjoyed it. After her friend had gone home, Cynthia had gotten a lecture on table manners followed by an impromptu etiquette quiz. She passed the test her friend had failed. Their friendship was terminated. The following year, Cynthia was placed in a private academy.

On the tails of this memory came a thought that bothered her far worse than the sound of Byron's airy discharge. The instant displeasure at such a boorish act had not been in the voice of her mother, but in her own, which proved she was becoming very much like the person she wished in this area to never emulate: Mrs. Anna Marie Hall.

Eewww.

"What?"

She looked up, until now unaware of her expression. "Oh . . . nothing."

"Then why are you frowning? This wine is pretty good, not like what my mom gets at the grocery. Can I get another glass?"

Cynthia reached for the bottle, emptying almost all of it into Byron's glass. Who cared that he'd just chugalugged a sixty-dollar wine? For what he'd done last weekend and would likely do tonight, he was worth the whole case . . . and more.

23

He'd asked for a second glass of wine, so when she handed him the glass and he set it right down, it surprised her. Even more confusing was when he gently took the glass out of her hand and placed it on the counter.

"Why'd you do that?"

"So I could do this."

The next thing she knew, Cynthia's butt was on the counter, her legs were in the air, and her eyes were even with the backsplash peeking through a stainless-steel toaster and a bowl of fruit.

"Byron! This granite is hard. What are you doing?"

He answered by releasing the single button at the top of her jeans and impatiently tugging them off her. Her panties dangled off her right ankle. He bent his head, pushed wide her legs, and proceeded to lap, lick, suck, and sip until the only thing Cynthia felt was the party happening between her legs. Granite, what?

The orgasm that resulted from this oral assault

sent her bucking off the counter into Byron's arms. The only thing missing from the scene was a judge with a card, holding it up and shouting, "Ten!"

He walked out of the kitchen. Cynthia placed noodle-limp arms around his shoulders. Before she could recover from the unexpected kitchen encounter, she found herself being tossed over his shoulder like a bag of potatoes as he mounted the stairs.

"Byron, put me down."

Pop. The feel of Byron's firm hand on her bare behind sent unexpected tingles through every part of her body. Her first thought: *Did you really just smack my ass?* Her second: *Can you please do it again?*

Ping!

"Ow!"

This tap was a little harder, the thrill a little higher. His hand ran lightly over the trail of goose bumps caused by such unexpectedly sweet torture. He popped the fleshy part of each fleshy cheek one more time before they reached the bedroom. Cynthia was so totally and thoroughly stimulated that when he laid her on the bed, she nearly pounced.

"Get your clothes off," she demanded, reaching for the buttons on his shirt with focused determination.

"Whoa, wait a minute, girl!" Byron laughed, happy to see the ever-so-composed Cynthia Hall—hair tousled, eyes fixed, ass blushing—meeting this part of herself.

"No," she panted. "You did this." Last button

conquered, she pushed the shirt away from his chest, nearly tore off the undershirt and fairly pushed him onto the bed. "Wait, baby, where's the con—" *Well, damn!*

Cynthia had jumped on his strong erection with the precision of a bucking bull rider at a Bill Pickett rodeo. Head thrown back, mouth slack, eyes closed, she went in search of magic buttons and back-to-back orgasms.

"Ooh . . ." she moaned, her body in motion. Had there been a twerk competition right about now, she would have won hands down.

"Eek!" Faster and faster she twirled her pelvis as a seismic explosion built in her core. Seeing her fast-approaching nirvana, Byron grabbed her hips and pushed upward, tilting his pelvis—left, right, front, back—until she erupted. In mid-climax he flipped them over as if they'd practiced the move for *America's Got Talent* and grunted out his own primal release.

"Oh, my word, oh, my goodness . . ." Cynthia took in quick bursts of air, trying to recover. She'd heard of people having heart attacks during sex. Now, she knew how such a thing could happen. Orgasmic aftershocks produced slight jerking motions, encouraged by Byron's magic wand, still hard, still inside her.

After several minutes passed, she looked over at Byron. "What just happened?"

Byron, on his back with an arm thrown over behind him, didn't open his eyes as he answered. The workout had obviously been good for him, too. "I think," he began, continuing to force slow, even breaths from his body. "I think I just served up a Carter classic."

With breathing finally under control, Cynthia rolled to her side and propped up her elbow. "Where'd you learn to . . . do that?"

"Do what?"

"You know, everything you just did, throwing me over your shoulder and spanking my behind."

Byron opened his eyes and slid his gaze over to meet Cynthia's inquisitive eyes. "I haven't been practicing the move on a dozen other women, if that's what you're wondering." He reached over, grabbed a lock of hair, and twirled it around his finger. "I guess you bring out my mannish."

"What?"

"My mannish, you know, like me Tarzan! You"— he looked over, waiting for what should have been a no-brainer response. "What? You're going to leave Tarzan hanging?"

"Isn't that what he does?"

He cocked his head the way a dog might, and bugged his eyes. Cynthia laughed, a deep belly laugh that was patently unladylike, yet couldn't be helped. His facial expressions were priceless. She adored him.

He rolled to his knees and pushed out his chest. "Me Tarzan!"

She tried to hold it in, but the laugh escaped through her nose in an unrefined snort. "You're silly."

Beating his chest, he went deeper into the impersonation. "Me. Tarzan. Who are you?"

Shaking her head, she continued to laugh.

"Oh, you're not going to say it? You think

you're not going to say it?" He pinned her to the bed with his body, found her rib cage, wiggled his fingers.

"Stop! That tickles! Byron, stop it!"

"Who are you?"

"Cynthia!"

"Who? Me Tarzan. Who are you?"

She howled. "Byron, stop it! You're going to make me urinate on the sheets!"

"Me. Tarzan! Who are you?"

She was now in an all-out guffaw. "I'm . . . I'm Jane."

Byron jumped up, beat his chest, and bellowed. Tarzan would have been proud.

24

It rained all weekend, but by Monday, Memorial Day, the clouds had disappeared and the ground was dry. Byron turned up the volume on the Hip-Hop/R&B 2000 station he'd personally programmed to blast from the speakers of his SUV. The Wu-Tang Clan went Outkast while Common compared water to chocolate. After stopping at a neighborhood grocery chain store for the cans of soda and other drinks he'd promised to bring, the holiday car concert continued with Marshall Mathers using country grammar to ask the real Shady to stand up, Destiny's Child paying homage to independent women, and Shaggy swore that it wasn't him. He neared the street for the block party and turned off his stereo. Even Bow Wow's bounce couldn't compete with George Clinton's "Atomic Dog," especially when played on Uncle Johnny's jimmy-rigged sound system with a woofer the size of Byron's first car.

Said uncle lifted his red plastic cup as Byron

turned the corner, doing a wobble inspired more by what was in the cup than on the stereo.

Clearly, the seals had been broken and the liquor was flowing. By the time he'd navigated around the citizen-erected barricade, playing children and waving neighbors, to park his car in front of his parents' house, he was pleased to note Cynthia's face had gone from looking nervous to looking startled. He could handle that reaction. The Carter clan alone was enough to scare anybody.

He turned off the engine and reached for her hand. "Remember what I told you. My daddy's slow, my mama's a trip, and my whole family's crazy. So don't take anything personal. They love anybody who loves me. You do love me, don't you?"

"I don't recall ever making that declaration."

His eyes swept her body. "You may not remember, but your body told me last night."

"You wish." Said even as a nice flush of embarrassment crept from her neck to her earlobes.

He reached over, ran a soft forefinger down her cheek. "I did . . . and it came true." Her eyes darkened with the pleasure his statement aroused. This noted before his gaze slid to her succulent mouth, and his body leaned forward of its own volition to initiate another tantalizing tongue tango. . . .

"Byron! Get your ass out that car and bring the drinks over to the tub. That spit-swapping is probably why you're just now getting here." Liz was a tornado in motion—voice booming, hands gesturing—as she moved across the lawn. Byron and Cynthia dutifully obeyed Liz's command.

Liz stopped a boy on the sidewalk. "Baby, go get your cousins to help carry this soda and ice over to the tub. Nothing in there now but water, wine coolers, and Colt 45, and Johnny don't need to drink a damn thing else. Even though it's hotter than hot grease next to a straightening comb."

She reached the car. With eyes trained on Cynthia and one brow arched, she launched into a ping-pong monologue, splitting her attention between her two-person audience with the skill of an actor onstage.

"Hi. I'm the mama of the man who made you late. Boy, you didn't tell me you were peeing in high cotton. I see why you didn't want chitterlings. You are one beautiful girl. I bet you hear that all the time, huh? How in the hell did you get her to come with you, kidnap her or something? Baby, if you're here against your will, I'll take you home. We don't want any trouble today."

"Mama, stop!" Byron could barely talk for trying to keep from laughing. In Liz Carter's presence for less than a minute and Cynthia's expression conveyed shock and awe. "Don't tease her like that when she barely knows you."

Liz gave Cynthia another dubious glance. "Are you sure she's ready for this? You know how Johnny is once his Henny gets to seeing, and Della's brandy-laced coffee had her turned up at ten a.m."

"No worries, Mama. I already warned her." He placed an arm around Cynthia's shoulders. "This is Cynthia Hall, Cynthia, my mother, Elizabeth Carter."

"It's a pleasure to meet you, Ms. Carter."

"That's Mrs., honey, not Ms. I worked too damn hard at trapping my husband for you to not put an *r* between those letters."

"Oh, please forgive me. In today's society—"

"Baby, don't try and explain yourself. She's just messing with you." He tried to scowl, but Liz's twinkling eyes smoothed his face's rough edge. "It goes this way with all of the people she feels good about meeting." He reached for Cynthia's hand. Her stepping away was a reminder of the holiday rule he'd sworn to follow, one that would be hard to remember—no touching. When Byron told Leah about Cynthia coming, his niece hadn't reacted. People from all over came to this celebration. However, if Leah caught them showing affection, that would be a different situation.

They reached the corner in front of the Carter house. "Mama, where is everybody? I want Cynthia to meet the fam."

"They're around here somewhere. Except Barry, who's got his nerve to be at somebody else's picnic. I told him their enchiladas weren't going to compete with my ribs."

"Where did he go?"

"To some park with the family of the client he's 'training.'" She used air quotes. "He's probably using something besides a treadmill to lessen the curves on that moon over *muchacha*." Byron's brow creased in confusion. "A pretty Mexican girl with a bright smile and a big ass."

Cynthia couldn't hide her shock at the unexpected response.

Byron's mouth twisted in annoyance. "Dang, Mama. Go easy. Cynthia just met you."

"And? She might as well know the truth from jump street. No matter who's around me, baby, I'm Liz Carter all day long."

Liz went into the house while Byron and Cynthia walked toward a group of men in lounge chairs under an awning erected for shade.

Byron gave a general greeting before addressing his dad. "Dad, this is Cynthia Hall, Leah's counselor and my guest for today. Cynthia, this is Willie Carter, my hero."

"Boy, get on way from here with that foolishness." His voice was gruff, but Byron knew these words made his dad's heart soar. "You must be needing a loan sometime soon." Reaching out his hand, he added, "A pleasure to meet you, miss."

"Likewise," Cynthia said, giving his a firm handshake. "It's easy to see why Byron has such great character, Mr. Carter. He tells me you're an army man as well. Thank you for your service."

"You're quite welcome. So, you're taking care of Leah, huh?"

"We're working together to secure her bright future."

"That's good to hear. So thank you for *your* service." He sat down just as a strong hand clamped

Byron's shoulder. He turned around. "What's up, Dougie Stale?"

Douglas laughed at this childhood throwback. "It looks like you, man." They did a shoulder bump hug. "For real."

Byron knew that Douglas's words were for him but saw his eyes were on Cynthia, as were those of all the men sitting in the shade.

"Hello there, lovely," Douglas said, stepping over and reaching out to take Cynthia's hand. "My name is Douglas, the brother who signed the papers to let Byron out this weekend and talked the staff into exchanging his straitjacket for civilian clothes."

Her smile widened. Byron's family was simply . . . indescribable! "Hi, I'm Cynthia."

"Well, uh, Cynthia . . . it appears you're new to the neighborhood, so why don't you let me show you around."

Byron's look was WTH. "Really, bro?"

"Hey, I'm just being friendly to Leah's counselor." He turned to her. "That is why you're here, right, because you know Leah?"

"Yes, I work with Leah and met Byron when he escorted her to a session."

"That's what I thought," Douglas said, his voice casual and smile telling as he winked at Byron and took Cynthia's arm. "Hey, man, Marvin was looking for you earlier. Why don't you go and try to find him. We'll be back."

Byron watched them walk away, the humor at Douglas's audacity showing on his face. They'd had a conversation about Cynthia being there, and how the two of them would have to appear as nothing more than friends. Making a mental note to later punch out his younger brother, Byron turned and went in search of Martin.

The day became a whirlwind. After tracking down Marvin, the two rejoined Cynthia, Douglas, Ava, and about a hundred other people socializing up and down the block. Neighbors who'd known Byron since childhood were more than happy to enlighten Cynthia on his boyhood exploits. Older men flirted and younger women threw shade. Leah joined the other teenagers who, in typical nonconforming, no-socializing-with-adults fashion, congregated at the opposite end of where old school ruled, rocking their new beats while some sneaked illicit sips and tokes. Kids were everywhere—laughing, fighting, screaming, crying—watched by adults who cracked jokes, argued, reminisced, and played games. Cynthia's feelings went from appalled to amazed, and from uncomfortable to relaxed. When she informed Liz that she didn't like greens, she learned about a black card that had nothing to do with shopping, one that Ava said she'd lose, along with her mother's good favor, without putting at least a forkful on her plate.

After a fun-filled day and lots of hugs, Byron and Cynthia wished his family good night. The barricade had been moved, making it easy for him to head down the block and reach Slauson Avenue, a direct route from Inglewood to Culver City, within minutes. As he turned from one block to another, making small talk about the day, Cynthia remained quiet.

"Cynthia, what's wrong?"

"Just thinking; taking the opportunity of not driving to survey my surroundings."

"You're probably shell-shocked. I told you my peeps were full throttle."

Her smile was brief but genuine. "The behavior was not that of which I'm accustomed . . ." She looked away from the passing scenery and focused on him. "But I think your family is wonderful. I had a great time."

Byron let out a relieved sigh. "You don't know how happy it makes me to hear you say that." He reached for her hand. "I thought they might send you running away. I like having you around."

"We're very different, Byron. Our backgrounds are worlds apart. Still, I find myself attracted to you. Those differences are probably some of the reasons why."

"Explain that."

"You're very comfortable in your skin and move through life with an ease that I've never experienced. Your family is loud and rambunctious and carefree, where mine is conservative and quiet, very aware of and beholden to societal standards. That's how I was raised as well. To scream like your mom did when they were playing cards and she went to Baltimore? Totally unacceptable."

"Baby, that's Boston. Please get your card-playing cities straight."

"Whatever city it was made her superexcited. My mom would die if I did that."

"Mama loves bid whist. She loves life, period, and is Liz Carter all day long!" His was a very close imitation.

"I like her. It was an adjustment, but everyone was friendly and made me feel welcome."

"You know that makes me feel good. There is one thing, though."

"What's that?"

"To hang with my family, you're going to have to urban up a bit."

"What does that mean? Oh, wait, I know. Drop the proper English that cost my parents thousands and replace them with words like muh-fuh?"

"It's muh. Fuh." Byron shook his head in exasperation as she slaughtered the lingo some used to replace the harsher MF. "Girl, we're going to have to work on your slang skills."

Cynthia gave him the side eye. "I'm not sure I'll ever master muh-fuh, but I do like diddly-squat."

"Ha!" So shocked was he at hearing one of Willie Carter's favorite sayings spill from her pearl-pink lipstick-kissed mouth that Byron was silent for the next two miles.

Music filled the void as he absorbed all of what Cynthia had said. That she was attracted to him. *I knew that.* That she'd had a great time. *Of course, she was with me.* That she thought his family was wonderful. *That sounds nice but is a bit of a stretch.* Byron adored his family and embraced his neighborhood, but he had no illusions about the difficulty of Cynthia ever totally fitting into his

world. She'd already made it clear that she had
no plans to remain in his.

This isn't a relationship, remember?

That was her story, and she'd stuck to it. As
long as they kept seeing each other, he didn't
care what they called it.

25

The following weekend, Cynthia and Byron
headed to an art show in Santa Monica. Earlier that
week, she'd performed the rare act of RSVPing to
one of many invitations that as a member of the
Arts as Healing Foundation she received. Tonight
the founders, Dr. and Mrs. Gregory Morgan,
were conducting a fund-raiser for a project he
spearheaded, one in which the use of art as an
intrinsic component in healing brain and other
organ injuries played a major role. All of the pro-
ceeds would go toward this continued research.
The cause in itself was worthy enough. That his
wife, Anise, was the featured artist, and that
Cynthia had been wanting original pieces for her
dining room and bedroom made the affair all
the more special.

Given what she'd seen last weekend, Cynthia
had vacillated in asking Byron to be her escort.
He wasn't upper echelon or from a slice of society where there were rules and standards, where
people were routinely judged and either accepted

or dismissed by what they wore or how they spoke, where they worked or went to school. As far as she knew, she'd been accepted by his family, their neighbors and friends. Byron wouldn't have it so easy. Her girls, except Lisa, were constantly giving her flak, turning their last two Sunday chats into "save Cynthia" sessions. A readily apparent good mood had aroused her mother's suspicion and Jayden had returned from New York with the news that "Uncle Jeffrey has a girlfriend. She's really pretty, is an attorney like he is, and lives in a cool house with a pool on the roof!"

"How nice for Uncle Jeffrey," Cynthia had replied with a smile, successfully removing all traces of sarcasm from her voice. She dearly loved her brother, who couldn't help that he was the golden child. He had always been his parents' favorite and, after the error that sullied her mother's social standing and the Hall reputation, was the only perfect one as well.

All of this, and Cynthia continued her time with Byron. It was the most irrational, defiant thing she'd ever done, yet she'd never before felt so special and free. She'd decided to limit the discussion of those against him and deal with any fallout if and when the time came.

A valet service had been hired for the evening. Cynthia and Byron exited her car. He came around the car to shield her from oncoming traffic and placed a light hand at the small of her back as they walked the short distance to the Samuel Morgan Trauma Research and Health Center entrance. Near the door, Cynthia stopped abruptly. She looked down the street, and across it.

"What is it, babe?"

"Did you hear someone call my name?"

"No, did you?"

"I thought so." She gave another quick scan of the area. There was no one she recognized, no one looking in her direction. Shrugging her shoulders, they went inside.

The medical and research offices had been transformed to resemble a chic art gallery. Office equipment sat hidden beneath skillfully constructed boxes covered in faux marble, wood, and satiny skirting where sculptures and smaller pieces of Anise's art sat in easel picture frames. Billowy folds of navy voile drapery sheer hung from the ceiling, adding warmth and intimacy, as well as a fitting backdrop for LED fair lights that twinkled like stars. Faint strands of classical music wafted over the heads of the patrons, enveloping them effortlessly like a warm breeze.

Cynthia recognized the composer at once. *George Frideric Handel.* Her mom's favorite. Accepting a flute of champagne from the passing waiter, she casually eyed the designer-clad women and well-dressed men. The two days it had taken her to talk Byron into wearing a rented tuxedo (he refused to even think about buying one) had been worth her while, as had her suggestion before his trip to the barber to lose the mini-afro, and gentle teasing that he trade in ashy knuckles and hang nails for a buffed manicure. As a sip of vintage bubbly danced on her tongue she breathed in the familiarity of cultured refinement, now keenly aware of a lifestyle she'd not known that she missed.

"Let's work the room," she murmured softly, turning just as Byron gave his bowtie a nonsubtle tug.

"Honey, careful! It took us forever to get that tied."

"Yeah, and it'll take about a second to untie it, which is exactly what I'm about to do."

"Why?"

"It's uncomfortable! I haven't felt anything this tight around my neck since Douglas tried to choke me 'cause I broke his Nintendo!"

"Well, suffer in silence. You look the part of a man who belongs here."

She started down the hall next to a wall boasting large, unframed paintings.

Byron snorted. Cynthia gave him a look. "Baby, I belong wherever I am."

She patted his arm. "Of course, dear."

She stopped in front of a large, abstract drawing loosely resembling clouds, the ocean, or a combination of both, with errant streaks of bold, primary colors. Words—divine healing, perfect flow, body beautiful, peace, love, joy, and gratitude— were printed and repeated enough to frame the entire picture in stark, block letters.

Cynthia sighed happily as she imagined this in her room. "Isn't it stunning?" Byron didn't answer. "What does it look like to you?"

"Like something Tyra could have painted at the age of two."

"Then Tyra must have been a talented toddler indeed."

It took thirty years of discipline for Cynthia not to flinch and whip her head around to confirm the speaker of these words. She recovered her poise within seconds, and with a smile slowly turned while thinking, *Please, don't let it be her.*

It was.

"Pay him no mind. The painting is breath-taking."

"Not half as much as this bowtie," Byron mumbled, giving the offending piece of cloth another tug.

"Cynthia Hall!" In trying to cover his gripe, she spoke louder than intended, and cringed inside.

"Anise Morgan," the woman said, her eyes twinkling with mischief as she held out her hand to Cynthia but focused on Byron. "Painter of these childish doodles and co-host of this event." She turned to the handsome man beside her. "And my husband, Dr. Morgan."

Cynthia held out her hand to him. "It is my pleasure to meet you both, and to not only support this worthy cause but to place a stunning piece of artwork on one of my very bare walls."

"We appreciate that," Dr. Morgan said. "What do you do?"

"I'm a manager at the H.E.L.P. Agency."

The doctor nodded. "I'm familiar with that agency, and have heard good things about it."

The artist turned to Byron. "And what about you?"

"He's a director for the Los Angeles Department of Transportation," Cynthia interjected.

Byron's eyes narrowed as he met Cynthia's gaze. "Yeah, right." His attention shifted to Anise. "I direct a big bus down Central Avenue, the number 53, using a steering wheel, gas pedal, and brake. Some people call that a bus driver."

The doctor chuckled. Anise's smile widened.

As did Cynthia's eyes as she spoke lowly through gritted teeth. "Byron!"

"What? You thought I was going to go along with that director bullshit? Carters keep it real all day, every day. I'm not ashamed of my occupation. It pays the bills and transports clients who probably can't afford the supplies it took to draw one of these paintings, let alone buy the finished work."

Cynthia hung her head, shoulders heaving. Whether from embarrassment, anger, shame, or all of the above, Byron couldn't tell which. Nor did he care.

"I hear ya, man." The doctor surprised both Byron and Cynthia by easily switching from the proper tone of an esteemed expert in the medical field to a homeboy. "Long Beach right here, brothah. Grew up in the thick. North Side, podna, ya heard?"

"That's what I'm talkin' 'bout." Byron's smile widened and eyes gleamed with newfound respect as he clasped the doctor's hand in a soul shake. "The Wood, dog, Seventy-Seventh."

"Aw, yeah? One of my brother's best friends-turned-business partner grew up in Inglewood. Where you from?"

"Man, I'm from the Carter crew led by gangstas Willie and Liz. Mama didn't allow no bangin'."

"Does she know a gangsta named Jackie?"

The two men laughed as they gave each other dap.

Anise crossed over to Cynthia, and whispered, "While they're in the throes of male bonding, why don't you show me which pieces you like."

A steady flow of small talk, networking, and art shopping kept an underlying tension at bay, but once sitting on the plush leather of Cynthia's car, the huge elephant's presence could not be denied.

"What was tonight about?" Byron turned from looking out the window to see Cynthia's face.

"It was about supporting a worthy cause," Cynthia replied after a brief pause. "And purchasing some very nice art pieces. I think I'll give one of the pieces to my friend Gayle, in Chicago. She's a connoisseur and will appreciate Anise's aesthetic."

"Is that another word for artwork?"

A soft sigh and then, "Basically."

"Look, if you're ashamed of me or consider being with me as dating down, just let me know and I'll be out your way. But what I won't do is be with anybody who thinks I'm less than they are, because I can assure you that I am not."

"I never said you were."

"Words, whether or not I know their meaning, are not our only form of communication. I've been getting this message ever since you got on my bus."

"What message is that?"

"That you're better than or higher than because of what you do and where you came from, or where you live or how much you've been educated. But at the end of the day it don't matter that your panties are silk and came from Victoria's Secret. They basically do the same job as the ones on a homeless woman, even though hers are cotton and from the dollar store."

Several long seconds passed and not even the "Happy" song could lighten the somber mood.

Cynthia reached over and turned off the stereo. "It's not that I feel better than you or anyone else."

"Then what is it?"

"I was taught that there is a time and place for most things, not everything, and that there is a way to behave in certain social settings and among a particular group of people. One should observe and adapt."

"Oh, like you adapted the other day at the block party? I don't recall seeing you accept Ava's invitation to a game of spades, or chugging back a cooler out the bottle. I would understand if it had been chitterlings, because they're an acquired taste, but you're the first black person I've ever met who didn't like greens or black-eyed peas. And who in the hell, besides you and I guess your mama nem, takes meat off a rib using a knife and fork?"

"I was taught that one should not eat with their hands." Cynthia talked, but heard her mother's voice in her ears. She couldn't help it and, in this instance, didn't want to. This was who she was and how she lived. "If you believe it's okay for you to be Willie and Liz's gangster son, part of the

Carter crew, then it should be acceptable for me to be who I am."

"It is, except for when who you are feels the need to lie about who I am."

His words gave her pause and erased all quippy comebacks. How could she defend actions that happened almost subconsciously against his truthful statement?

"Why did you do it?"

"Honestly, I just asked myself the very same thing."

Once again silence descended. Cynthia switched back on the radio. An appropriately melancholy Sade song surrounded them like a low, dense fog, wrapping them both in the reality of what may very well be an impossible situation.

When they reached Cynthia's condo, Byron asked to be let out next to his SUV.

Her surprise was obvious. "I thought you were going to spend the night?"

He opened the door and for several seconds sat in silence, staring straight ahead. Finally, he turned to her, and said, "So did I."

"I think we should talk about it!" she threw at his back.

"Maybe later," he responded, without turning around.

Entering her home, Cynthia tried to figure out how an evening filled with such promise had turned into a total mess. *You know why.* Anna Marie, in her ear once again. Ever since meeting his family, Cynthia had been plagued with the likely reactions if Byron met hers. Total nonacceptance from her mother, and that would be even before

his atrocious—again, Anna's voice—social manners
were unveiled. Her father would be more forgiving
but afterward, in his study that smelled of aged
brandy and expensive cigars, she'd be gently per-
suaded to widen her pool of eligible candidates,
preferably with the son/cousin/brother/friend of
a valuable business associate. Jeffrey would jok-
ingly tell her she'd gone slumming, but would
then get serious and tell her to go for love.
They'd both lived in a household without it, and
had vowed a different type of marriage for themselves. And the girls? Lisa would back her. Eventually Dynah would come around. Gayle would
be the holdout. But for love, losing one best
friend out of three wasn't bad. *Love?* No. It was
too early to use this word to describe what she felt
for Byron. Wasn't it? Given that it hadn't been
too early for him to risk his life to save hers . . .
maybe not. She'd called it lust when describing
her feelings in the Sunday phone chat, but after
spending the day with his family and her continued deepening feelings, she knew whatever was
happening between them went beyond that. Her
lust for Byron Carter had turned into something
much deeper—a feeling that had her questioning every rule she'd ever created or followed.

Cynthia showered, checked on Jayden at his
buddy Bobby's house, scanned her e-mails, and
climbed into bed. Sade's music still looped in her
conscience, the question she asked swirling with
others that spun in her head. Was it too late for
Byron to know that she loved him? Was it possible that he felt the same? What was it that caused
her to define Byron as a transportation director

rather than a bus driver? What made her wary of telling her parents about him, let alone arranging a meeting? What made her hesitant to admit that she loved him? Was it her own beliefs that he didn't measure up? Was it her upbringing? Was it her pride? And if so, was love really stronger?

26

It felt like a Monday. Not only because she'd not seen Byron for the rest of the weekend and her phone calls were responded to by text, but because Jayden had returned home with some type of virus. She'd split her Saturday and Sunday between sitting in emergency, wiping up vomit, and worrying herself to the point where she herself felt ill. After tossing and turning half the night, she got up early and phoned the regular babysitter, Tanishia, who was home from college, to ask if she could look after Jayden. The sitter had agreed to come over right then. Cynthia had jumped into the shower, and for the first time in months arrived at the office before her assistant, Ivy, at exactly 7:15. She wasn't so much excited to dig into the overflowing workload as she was to escape her incessant thoughts.

"Oh!" Cynthia's hand went to her chest as she expelled a relieved breath. She'd gone to the break room for the requested extra sugar that the coffee shop employee had failed to add to her order. Had she known it was occupied, and especially if she'd been privy to who, she would have drank the joe black. "I didn't expect anyone else in this early."

"Well! I certainly never expected to see *you* before nine or after five. I don't know how you manage to accomplish so much in so few hours. I seldom leave before seven each evening and still have a ton left to do." Margo eyed Cynthia's perfectly tailored ivory skirt suit, smooth bare legs, and four-inch heels with a mixture of envy and contempt. "Whoever gets the director job will have to be totally committed."

"I agree." Cynthia's voice rose with enthusiasm, as if talking to a best bud. "She also must be well-organized and able to work effectively in a timely fashion."

A subtle shade of red rising from Margo's neck upward was the only outward sign that the words had hit their mark. Even so, a smirk settled on Margo's face. "How was your weekend?"

As if you care. "It was very nice, thank you. And yours?" Cynthia reached for a packet of raw sugar.

Margo's fake laugh was like nails on a chalk-board. "Very nice, thank you," she repeated. "A girlfriend and I went to the promenade in Santa Monica."

Cynthia was glad her back was turned. She slowly opened and poured the packet of sugar, forcing calmness into her voice as she reached for another. *Is she the voice I heard that night? Of course not. In a city as large as Los Angeles, what are the chances?* None, but Cynthia focused on this verbal spar as a fencer would his conversation. "I love that area, and would live there if it weren't so expensive and more child-friendly."

"Have you been there lately?"

Antagonism, like thick, black oil, oozed through the cheerful tone of the question. *She knows.* Picking up her cup, Cynthia took a carefree sip of coffee as she turned around. "As a matter of fact, I was there this weekend, just like you."

"You're kidding? What a small world. Had I known that we could have met for drinks."

Not if hell had frozen over and you had the pick for our escape. This thought was hid behind a patient smile.

"Were you on a hot date?"

"Hardly; I attended a fund-raiser for medical research."

"Ooh, that's a smart way to snag a doctor," Margo teased, wiggling a manicured finger. "Of course, to do that, you'd have to go alone."

"If that were one's motive, arriving alone would be best."

"So, did you?"

"Did I what, snag a doctor?"

"That, too, but did you go alone?"

Cynthia reached for a napkin. "Margo, it is truly too bad we didn't run into each other this weekend. It was an invitation-only event focused on art, but given the handsome doctors in attendance and your considerable interest in medicine, I think you would have had an enjoyable time." She headed toward the door but was stopped by Margo's question.

"Did you purchase any?"

"A couple pieces," Cynthia said, turning around once more.

"Wow, you're a gambler."

"Not really. This type of art is a pretty safe investment."

"Perhaps, but I was talking about spending money frivolously when you'll soon be out of work."

"Oh, I missed a memo?"

"Let's face it, Cynthia. You're a pretty girl, but it's going to take more than looks to head up this agency. I'm simply more experienced and better qualified to do that than you."

"Then it's clear why you're not worried. That being said, I think I'll wait until the official announcement to clear out my office."

The smile remained on Cynthia's face until she reached her office and closed the door. Unfortunately, her peace didn't last. Between a manager's meeting and a case involving a mother and her teenage daughter that they had to work on together, Cynthia was forced to interact with this walking irritation for most of the day. Even more, the snide comments Margo made about Santa Monica continued to bug her. She'd not given much thought to Byron being related to her client, hadn't believed their coffee date would go beyond that. Given that her position was already tenuous, the possibility of their being a conflict of interest, even improper if reported by a certain competitor, had to be explored. Then again, Byron hadn't called. Perhaps there was no longer a problem to worry about.

Even if there were, it took a back seat once she'd arrived back home from work. Jayden said he no longer felt sick, but lying in bed most of the day had obviously given him time to think.

"Mom."

"Yes, Jay."

"Who is my dad?"

The question caught her off guard. But not as much as what she saw when she turned to face him. They were in his bedroom where he reclined against a pillow, his fingers latched behind his head, looking very much like the person in question.

"Why all of these questions lately about your father?" Her voice was light as she came to sit beside him, an exact opposite contrast to the weight of her heart. "It's been a while since you've thought of him."

"No, it hasn't. I just don't tell you."

It was hard to absorb these words with a nonchalant face. "You're getting older. It's only natural you'd be curious."

"Who is he?"

"I don't know where he is." Not quite an answer to the question but at least not a lie.

"Why not?" He sat up, and met her eye-to-eye.

"As I've told you before, once he and I were no longer together, we both moved on with our lives."

"He's no longer your boyfriend, but he's still my dad!"

This was different. When discussing Jayden's father with him she'd seen curiosity, sadness, even longing. But she'd never seen anger. *What brought this on?*

"Did something happen today that made you want to see your father?"

"Doesn't every child want to see their dad?"

The question pierced her heart. "Yes."

"I've asked you before, but you never tell me anything about him. You won't even tell me his name and now I know why. Because you know I'd search for him on the Internet. And I'd find him, too."

"I know how difficult this must be for you—"

"How can you say that when you know Grandpa?"

"Yes, I know Dad. I'm speaking of the difficulty of this whole situation. It's very complicated, Jayden, which is why I'll explain everything when you're older. Not now."

"That's not fair," he said, tears welling up in his eyes. "Bobby's got a dad. Zachary's got a dad. Joshua's got *two* dads!"

"Does he have a mom?"

"No, but he's got a dog!"

Cynthia would have chuckled, had the light in her child's eyes not dimmed so quickly. And if not for his next question.

"Do I look like him?"

"You're way more handsome." Silence. "You have his eyes, and body structure. When you smile, there's a hint of a dimple in your right cheek, just like him."

Her voice broke, and Cynthia fought for restraint. Unresolved feelings and prolonged guilt is only part of why Cynthia had hoped Jayden would outgrow the curiosity about her first love, and biggest mistake. Clearly, this was wishful thinking. The questions wouldn't get easier. For her and Jayden to move peacefully into their future, she'd have to step back into a tumultuous past.

Once in her room, she went straight for her cell phone and tapped her thumb on the face she'd snapped of Byron when just before leaving for the art show in Santa Monica, he'd done the same. Just seeing his smile calmed her spirit. Love might trump pride after all.

27

"I've been thinking about you," is how Byron answered his phone.

"But you didn't call."

"No."

"I understand."

"Do you?"

This evoked an unlikely snort that would have made Anna swoon. "For the second time tonight, my ability to understand has been questioned."

"Perhaps there's a reason."

"There is, and I'd like to tell you about it."

"I'm listening."

"Not over the phone."

"It's late, and a weeknight. Tyra's already in bed."

"I'm . . . it's . . . ." The dam of restraint tethered to resignation slipped. She closed her eyes to staunch tears, held a sob behind clenched teeth, straightened her spine, and swallowed pity. "It's okay. I'm sorry to have bothered you. Good night."

"Cynthia."

"Yes."

"Give me a half hour."

"Don't ring the bell. Call when you get here. I'll let you in."

Forty-five minutes later, her phone face lit up. She tipped down the stairs and opened the door. "Hello," she whispered, before placing a finger to her lips and motioning him inside.

They were quieter than cat burglars as they returned to her room. She closed the door and visibly exhaled. "I can't believe I'm so nervous. He's a very sound sleeper."

"If he knocks on the door, I'll jump in the closet."

"That's a good idea!" She attempted a smile and failed miserably.

Byron's eyelids lowered along with his already soft voice. "Cynthia, come here."

She fairly ran into his arms. Tears followed suit and ran down her face.

"Shh. It's okay." He looked around. "Let's go over here and sit on this big chair."

Chaise, she thought automatically but didn't correct. As long as he kept his arms around her, she didn't care what he called it.

He sat down and settled her between his legs, gently rocking her silent but shaking body as the tears flowed. After several long moments she pushed away from him, and got up to blow her nose. "Would you like something to drink?"

"No, I'm good."

"Well, I'm in need of liquid courage. Be right back."

Byron watched her leave, then looked around him. His brow furrowed as he thought. *What in the world has happened?* It had to be serious for her to invite him here. He rested his head back against thick, plush fabric, noting how the chair almost conformed to his frame. Everything around him matched and looked expensive. As was the case on his other lone visit, not so much as a piece of paper was out of place. Yet his being there alone was proof of a mess somewhere.

Cynthia returned. Still shaken, but composed. "I brought the bottle and an extra glass in case you changed your mind." She placed the tray on a table beside the chaise. "There's a savory trail mix as well, so please, help yourself."

She sat at the end of the chaise facing Byron and took a couple sips of wine. "Where's Tyra?"

"My neighbor came over to watch her."

Now, Byron watched Cynthia. And waited.

She drank half of the wine in her glass. "Jayden asked about his father."

"Not an unusual question, especially for a boy his age." She nodded, took another sip. "What exactly did he want to know?"

"Where he lived . . . and his name."

"He doesn't know his father's name?"

Byron hadn't meant to sound so incredulous but . . . for real? *Stay calm, man. This is hard enough for her as it is.*

Cynthia finished her wine and set down the glass. She took a deep breath and spoke without emotion. "I was seventeen when I met him, the summer before I left for college. He was thirty-one, an investment broker doing business with my father. I was hanging out with friends by our pool when he arrived, had no idea he was there. We were playing around and one of the guys started chasing me. I ran into the house in nothing but my bikini, hair plastered to my body, something I'd done countless times. Only this time, I ran straight into him.

"I looked up and into the eyes of the most amazing man I'd ever seen—in person, at the movies, on television . . . ever. Looking back, I think I fell in love right then. But, of course, I denied it. Especially when my dad came out of his office and sternly commanded I change out of my wet suit."

"What did this guy do?"

She shrugged. "Not much. It happened so fast. He said, 'whoa,' or something like that. We looked at each other and then I heard my dad. When I came back out of my room, he was gone. It would be four years before I saw him again."

Cynthia stood, walked over to the table, and poured wine into two glasses. She gave one to Byron, who held it but did not drink.

"I graduated from college with a degree in sociology, and decided to take off a semester before returning to get my master's degree in business administration. It hadn't been easy maintaining a 3.8 GPA and I was burned out. One night I went into the city with some friends, to attend a private party."

"The city?"

"Minneapolis. That's about an hour away from where I grew up. It had been awhile since we'd all seen each other and we were ready to cut loose. We rented a limo that was stocked with champagne. Brought the party *to* the party." Her smile was bittersweet. "We were young and carefree, had the world by the tail. We knew several of the other guests. The house was huge, a mansion, and soon we'd all gone our separate ways. Eventually I got tired of dancing and went outside to get some fresh air. And there he was."

"Why won't you say his name?"

"Because it feels like I'll choke on it." She came back to the chaise, sat close to Byron but with her back to him. "Stewart Monihan. That's the name I haven't spoken aloud since Jayden was two months old, which was also the last time I saw him."

He slid his hand across the downy material near her leg, but not touching. She reached over, clasped it, and continued. "He seduced me that night. It wasn't hard. The relationship I'd entered during my sophomore year in college was one I knew wouldn't last. After graduating, we wished each other well and went our separate ways. A few years ago we reconnected on Facebook. He's married, has a daughter, doing well.

"After that amazing night with Stewart, I thought I was doing well, too, incredible, in fact. We had an intensely torrid love affair, clandestine because I was sure Dad wouldn't approve. A little more than a month later, I found out I was pregnant, and he was married."

"Damn."

"Exactly. As bad as that sounds, it wasn't the worst mistake. No, that happened three days later, when I told my mom."

"How was that worse?"

His voice was soft, laced with concern, as he disengaged his hands from hers and ran them up her arm to squeeze her tense shoulders. She leaned back against him and picked up the glass of wine he never drank.

"From the way my mother reacted, you would have thought I screwed the pope. I think to have murdered someone would have been a lesser crime. Somehow the fact that I had no idea he was married got lost along with the lucrative business deal my dad could no longer continue. I thought to get an abortion."

"Why didn't you?"

"Because of Stewart, and the promises he made: to leave his wife, get a divorce, marry me and carry me and our child off into the happily-ever-after sunset. By the time I realized he had no intention of leaving his trust-fund darling, I was almost seven months along, and not at all happy."

"What did you do?"

"Get shuttled off to upstate New York and an aunt I barely knew. I had Jayden and returned to Minnesota, a near prisoner in my parents' home. It's pathetic, but I still believed there was a chance with Stewart, that after seeing how beautiful our baby was he'd choose us and leave her. He didn't. Within a week, I'd packed up my life and returned to Chicago, where I'd gotten my undergrad degree. I hired a live-in nanny, threw myself into work and school, got my master's degree, took specialized certification classes in various types of counseling, and built the reputation that led me here."

Finally, she turned and looked at him. "I am my mom's most profound disappointment. She never lets me forget it, and I'm always trying to live up to her high standards. It's why the other night you couldn't be a bus driver." One lone tear began a soulful journey down her cheek. "I was practicing the lines I'd use if you met her. I was lifting you to the standard that I know she demands."

She rested her head against his chest. He caressed her tenderly, kissed the top of her head. She ran a hand up his arm, much as he'd earlier done to her. He inhaled her perfume, the scents of jasmine and citrus mixed with vulnerability and relief. Her hand moved to his cheek, as her lips grazed his collarbone. Her tentative movement unleashed something deep inside of him. A desire, no, a mandate that he shield her, protect her, make sure her heart was safe. His plan was to simply comfort her. Cynthia had other ideas. She turned and covered his lips with her own. The kiss was deep, wet, hungry, and haunting. Soon clothes were off and bodies touched, hands groped and found and caressed the other's sex.

"Do you have condoms?" Byron urgently whispered.

Cynthia scrambled off the bed, retrieved the foiled protector, and returned to the bed. Byron was as impatient as she, pulling her to him, teasing his tongue over every inch of her body before lapping the nectar from her private paradise.

"Now, I need you inside me."

Byron needed that, too. Within minutes he had her mewling. She grabbed a pillow, pressed it to her mouth to stifle the screams. He loved her once, twice, three times before morning. She woke up feeling satiated, and free.

After a quick shower, Byron and Cynthia tipped down the stairs to her front door.

She gave him a last quick kiss. "Thank you."

"You're welcome. I'm glad that you called."

She opened the door. He stepped out, then turned around. "Tell your son about his father. The circumstances can remain hidden, but the father's identity is part of your son's identity, and is something he needs to know."

As he walked to his car, those words rang in his ears. Tanya continued to insist he was little Ricky's father. Which meant there was another little boy who needed to know the truth about his father. Byron needed to know this, too.

28

It was going to be a long day. Cynthia knew it as soon as she stepped into the H.E.L.P. Agency offices, before she reached her area, turned the corner, and saw trouble. There sat Leah, an hour early for her appointment, talking to Margo, who had no business with her client. After last night's revealing talk with Jayden, painful disclosure to Byron, and two hours' sleep, she was not in the mood.

She walked over to Margo. "May I help you?"

Margo stood. "Good morning, Cynthia. I was walking by and saw this pretty young lady sitting here all alone. Your assistant is nowhere in sight, so I stopped to ask if I could help."

Cynthia was about to inflict a verbal slice and dice, but she noticed the strain on Leah's face. This young adult lived in a world of drama. She didn't need to see it in the place she came for help. She owed Margo nothing, least of all an explanation on the goings-on of her department.

"Good morning, Leah. Let's go in my office."

Cynthia left Margo standing in her department's reception area, not even looking her way as she closed the door.

"Would you like something to drink?"

"No, I'm fine." The troubled countenance and low, tremulous voice told Cynthia that Leah was anything but.

"You're early."

"Yeah, I got dropped off."

"Okay, no problem. Rather than have you wait an hour, let's go ahead and get started. We'll sit over there." Cynthia nodded to the sitting area. Leah walked over and plopped down on a tan-colored leather chair that matched a blue, tan, orange, and ivory striped love seat. Two square cubes were arranged to form a coffee table. Atop it were a small bamboo plant and a set of slate coasters boasting positive messages such as believe, dream, and gratitude. A large potted plant set in the far corner. In the corner behind Leah was a tall, three-tiered table housing magazines on the bottom, an iPod and dock on the second shelf, and a combination serenity fountain and candle holder on top. The fountain was turned on, providing the soothing sounds of a softly babbling waterfall. Leah seemed oblivious to the attention placed on providing an ambiance of peace and calm. Her eyes were glued to the cell phone she held, her thumbs in synchronized movement as she typed.

After setting down her bag and retrieving her iPad, Cynthia walked over to the sitting area. She placed her large coffee with a double shot of espresso on one of the coasters and then walked over and turned on the iPod. Soft strands of a new age instrumental played with a soothing combination of piano and strings swept through the room like a warm summer breeze. She turned and witnessed Leah's tense shoulders relax.

Good. Cynthia took a deep, clearing breath. It was time to put aside every personal situation and focus on her client's needs.

She sat in the middle of the love seat, close enough for their conversation to feel intimate, yet far enough away to give Leah her personal space. The iPad remained on the table. She picked up her coffee, leaned back against the sofa, and chatted as though she were talking to a friend. "So . . . how is school this week?"

"It's all right."

"Leah, would you please put away your cell phone and give me your undivided attention, the same as I'm giving you?"

A few more seconds of typing, a healthy sigh, and then Leah complied with Cynthia's request.

Aware of Leah's need to feel in control of some aspect of her life, Cynthia took another sip of coffee, and another deep breath. "Is there anything specific you'd like to talk about today?"

"Not really."

"Why don't we start with what has you unhappy."

"I'm not unhappy," she mumbled with a scowl.

"Then you should let your face know." Cynthia glimpsed a wisp of a smile. There was hope.

"How does that woman know my uncle?"

Now it was Cynthia's turn to scowl. "What woman?"

"The woman who was with me when you got here, trying to get all up in my business. I can't stand when people do that, acting all fake like they really care."

Except for a slight narrowing of the eye, Cynthia did not react. Oh, but she wanted to. She wanted to react all over Margo Edwards. *Do not curse. Do not get up. Do not behave as your dear friend Lisa would, leave this office, find Margo, and slap her sideways.* She looked at the coaster on the table. *Breathe.* She decided this was a good idea and in mere seconds could speak without yelling, which would be most uncouth.

"What did she say?"

"Something about him looking familiar. She asked where he lived."

Why would she want to know that? "Did you tell her?"

"Why would I do that? I don't know her. So I just said south central."

"Hmm."

Cynthia picked up her iPad, giving herself time to take her attention off of Margo, for the moment, and put it back on her client. And giving Leah an opportunity to gather her thoughts and take the lead in their discussion. Many counselors with whom Cynthia trained talked constantly—probing, asking, digging. These methods were often successful. But Cynthia believed that sometimes silence was the space that people needed in order to open up.

Several minutes passed. Music played. Water

flowed. Cynthia sipped coffee and made notes on her pad.

"His birthday's tomorrow."

Wow. A breakthrough. "How old would your brother have been?"

"Twenty-one."

"Ah, that makes him a Gemini. So is my father."

"When's his birthday?"

"This coming Saturday." Cynthia almost added that he'd be sixty years old, but stopped herself because that was an age Leah's brother would never reach. "What did Lance normally do on his birthday?"

"He liked to go to the ocean."

"Really? Where would he go?"

"Dockweiler. It's a beach straight out Manchester. You can take the bus there."

"Do you like the ocean?"

She shrugged. "He didn't want me to go with him. He'd always take his friends."

"But you've seen it, right? You've been there."

"A couple times."

"Do you think that's something you'd like to do on his birthday? Maybe go to the one Lance enjoyed and experience what he loved?"

"I don't know why they had to shoot him. He was minding his own business, just walking down the street." A tear escaped each eye. She angrily wiped them away.

"It's a horrible thing they did to your brother. Not only him but you, your mom, uncle . . . everyone in your family. Sometimes bad things happen to good people, for no reason at all."

"It's not fair."

"No, it's not."

"He used to always tell me not to get caught up with the boys on the block."

Cynthia put down the iPad and sat back. "Sounds like a smart brother to me."

"He was really smart, wanted to be either a computer scientist or an engineer."

"What do you want to be?"

Her voice dropped. She looked directly at Cynthia for the first time since entering the room. "For real? I just want to be alive."

29

There were some situations that couldn't wait until Sunday. So shortly after her session with Leah, Cynthia told Ivy that she had to run an errand and would be back in half an hour or less. She reached the building's lobby, walked outside and into a corner restaurant. After ordering an orange juice and small salad, she retrieved her cell phone and dialed Gayle's number.

"Hello, Gayle. It's Cynthia."

"Hello, Cynthia. This is a surprise."

"I know. Middle of the workday calls are rare. Are you busy?"

"Of course, but there's always time for you."

"Good. Can you hold for a moment?" Cynthia tapped the contact icon and then Lisa's face.

"Hey, chick!"

"Hello, Lisa. I've got Gayle on the line. Let me merge the calls." She did. "Gayle, are you there?"

"Yes."

"Can you call Dynah and conference her in?"

"Is everything all right?"

"Obviously not, Gayle," Lisa replied, "since Cynthia's trying to have a Sunday girl chat on a Tuesday."

"I'd just like all of your perspectives on a situation."

"With that sow Margo?"

"Gayle, can you please—"

Gayle interrupted. "Hold on."

Lisa kept talking. "I'm right, aren't I?"

"Yes."

"What happened?"

"Let's wait until Gayle gets Dynah so I don't have to repeat myself."

"Cynthia?" No idea what was happening yet already Dynah's voice was filled with concern. "What's going on?"

"Okay, ladies, here's the deal. And since time is limited, let's not make this about whether or not I should be dating someone like Byron."

"Did you hear that, Gayle?"

"Did you hear me say anything, Lisa?" A beat and then, "Cynthia, this isn't about him, right?"

"Yes, and no," she began, and then gave a brief overview of what all had transpired. About going out with Byron Friday night (a fact that she'd pointedly not shared on Sunday), feeling as though someone was watching her (while at the art show with the man whom she'd chosen not to discuss), but not seeing anything out of the ordinary. She continued with Margo's cryptic comments yesterday and the questions she asked Leah today. "I think she saw me with Byron, remembered him from the day he was in our office, and has put two and two together."

"And come up with what?" Lisa asked, irritation obvious and patience short. Lisa was always ready to kick butt first and ask questions later. "Is it against the law or your company's rules to attend an art show with a client's uncle?"

"No, but depending on the circumstances, it's also not necessarily a good look. Margo and I are the only ones being considered for the director position. Since the company is being restructured, other titles will shift as well. On paper, we're almost even. She has more experience, but I have a master's degree. We both bring a unique skill set to the table. For me, it's a diverse perspective and book knowledge. For Margo, it's the fact that as a troubled teen, she received similar counseling to that which she now discharges and can relate on another level with both teens and adults."

"What about the board?" Gayle asked. "They're ultimately the ones who decide, correct?"

"That's a good question, Gayle. Yes, the ten members who make up the board will choose who heads up the agency."

"Any idea which way they are leaning?" Lisa asked.

"I'm almost certain of four members who will vote my way and equally sure of four who will most likely pick Margo. That still leaves two people undecided. The vote can go either way. What I believe the choice will come down to are personality and behavior, which is why any type of

professional impropriety against me right now,
no matter how small or even imagined, could
make the difference between having a job or looking for one."

Her friends knew Cynthia's family was financially comfortable, which meant she wouldn't be
homeless or starve. Still, no one liked the possibility that she could be forced out of a position
she loved.

"I haven't heard from you, Dynah? What are
your thoughts?"

"Cynthia, you know what I'm thinking and you
know what to do. End all contact with Byron immediately, personal or otherwise."

"I agree," Gayle quickly added, as though she'd
waited the entire conversation for an opening to
speak what was really on her mind.

Dynah continued. "Where personal relationships are concerned, you know that the ACA's
Code of Ethics is similar to that of the ASCA."

"Okay, y'all just dropped me into a bowl of al-
phabet soup. What in the hell are y'all saying?"

"Never mind that, Lisa." Gayle had a meeting
in ten minutes and needed the conversation to
stay on point. "Cynthia, what is the code pertain-
ing to this type of situation?"

"Intimate and/or sexual relationships between the client or their family members is
prohibited—"

"Then case closed!"

"Bam!"

"I think your question is answered."

Everyone chimed in at once and over each other.

"But!" Cynthia continued. "The definition of family is not clearly defined and is at the discretion of the counselor based on what, if any, harmful effects said relationship could have on a client—which in this instant is none because she is not aware of the intimate relationship—and how said relationship potentially affects a counselor's ability to maintain a professional and separate relationship with the client. The client's welfare and best interests have always been and will remain my primary focus, no matter what."

"Great argument, counselor," Dynah said softly. "Was it convincing enough to believe that what you're doing is correct?"

"I've got to run." Gayle's brisk tone suggested she was already mentally down the hall. "But let me say this. You've already spent too much time with a man who's not a DHOP, marriage material, a career enhancer, or has any networking benefits. He's a bus driver, Cynthia. And unless you want to be riding in it with him instead of driving your Lexus, I'd delete his number as soon as you end this call. Ciao, ladies."

"I have to go, too," Dynah said. "And while my reasoning is different from Gayle's position, the end result is the same. Cut ties with Byron immediately and hope that Margo had nothing concrete to back up whatever accusations that may come up. We all want love, Cynthia. It's maddening to be in a position to demand the best, when the best seems scarce. But you deserve the best, someone who can at least do for you what you can do for yourself. And that's not Byron. I love you, girl."

"Love you, too." Cynthia placed a bill in the receipt holder and headed out of the restaurant. She'd been gone fifteen minutes and judging from Margo's underhanded actions, that may be fourteen minutes too long.

"All right, Lisa. I'm headed back to the office. Thanks for your input."

"You're welcome, but I haven't inputted yet."

"Your straightforwardness and humor are as valuable as anything else I heard just now."

"Then humor me, and hear this. When you're on your death bed, it probably won't be a client who comes to see you and help you cross over. If you're lucky, if you're smart . . . it will be your man."

The elevator door closed, effectively ending a conversation that was already over. In hindsight, Cynthia wondered what the heck she'd been thinking. That this wasn't an obvious no-brainer points to just how off-kilter were her priorities.

She would end things with Byron tonight, if possible, no later than Friday and her trip back home. A shame that it had taken his being forcibly removed from her life for her to realize how much she wanted him in it.

30

He'd thought about her all day long, and by the time his shift ended, Byron had designed the perfect evening to make his girl feel better. Okay, admittedly with a little help from his little brother, Barry, the family's Romeo. If Byron could do anything, it was give props where they were due. There was no way he would have come up with the idea to book an in-home spa treatment for Cynthia, along with a personal chef to prepare her and Jayden's dinner. His first thought would have been that he couldn't afford it and wondered how his barely working brother even knew of such things. With Byron's knowledge and connections, however, the entire night had cost him less than two hundred dollars. Cynthia opening up to him last night had reeled him in all the way. That she would tell him what hadn't even been shared with her girls showed a rare confidence in him as a man, and a friend. It was the kind of vibe that existed between Willie and Liz, where attributes such as love and loyalty existed without question and beyond all doubt. He couldn't count the number of times when during a disagreement with his mom, he'd enlisted the help of his father and heard, "Watch yourself, buddy. If I hadn't known her, then I wouldn't know you now. That's the order in this house. She comes first."

Byron would slink to his room, mumbling about his poor, arduous, unfair life. But on occasion, he'd stay around long enough to witness the light his father's declaration put in his mother's eye. And he'd vow that when he had a wife, he'd say the same thing.

He got into his SUV, turned it on, and turned on the air conditioner. Then he pulled out his cell phone to put tonight's plan in motion. The call went to voice mail. Disappointed, but not deterred, he left a message.

"Cynthia. Hey, baby, it's me. I was hoping to catch you, find out how you're recovering from our after-hours rendezvous. I hated to leave you and found myself thinking about you all day, and how it would be to wake up to your beautiful face more often.

"I know last night was an exception; plus, we both need our sleep. So as much as I'd like to see you tonight, I know it's not possible. But I still wanted to be a part of your evening, so I hope you get this message before taking Jayden out to eat. I've made arrangements for you to, uh, to have y'alls' meal delivered tonight. So call me when that happens. Matter of fact, call me when you get this. I want to hear your voice. You've got me gripped, girl. All right, then. Bye."

A short time later, he pulled into his driveway. His neighbor, Miss Margie, was busy in her flower garden, pulling the weeds away from "her babies."

"Hey there, Miss Margie."

She stood straight and removed a worn straw hat to wipe her brow. "Hey now, Byron. What you know good?"

"Another day, another dollar."

"After the tax man gets it, you'll only have fifty cents."

"Ha! That's about right. Tyra inside?"

"Yeah, she wanted to stay out here with me and plant her namesake. But I told her she wasn't going to use me as an excuse for why her work wasn't finished. Kids think they're the first ones to try and run game. I've forgotten more ways to get over on folks than she'll ever know."

Byron walked over to inspect her vibrant flower bed boasting a variety of colors: red, yellow, purple, pink, lavender, and hearty green. "One of these plants is called Tyra?"

Miss Margie smiled. "Well, not quite. But these"—she pointed to a grouping of beautiful burnt orange flowers with magenta spots or yellow starbursts at the root—"these are called tiger lilies. I just renamed them Tyra's lilies."

Byron reached over and gave his neighbor a spontaneous hug. "Thank God for you, Miss

Margie, seriously. Being the primary parent isn't easy. I don't know what I'd do without you."

"I know what I'd do."

"What's that?"

"I'd spend more time courting that pretty lady who came over one time in that fine silver car and didn't get back to it until two days later."

The good thing about nosy neighbors? They saw everything that went on around them, which was also the bad thing about them. Unable to think of an appropriate response to this comment, Byron became very interested in Tyra's lily.

"Look, I wasn't always old and wrinkled. Been married four times and have five kids."

Byron didn't try and hide his surprise. "You have kids? How have I lived next to you all these years and not known that?"

"Probably because they're not worth the energy it took to push each one of them out. I love 'em all, but except for my two youngest, a son in the air force and a daughter married and living in Hawaii, they're worthless. One's in jail, one's in hell—though she calls it marriage by common law. And my oldest is in a losing battle with a crack pipe. And you know what? If the right man came along and asked, I'd go for number five."

"Ha!"

"I'm saying all that to say you're young, not bad looking, and you're a good man. Too good to spend so much time by yourself, just you and your daughter. I know you've got your family, your brothers and all. But every man needs his own kingdom, know what I mean?"

"I believe I do, Miss Margie. That's good advice. I think I'll take it." He started across the lawn to his house.

"Just make sure I'm invited to the wedding."

"That's a bet! You'll sit with the family!" He entered his home. "Tyra!" Stopping to remove his tennis shoes and crew socks, he hollered again. "Tyra! That girl and those headphones." He marched toward her bedroom but halfway there stopped, and tiptoed the remainder of the way.

Reaching her open door, he stood there, watching her. Back to the door, textbook on the floor next to the iPad that along with the pen she held passed for a drum set. Headphones over ears, with the music so loud he could make out some of the words.

How in the world can she study with the music so loud?

He took three steps and grabbed her shoulders.

She jumped so high and screamed so loud he almost felt badly.

Almost, but not quite.

"Daddy!"

He tried to answer, but couldn't for laughing.

"That's not funny! I almost peed my pants!"

"Uh-huh, would have served you right. That's what happens when your music is so loud you're not aware of your surroundings. What if it had been a burglar instead of me tapping you on the shoulder? What would you have done?"

"Definitely peed my pants, for one. And then . . . I don't know . . . tried to get away I guess."

This just got real. Her answer showed unpreparedness should—God forbid—an event like that occurred. *What would she do? Hell, what would I do for that matter?* What began as a fun antic was now a learning moment . . . for both of them.

He sat on her bed. "You know what I just realized?"

"What?"

"I'm not sure what I would do or what you should do if that ever happened. Grab your iPad."

She picked it up, then came over and sat beside him.

"Type, uh, never mind, give it to me." He sat there a moment, shrugged, and typed, "what a child should do if a stranger enters home."

Several sites came up but none that looked to have the information he sought. He replaced the word *stranger* with *intruder,* and got better luck.

"All right, let's see what's up."

Tyra leaned over, to read for herself. "Think ahead."

He nodded. "So far, so good. Your daddy's smart, isn't he?"

"Yes."

Boy, do I have this kid fooled. He scanned the article, which turned out to be more about burglaries and intruders being in a different part of the house. Several more sites offered more of the same, and included suggestions for security systems and what breeds made good guard dogs. He finally found a Web site with a couple of helpful tips. "What does it say?"

"Have a list of phone numbers . . ."

"Start right here."

"Okay. Keep your phone close so you can dial 911." She looked at Byron. "But he'll hear me!"

"Not if you're quiet. But I saw this show once, where the girl dialed the police without the guy knowing. That's what you should do. Dial 911 and then put down the phone so he doesn't even know it's on. That way the police can hear what's going on."

"And do what?" *Dang, good question.* "Oh, I know. Yell, 'There's a stranger in my house! He's coming after me!'"

"No, you should stay calm, and ask, 'Why are you here at my address? I'm Tyra Carter. I'm not your child.'"

"Why would I tell him my name?"

"You're saying your name and address so the police will hear, and be able to help you."

"Oh! Cool!"

Byron rolled his eyes. Here his daughter was, looking at an intruder encounter as one would an adventure while he was about to have a heart attack and go load his gun!

His phone rang. He looked at the ID, smiled, and stood. "All right, kid. That's lesson number one." His tone went from studious to sexy as he walked across the hall and closed the door to his room. "Hey, you."

"Hello, Byron."

The clipped, professional voice stopped him dead in his tracks. He looked at his watch: 6:25. "Are you still at work?"

"No, I'm home."

He relaxed. "Oh, okay. Did you get my message?"

"Yes."

He was expecting a more enthusiastic reaction but . . . okay.

"Did you eat yet?"

"No, and that's one of the reasons I'm calling. I'm sure that you meant well, but you didn't have to go to the trouble of ordering dinner for me and my son."

"It's what I wanted to do."

He heard her sigh into the phone. *Did she just sigh into the phone?* He looked at the phone, as if it had answers.

This exchange is nothing like Barry said would happen. At all.

"Is there any way you can cancel the order?"

Byron's mood was quickly moving from feeling amorous to being annoyed. "Cynthia, what's going on?"

"We really shouldn't have this discussion over the phone."

This did not sound good. "What discussion is that?"

A long pause and then, "The one where I explain that because of what in our code of ethics is defined as a conflict of interest regarding a client, I can no longer see you . . . in any capacity."

"You're kidding, right?"

"I am very sorry. Ending any kind of personal liaison by phone is the epitome of churlish behavior . . ."

"Did you say childish?"

"Handling this remotely is in very poor taste, though it would be even more difficult to do in person. Considering the circumstances, this inappropriate, unfortunate ending is for the best."

Byron had shifted from his position of romantic repose to now sit on the side of the bed wondering where was Cynthia—the one who less than twenty-four hours ago had cried on his shoulder, spilled out her heart, and cried out in throes of ecstasy—and who in the hell was this cold, robotic imposter, trying to tear his heart straight out of his chest?

"Cynthia. Tell me what happened. I know something did because you and I together are magic. Real talk."

"What's relevant is that which never should have happened, what I never intended would happen. And that's a personal affiliation with you. It is ethically improper and I am truly sorry for any hurt I've caused you by crossing the line."

"This is about your job. Either someone found out, or is suspicious. And rather than take a risk on the relationship, on me, you're choosing your job. How's my assumption so far?"

"Good-bye, Byron."

"No, Cynthia, don't—"

But she did.

She'd ended their affair, provided an unflappable explanation, apologized for any inconvenience, and hung up the phone.

Cold, curt, professional, not like the woman he held last night, but the one who'd boarded his bus.

31

Cynthia ended the call and wanted nothing more than to run to her room, assume a fetal position, and enjoy an all-out boo-hoo. Instead, she turned around and met the curious eyes of her observant son.

"How long have you been standing there?"

"Just now. What's wrong?"

The doorbell rang.

"I'll get it!"

"Jayden! No, let me." Cynthia walked to the door and after looking through the peephole placed her head against the wooden door. *A chef? The man with whom I just ended all contact has arranged for a chef to cook in my home?*

She opened the door, feeling lower than the sole of a shoe.

"Ms. Hall?" the man asked, in a tone that suggested he ate happy for breakfast, zeal for lunch, and chipper as a pick-me-up before in-home appointments.

"Yes, I'm Cynthia." She wanted to tell him to

go away, direct him to Inglewood to fix a meal for Byron and Tyra. She opened her mouth to do just that but "please, come in" came out instead.

"Thank you!" He stepped inside. "Wow, this place is amazing! I'm Chip, professional chef and owner of Chip's Choice Cuisine. I'd love to shake your hand, but mine are full."

"Oh, of course. Come right this way."

He followed her to the kitchen, placed a large recycle bag on the island, and unzipped a carry-on style case containing cooking utensils. All while talking nonstop. "I was so excited to accept this assignment. Your friend thinks you're amazing. He went on and on about how much you deserve to sit back, relax, and have someone serve you for a change. He thinks you work too hard and says you're . . . navigating a few challenges. I told him I had the perfect menu to relax you, rejuvenate you, and make your body feel good."

Seriously, the man was a walking infomercial.

He turned to place a pot on the stove, and spotted Jayden eyeing him intently. "Oh, hey, buddy! How are you?" He walked over to the boy, hand outstretched. "My name is Chip. I'm a chef. I came to cook for you."

"What are you going to fix?"

"What do you like to eat?"

"We're not choosy. Italian, Mexican . . . tonight we were having Chinese. But I guess we're not going out since you came to our house. Mom, who is your friend that sent him over here?"

"Someone you haven't met, Jayden. Give me a moment so I can make sure Chip is squared away." She turned to him. "I don't cook much. What type of equipment do you need?"

"I bring everything with me except a refrigerator and stove. Actually, that's not quite true. I have a mini-fridge and hot plate inside my van."

"You cook in your car?"

"Absolutely! You don't?"

"How old do you think I am?" Jayden asked, finding humor in the man's obvious ignorance.

"I don't know . . . sixteen?" Chip winked at Cynthia.

"I'm eight! Too young to have a car."

"Then that presents a problem for cooking in one." Chip reached into the case's side pocket and pulled out an iPad. "Cynthia, I was told your tastes are quite varied, as Jayden here pointed out. So I designed this menu." He offered the iPad, which she accepted. "What do you think?"

Cynthia read aloud. "Tomato bisque with cheese poppers." *How did he know this is my favorite soup?*

"Are those like jalapeño poppers?" Jayden asked.

"Exactly," Chip answered, "but not as spicy."

"Oh, good. Because Bobby's mom makes the kind that are hot. Why are you serving them with biscuits?"

"Jayden, don't ask so many questions."

"I totally don't mind," Chip readily assured her. "In fact, I was about to ask if I could interview this young man for the position of sous chef. Just for the evening, of course."

"What's a sous chef?"

"The sous chef is second-in-command, and helps the chef pull off a fabulous meal."

"But I don't know how to cook."

"I have a feeling you're a quick study."

During their chat, Cynthia had quickly scanned the rest of the meal: Farmers Market salad, grilled lollipop lamb chops paired with a potpourri couscous, and candy sprinkle-covered ice-cream cones for dessert.

He was thinking of Jayden. While discussing possible choices with the chef, Byron had kept her son in mind. This simple gesture proved he'd listened during their conversations and understood the elevated position Jayden occupied in her life. The truth of it took her appetite, along with the certainty in the rightness of her decision.

It took willpower, but Cynthia made it through Jayden's newfound love for cooking, Chip's incessant conversation about cooking, and what turned out to be an amazingly delicious meal. With the last of her control she bid Chip goodbye, got Jayden to bed, and had just poured a glass of wine to take to her bedroom when the doorbell rang again.

Crossing the room, she looked at the counters for what the chef must have forgotten. She looked through the peephole. It wasn't Chip.

"May I help you?" she asked through the closed door.

A soothing voice with an accent answered. "I'm looking for Cynthia Hall. My name is Thilago. I was hired and sent by a Mr. Carter to provide you relaxing massage."

As proof, he held up a bag in one hand and masseuse certification in another. "You can call him to confirm this. I am happy to wait."

"Um, give me a moment."

With the door once again her support, she placed her head in her hands, stunned beyond words. *First a five-star quality dinner and now a personal masseuse?*

Cynthia no longer thought she'd made the wrong decision. She was sure of it.

32

Since giving Tyra a good night kiss an hour ago, Byron had sat in a darkened, quiet living room watching the face light up on his silenced cell phone: Tanya, Barry, Douglas, Tanya (for the umpteenth time), Ava, Mama, Nelson, and just now Barry again. If it weren't for the fact that he hadn't heard from his dad or Marvin, he'd have sworn that Liz had sent out a Code 3C—Carter Call Circle—a tag team–styled communication system his mother had implemented and kept in place since childhood. There needn't be an emergency to have this plan implemented. In fact, at times the Carter Circle had been summoned for something as trivial as the answer to a Daily Double on *Jeopardy*. Liz had encouraged—translated, demanded—a transparent, close-knit family unit. It wasn't unusual to speak with one or all of his siblings on any given day. Never more than a week passed without some type of communication. There were no secrets between them. "On some days all we'll have is each other," she'd tell them. "And on those days each other will be all we need."

Right, but what about those days when all we want is to be left alone?

He'd been preoccupied yesterday, other more poignant thoughts blocking out the phone call that had upended his world. The family had gathered at their parents' house in Inglewood to celebrate the tragically short life of Lance Montell Thompson. Once home Byron had made a final call to check on Ava to see how she was really holding up. A good thing, too. In the privacy of her bedroom, she wasn't holding up all that well. She talked, he listened, until 3 a.m.

But tonight, there was nothing to obscure the stark reality that the woman of his dreams had come and gone from his life. *Was it only six weeks ago that I met her?* A series of failed relationships had made him a skeptic when it came to true love like his parents had existing anymore. And most definitely would have balked at anyone claiming to have fallen in love this quickly. He thought that crap only happened in movies. Now he knew it could happen for real. It had happened to him.

The doorbell rang, jolting Byron out of his pondering. He begrudgingly got up and walked to the door. *I know this fool Barry didn't come over here to . . .*

Halfway to the door another thought stopped him in his tracks. *What if it's not Barry? What if it's . . .* He stepped close to the window that faced the street, then leaned over slightly to peek outside without being seen.

The doorbell rang again. He hurried to open it.

"Ava. What are you doing here?"

"From that look on your face you were obviously expecting someone else." She stepped inside. "Is that why the lights are off? To set the mood?"

They shared a hug and then walked into the living room. He turned on a lamp. Both sat on opposite ends of the couch, facing each other. "Did Mama send you over here?"

Ava shook her head. "I haven't talked to her tonight. Douglas called, though, said him and Barry had called and both gotten voice mail." Ava had brought in a bottle of juice, which she set on the coffee table. "That's not why I came by, though. I could tell last night that something was wrong. What's up?"

He shrugged. "Same old, same old."

Ava cocked her head and gave him a look. "You are so not telling the truth right now! You've always been a bad liar. I don't know why you keep trying."

"It'll be all right."

"Though dealing with my own pain yesterday, I noticed you were hurting as well. At first I assumed that, like everyone else, it was about Lance."

"It was, partly."

"But not totally. What's going on, Byron?"

"Aw, man. I guess I should talk about it with somebody; about to drive myself crazy with this one-sided conversation going on in my head."

"Let me guess. The beautiful and refined counselor got tired of the hood and decided to go back and play in her own yard?"

Byron shot her a hard gaze. "If you came over

for 'I told you so,' I'm not in the mood. I don't need help feeling bad."

"No." Ava softened her tone. "I came over to support you like you did me last night." No response. "So, what happened?"

Byron shifted his position and began idly moving around the junk on the table. "According to her it's a conflict of interest; that she is prohibited from having personal relationships with the family of her clients."

"I thought you met her before you even knew she worked with Leah. Plus, if she knew this, why'd she go out with you in the first place? Wait, does she know that I'm your play sister, that we're not actually related?"

"Ava, you're as much my sister as if Liz Carter had carried you in her womb."

"But she didn't carry me."

"You're still family."

"You know I feel the same about all of you. Being an only child, having your mother basically adopt me after y'all moved next door is one of the best things that's happened in my life. But if she knew we weren't blood-related, that might change things. That's if Leah being her client was the only reason."

"What other reason could there be?"

"Who knows? But it sounds like you should have asked more questions."

"It was a rather one-sided conversation. Before I could ask her too much of anything, she'd hung up."

"Hung up! You mean she cut you loose over

the phone, didn't even give you the common courtesy to say good-bye in person?"

"That probably was a good thing."

"If you say so." Ava reached for the bottled juice, watching as Byron mindlessly took a pair of Chinese meditation balls out of a small satin box and began slowly rolling them around in his right hand. As he maneuvered them around and around with his fingers, soft ringing chimes and metal clinking against metal disrupted the silence.

"I can't believe how hard I fell for that girl." His voice was low. He looked at the balls instead of his sister. Rotating clockwise . . . three, four, five times, and then clumsily and with effort turning them the opposite way.

"I didn't even know you were into her like that. It definitely didn't show at the block party. But then again given what you said she told you, I guess y'all were keeping it on the low."

"I wasn't trying to. I mean, none of this was planned."

Ava's look contained a healthy dose of skepticism.

"Okay, I did go after her a little bit . . ."

"I know you did! She's cute and you're a Carter!"

"So are you, basically."

"Hey, I have no problem owning mine. Just sayin' . . ."

"Cynthia had no plans beyond meeting for coffee."

"And then you poured on the Carter charm."

"Every time we'd get together everything would just flow, it was natural. It didn't feel like there was this big difference between us, like she was on one level and I was on another."

"You were raised to believe that nobody is better than you."

"You felt that way, couldn't believe we went out more than once."

"That wasn't a reflection of how I feel about you, Byron, but how I felt about her. Don't get me wrong. As a counselor, I think she's very qualified. Leah likes her and I am seeing progress. Woman-to-woman, she seems friendly and genuine. But regarding the two of you on a relationship level, I just didn't see it."

"Well, we did. It was the first time I could imagine actually spending my life with the same woman."

"Dang, bro! You felt that way after what, a month?"

"Yes." He switched the meditation balls to his other hand, but after a couple turns placed them in the box.

"What was it, gold dust on her kitty?"

"Girl, you're crazy."

"Could it clap on cue or dispense money like an ATM?"

"Ha!" Byron cracked up, and realized it had been a minute since he'd enjoyed a hearty laugh.

"I'm glad to see you smiling." She reached for the juice bottle, took a drink, and recapped the bottle. "And not to wipe it off so quickly, but when was the last time you heard from Tanya?"

"She's called four times just today."

"Why?"

"Because I told her I wanted to have a paternity test done on little Ricky."

"And she didn't run right over to retrieve an old toothbrush or some of your hair? That's not your child, Byron."

"That's basically my thought. But I want to know for sure."

"I don't blame you." Ava stood. "We've both got to get up early, so I'm going to go."

Byron stood as well. "Yeah, and I'm pulling a double tomorrow."

"Why do you work so much? And you never take your vacation days. You probably have two months' worth by now."

"At least." They hugged. "I'm glad you came over, sis."

Byron took a shower and then climbed into bed, phone in hand, scrolling through missed phone calls, notifications, and . . . *wait a minute.* He scrolled back. What he thought he'd seen was confirmed. While talking with Ava, Cynthia had called.

He settled his head against the pillow and activated voice mail.

"Byron, I'm calling to thank you for the dinner and massage. That was very thoughtful and, obviously, totally unexpected."

A long pause, during which Byron wondered, *Is she crying? Changing her mind? Trying to find the right words to put their world back together?*

"You are a good person, Byron, and I . . . like being around you. I didn't expect that either. I'm not sorry for the time we spent together, but all things considered, this was probably the only possible outcome."

Byron's thumb hovered over the phone face. Save or delete? He tapped a button, deciding to do the same thing with the message that Cynthia had done to their friendship.

Delete.

He called Douglas.

"What do you want, dog?" is how his brother Douglas answered the phone.

"Ten million dollars and a getaway car."

"See, listen to you. Why do you assume the money would be illegal?"

"Because I know your mama don't roll like that."

"Ha! Daddy either." The brothers laughed, enjoying the easy camaraderie they'd shared for years. Unlike Barry, who Byron wanted to knock upside the head every other time they were together, Douglas was a lot like their father—steady, pragmatic, an upstanding man. "What's up, Byron?"

"I was calling to get the number of that attorney you told me about awhile back."

"Tony Jackson?"

"I guess so. I don't remember his name."

"Is this about Tanya?"

"Yeah, going through the courts to get a paternity test."

"For that, Tony is definitely the man to either do it or knows who does. I'll get it for you right now."

"I appreciate that, man."

Byron ended the call and after going to bed scrolled to where Cynthia's smiling face looked back at him, daring him to call her. He'd deleted her message but wasn't quite ready to delete her number. With a sigh, he placed the phone on the nightstand, turned off the light, and rolled over.

Leah, I hope you appreciate what all the people who care are doing for you.

33

She hadn't expected pain. Three days after what she'd hoped was a quick, clean break, the inevitable outcome of an imprudent decision, Cynthia felt loss, guilt, sadness, and an unrelenting feeling that she'd really screwed up. It wasn't just the dinner and spa treatment. It was the late-night phone calls she hadn't planned to miss, a memory of something silly he said, the nights of tender loving. It was the fact that the only person who could possibly make her feel better was the one she'd had to let go.

In deep thought, she barely looked at the clothes being thrown in the carry-on, used autopilot to add shoes and jewelry.

Did you really have to end it, Cynthia? And is the potential threat to your career the only reason?

She walked into the en suite bath and pulled her travel bag of toiletries from a drawer. *Whatever the reason, what's done is done.*

She went back into her walk-in closet, threw the toiletries into the case, and slammed down the lid. "Stop it, Cynthia." She angrily zipped the luggage and snatched it from the stand. "Enough is enough!"

"Mom! Can you come help me? I don't know what to wear."

Grateful for the distraction, Cynthia hurried from the room that seemed filled with the essence of her and Byron's last encounter. A short time later she and Jayden were in her car, headed for the airport. During the meandering journey from LAX's security area to the gate, she was determined to place her focus where it would be productive—her career, and her son, which meant coming to grips with her past so that Jayden could hopefully have a relationship with his father.

"The father's identity is part of your son's identity, and is something he needs to know." There it was again, Byron's voice, seeping into her consciousness. She willed her emotions to settle, her resolve to strengthen. This wasn't the first time she'd been forced to leave someone she cared for. There was enough of Anna Marie Hall in her to cut off unproductive feelings with a snip of reality and a clip of bourgeoisie.

The plane took off. Cynthia vowed that while she couldn't control thoughts about Byron, she would leave all feeling for him in Los Angeles. By the time they touched down in the City of Lakes, she felt she'd done just that.

"*Grand-mère!*" Jayden's excited shout seemed to reverberate in a house that was as quiet as a tomb.

Cynthia's first thought was of walking into

Byron's house to the sounds of a loud television, playing children, and his lively mother. She observed the thought as a magician would a rabbit before making it disappear.

"Hello, Jayden." Anna Marie knelt and gave her grandson a warm hug.

"Hello, Mom."

"Hello, dear." Another hug, but this one short and not quite as cozy. "Jayden, let's place your luggage in the guest room. And remember, while in the home of *Grand-mère,* please remember to use your inside voice."

Cynthia rolled her eyes as she also rolled her luggage down her mother's prized acacia walnut floors, part of a $40,000 renovation two years ago, and over a Persian rug runner that she felt compelled to explain had been hand-woven in a one-of-a-kind design. She tried to shake the aloofness of her mother's greeting along with the demand that she be called *Grand-mère,* not Grandma, a distinction still irksome after eight years. "Ma is the language of commoners," she'd explained, as if her ancestors arrived on Ellis Island and not Jamestown.

"*Grand-mère* is proud of you, *lumineux petit garçon,*" Cynthia heard Anna Marie say while passing the smaller guest room for the larger one she'd use.

"Excuse me, *Grand-mère?*"

"*Petit garçon* means 'little boy.' You've forgotten?"

Not surprising considering it's only heard once a year, at this house.

One of Anna Marie's proudest achievements was the ability to speak conversational French, an ability aided by annual jaunts to this favorite country and the help of a personal tutor.

That spattering of words is about the only thing French here, Cynthia mused as she emptied her carry-on and hung its contents in the closet. *Other than a loaf of bread on occasion. You don't even like fries!*

She turned from the closet to see her mother standing in the doorway. "Cynthia, I do hope you've brought something appropriate for the country club. I'm not sure I told you, but that's where the party will be held."

"Where is Dad? And Jeff?"

"Jeff is with his gorgeous, corporate attorney girlfriend—Fortune 500, mind you—showing her the town. I assured them that with seventy-five hundred square feet there was adequate room to house them, but they've opted for a suite at Four Seasons. It's obvious she comes from wealth and impeccable breeding." Anna Marie's eyes fairly sparkled. "I'd welcome her to our family with open arms."

Her face a mask of peaceful repose, Cynthia's answer was as bright, fake, and rote as a Stepford wife. "I look forward to meeting her."

In truth, she already envied the girl who in one visit received the one thing Cynthia had never gotten from Anna Marie: admiration.

"Carlton is on the golf course with Fred," Anna went on, "where he is some afternoons and most evenings."

"Always working on his golf game."

"Or so he says."

Cynthia ignored the comment. For as long as Cynthia could remember, her mother had insinuated her dad was unfaithful. Neither she nor her brother knew whether or not it was true, but after years of seeing him being browbeaten for the possibility, she no longer cared.

Less than ten minutes, and she'd already spent too much time with Mrs. Hall.

"Mom, may I borrow one of the cars? I brought something for the party, but something new would be nice. Plus, it would give you quality time with Jayden."

"That's fine, dear, though I wish you'd planned ahead. You're running the risk of being duplicated."

"Thanks, Mom."

Once in her mom's sedan, Cynthia felt she could breathe. She'd known what to expect from her mother and was angry for allowing the behavior to get to her. A subtle, gnawing tension, bubbling like molten lava, had existed between them for the past nine years. Unacknowledged anger. Unspoken words. Cynthia had a feeling that one day that volcano may explode.

Taking in the town's scenery along with blue skies and abundant greenery, Cynthia decided to heed her mother's advice and drive to Minneapolis to shop. It was late, but she knew just the place to go, a boutique where she could always find something simple and elegant. Just then, she reached the exit for the country club. "Maybe Dad's there," she murmured, deciding to run by there on a whim. While his personality was that of a quiet, introverted man, they'd always enjoyed a warm relationship, another reason for her mother's iciness, Cynthia believed. When she became pregnant, her father, though disappointed, never demeaned her but rather pragmatically helped her chart the best course of action. A hug from Carlton Hall was just what she needed.

She parked her car, walked up the familiar pathway to the country club, and went inside. No one was at the receptionist desk, so she continued down the hall to the restaurant. Her dad and his friends sometimes stayed there for hours, drinking, networking, or shooting the breeze. Halfway to her destination, a voice stopped her.

"Cynthia?"

No. Way. She slowly turned around and looked into the eyes of Jayden's father.

On the other side of the country, at this exact time, Byron turned off the bus to take his break. He pulled out his cell phone and called Cynthia.. He thought about her all morning and while he'd told himself he wouldn't, he decided to give her a call.

Voice mail. "That's no surprise." He pushed the pound key to bypass her message.

"Hey, Cynthia. Got your message. On my break and thought I'd call you back. I'm glad you enjoyed the chef and spa and whatnot. Had I known it was going to be my last supper so to speak, I might have just sent over a pizza, five dollars with everything on it, know what I'm sayin'?

On a serious tip, though, it's kind of cold how you called me and ended everything, like—bam—just like that. It's like what I was feeling or thinking wasn't important at all. That was just wrong, straight out.

"It's all good, though. You did what you had to, and now I'll do my thing. But if this . . . what did you call it?—transportation director—could offer a word of advice, it would be to look at everybody the same, treat everybody the way you want to be treated. I know you're a career woman and everything, but don't go so hard. Be gentle, like you were at around two, three o'clock the other morning. That's all. I wish you the best, baby."

As Byron ended the call, the phone vibrated. "Yeah, Tanya, what's up?"

"A little birdie told me you brought somebody to the block party."

He started the bus and opened the door for the waiting passengers. "You know what they say. Never trust a little birdie."

"I know I've been riding you hard for money, Byron, and I was wrong for that. But you know I've always been down with you. No matter what."

"Okay, that's good, but what is this call about? Do you need me to keep Tyra this weekend so you and Ricky can have some quality time?"

"I kicked him out, told him to come back when his act was together. I was hoping Mama Liz could keep her and you and I could go hang out somewhere."

"Have you sent the paternity results to my lawyer?"

"Forget you, Byron."

"It's a court order, Tanya. Get it done."

In a few short months, he'd found out a boy might be his, met the woman of his dreams, filed a paternity suit, had his first work-related accident in ten years, lost the woman of his dreams, and now had the baby mama of one and swearing it's two call to "hang out." Sometimes, life could be a trip.

34

"Thanks for agreeing to speak with me."

"Ha! Agreeing? That's a stretch." Cynthia looked at the closed door to one of the clubhouse's private rooms, imagining how it would feel to do as she desired—introduce the freshly poured lemon water to Stewart Monihan's face before running out of the country club screaming like a banshee. *The nerve of this man is beyond belief.* Here she'd gone looking for her father and found Jay's dad instead. There were so many thoughts and emotions running through her that the chance of keeping it together was fifty/fifty at best.

"Okay, you're right. When the manager stopped to chat, I knew it was my opportunity to finally have the conversation that's long overdue."

Cynthia's body fairly shook with anger. She clasped her hands together, speaking through lips that barely moved. Back straight, chin angled, anyone watching would see graceful poise. Another story if they were listening. "The only reason

I am sitting here is to gather my composure because I don't know what would happen if I moved, but I am fairly certain it would involve a physical altercation. In fact, moving that silverware may not be a bad idea."

Stewart laughed. Cynthia did not. His smile disappeared. She eyed the stark white linen napkin wrapped around a four-piece set of sterling silver flatware. He deftly reached over and pulled it to his side.

"You have every right to everything you're feeling. I just ask for five minutes. After that, if you still feel the way you do right now, I'll never bother you again."

Cynthia looked at her watch, and slowly relaxed against the chair back.

"When I found out you were pregnant, it was one of the happiest days of my life." Cynthia reached for her purse. "No, please. I'm begging you, Cynthia, just hear me out.

"Yes, I was married. Yes, it was wrong. I had every intention of telling you, was ready to end that miserable life. But when you got pregnant, your mom went ballistic. The next thing I hear is you've moved to escape me and I've ruined your life. Everything happened so quickly and involved so many variables: your parents, my family, the business deal with Carlton."

"And your wife, don't leave her out."

"By then she was the least of my worries, had been married in name only for years. We met as children. Our fathers had known each other since before either was married. We attended the same private school, traveled in the same circles. Our families spent vacations together. We were friends and then, as we got older, we were more than friends. I can't recall when the talk of marriage began, but by the time I'd graduated college and gotten my master's, the wedding was all but a fait accompli. I loved her, true enough, but it's one thing to be friends and another to be married. We should have stayed friends.

"Of course, I found this out after the vows had been taken and the wedding cake cut. Two years in, I'd had my first affair. The next year was her turn. Within five, we were sleeping in separate rooms. The kids came and we stayed together largely for their sake but for our families, too. Appearances, you know, and our social status and private club memberships. I was still making my way in the world of finance and image was very important. I'm not proud of it now, but back then I would do almost anything for a successful career.

"And then I met you. Actually, no, you met me, ran straight into my chest. A beautiful, wet, precocious, naïve wonder of the world. From that moment, I have thought about you every single day."

Cynthia looked at her watch, as cool as an ice cube on top of a glacier. "In the minute remaining, is there anything else you'd like to add?"

"Yes, a couple things, in fact. The only thing I regret worse than losing you and not knowing my son is that I took the deal your parents, mainly your mother, offered: a quarter million dollars and open access to your dad's business contacts to grow my clientele. In exchange, I agreed to exit my son's life . . . and yours."

Two hours later, Cynthia carefully navigated the side streets as she made her way back to the Hall manse. One might think it was because at the club she'd drank one glass of wine too many. No. It was the thought of returning to her parents' home. Had Jayden been with her, they would have headed straight to the airport and caught the first flight west. As it were, tomorrow, no, today was her dad's birthday and she was supposed to help him celebrate.

"I can provide the fireworks," she announced to the car's interior. "That's for damn sure."

She placed a hand to her mouth in surprise. *Did I just curse?* The thought amazed her, so complete had her mother's training—translated: brainwashing, browbeating—been on the absolute boorishness of a lady using foul language.

Would a lady pay the father of a child to abandon it? I'm surprised she can spell the word.

Cynthia reached her parents' home, pulled into the driveway, and cut the engine. She was desperate to talk this out with someone, to get the perspective of someone not involved. She thought of her girls, and wondered what they'd say about Stewart's story, and what they would do.

"I should have told them."

But she didn't. Following her mother's advice, she'd told no one. Until Byron.

She pulled the cell phone from her purse and called Byron without hesitation. *Don't send me to voice mail, Byron. If you do, I'll call again. And again and again until you—*

"Hello?"

His voice hit her like a hug and pulled the plug on steel will. "My life is so fucked up!" she managed, between sobs.

Two seconds passed. Five more. "Cynthia?" She covered her face and cried silently. "Cynthia, what's wrong?"

"I saw Jayden's father and he told me, he told me . . ." The crying began anew, this time with audio added.

"Stop!" The command was so forceful that Cynthia pulled half of the sob that had spilled out back into her mouth. "Pull yourself together and talk to me. I can't help you if I don't know the problem."

His stern directive was just what she needed.

"Okay," she mumbled, reaching into the console for a tissue. Never having been an emotional crybaby, she found her own behavior appalling, but then again, wasn't that the state of this entire situation?

She blew her nose, reached for the bottle of water she'd brought from the country club, and shared what Stewart had told her. "I didn't want to believe him," she finished. "But he had information that could have only come from them. Even more, in my heart, I feel it's true."

"Wow, babe. I don't even know what to say.

Makes sense that you'd have a drink or two after getting that news."

"How'd you know that?"

"Really?"

Cynthia's laugh held little humor. "I'm boozed like a muhfuh."

"It's Muh. Fuh. You can't hold your mouth proper and come correct with that phrase. You've got to relax." Instead of a response to his attempt at humor, there was silence. Both grappled with which thoughts to keep and which to share. "I'm sorry about all of this, Cynthia. It's a tough situation, something I thought only happened in movies."

"People would be surprised at what goes on in some gated communities; the length people will go to for the sake of appearances, societal standing, one-upmanship on their neighbors and friends. The term *friend* is used loosely here; they'll smile and give the biggest hug, then stab you while embracing. One of my dad's friends paid a poor cousin a boatload of money to take a sexual assault rap for his Ivy League–bound son. There've been abortions, secret adoptions, hundreds of thousands of dollars paid to make legal troubles go away or, in my case, a child's father."

Byron made a sound of disgust. "That's unbelievable. I can't even wrap my mind around how someone could do that to their own. What are you going to do?"

"Thanks to you, I'm not going to go in accusations blazing and start a midnight row. A part of me wants to confront them as soon as possible.

The other part wants my dad to enjoy his birthday. Whatever role he played was by my mother's insistence. I'm not sure I can do that, given what I know."

"I say take a little time to think about it, decide what it is you want to happen when you confront them. How will you react if they don't act the way you think they should? And most important, how this will affect Jayden getting to know his father."

"That's a whole other issue."

"Thank you."

"Oh, no problem."

"No, really. I treated you horribly. You're being so kind."

"Like I said on my message—"

"You left a message?"

"You didn't hear it? I figured that's why you called."

"I called because when I needed a safe place to land, the comfort of sharing with someone who cares about me . . . you're the first person who came to my mind." Silence. "I'm thankful we can at least have professional exchanges. It wouldn't feel the same to have you totally out of my life."

"Professional exchanges? Okay, I'll chew on that one. You get some sleep. And keep me posted."

"Thank you again. You're a really special guy."

"You're just now figuring that out?"

"Good night, Byron."

"Good night."

Taking Byron's advice, Cynthia crept quietly to the corner guest room, hurriedly undressed, and crawled into bed. Thoughts of the conversation with Byron brought a wisp of a smile, quickly chased away by what Stewart had told her. Not only about the unconscionable actions of her parents, but that he was getting divorced and ready to get back what was lost all those years ago, what he'd always wanted. Stewart had made it very clear that marriage was on his mind.

35

No one died. A day of hobnobbing, socializing, air kisses and fake smiles, and two nights of sleeping down the hall from the enemy, and Cynthia had not been arrested. Given the dark thoughts that crossed her mind, especially following one of her mother's snide comments, being free was not to be taken lightly.

Distance and distraction played a major role in peacekeeping. Along with Jeff and his flawless lawyer partner, Veronika, two other couples had joined the family for breakfast, making direct conversation with Anna Marie unnecessary. Only child Jayden was as happy as a clam in sauce while playing with several of the workers' children. Her best idea? Deciding to rent a car instead of rely on family. If a quick exit was necessary, she could go.

Fortunately, that was not necessary. The day passed, Carlton Hall's sixtieth birthday party was a hit, with Anna Marie the dazzling belle of the ball. If her mother noticed the chill index blowing from Cynthia's direction, she showed no signs. For her part, Cynthia spent most of the evening with her father, his friends that she knew, and a former neighbor who'd returned home and bought a house near their community, was married, and had a ten-year-old son. Jayden was at their house, with the sitter.

During a lull in the festivities, Cynthia spotted Carlton standing alone. She quickly retrieved her handbag before joining her father. "May I have a moment alone with the most popular, not to mention handsome man in town?"

"Why most certainly, my beautiful daughter."

"Good. Come with me." She linked her arm in his, enjoying one of a very few genuine happy moments. Speaking to someone on her left, she saw Anna Marie watching them, envy in her eyes. *How can she begrudge the relationship I have with Dad?*

When she started toward them, Cynthia hurried toward the hallway and a small private room just beyond it. She breathed a sigh of relief when Jeff clutched his mother's arm as she passed and spun her onto the dance floor. Once inside, door closed, her face crumbled.

"Are you all right, dear?" Concern creased her father's brow and shone in his eyes.

Cynthia noticed the deepening crow's feet around her father's kind eyes. They hadn't been there a year ago. She shook off the disenchantment from her and her mother's non-relationship, and smiled. "I'm well, Dad. A few concerns at work, but nothing important enough to be discussed on your special day." She reached into her purse and pulled out a small box, eloquently wrapped in black paper with a silver bow.

"What's this?" He cocked his head and looked between her and the gift. "I love the gifts received this morning, from you and Jay."

"I know you do. But that one has your name all over it. I couldn't resist."

Carlton slipped off the bow and quickly rid the box of its wrapping. "Oh, boy!" His smile was genuine as his eyes gleamed. "How'd you know I was thinking about getting a new golf GPS?" He looked again and noticed engraving on the platinum case. "You weren't kidding when you said my name was on it. 'FOR CARLTON HALL. BETTER THAN A HOLE IN ONE. YOUR DAUGHTER, CYNTHIA.' Thank you, sweetheart." They hugged. "This is very nice."

He placed the GPS device in the box, but instead of preparing to rejoin the party, he leaned against the wall. "I understand you went to the club yesterday."

"I should have known there'd be no keeping any event at the club from its unofficial mayor."

"You saw Stewart."

"I did. When did he move back?"

"As far as I know, he didn't. But his mother's ill. I think he bought a place to stay when he visits."

That her father knew about Stewart was somehow a relief. But she wasn't prepared to have an in-depth conversation about him.

Carlton's eyes were unreadable as he studied

her. "I understand the two of you shared the private room."

"Considering my scandalous secret, we felt it best." The truth was said without rancor. She placed a light hand on his arm. "Don't worry, Dad. I'm no longer that twenty-two-year-old college grad, naïve and unthinking. It was a civil conversation over a delightful meal. The contents of which will remain between Stewart and myself."

Any comment Carlton may have had was cut off by the abruptly opened door. Anna and her newfound BFF, Veronika, stood at the door. "Really, Cynthia, must you hide your dad and keep him all to yourself? I'd think you'd want to take as much time as possible to get to know your future sister-in-law. Look at her necklace. It's a custom Katz design."

An hour later, she didn't have to feign sickness to leave the party. Her mother was a pain in the behind. Snobbery, cattiness, and empty compliments that for most of her life had been the norm was now a pain in her head.

Using a last minute change in flights as an excuse, Cynthia awoke early, got she and Jay packed, and left for the airport five hours before her flight was scheduled to depart. To appease a sulking kid who hadn't wanted to leave, they stopped at the Mall of America, an incredibly large attraction just outside of Minneapolis. A good move. Jayden wore himself out and was asleep before the plane reached cruising altitude, giving Cynthia three hours and forty-eight nonstop minutes to figure out when this mass of muddled mayhem became her life.

They arrived home, showered, ate, and went to bed. Five minutes later, it seemed, the alarm sounded and it was time for work. Cynthia prayed this would be a calm Monday. Her frayed, over-worked nerves and Margo's haughty nosiness would not be a good mix.

One doesn't always get what they pray for. Ivy was on her as soon as she turned the corner.

"There you are! Is everything all right?"

Is the state of my life plastered on my face? Not even thirty seconds in and Cynthia was already frowning. "I'm okay. Why do you ask?"

"I've been trying to reach you; called your cell phone several times."

"Oh, shoot. I forgot to take it off airplane mode." Cynthia looked at her watch. "I usually arrive at ten on Mondays. What's going on?"

"You missed a meeting."

"Excuse me?"

Ivy gave an almost imperceptible nod toward Cynthia's office.

Cynthia got the hint and led the way into a more private space.

Ivy had barely shut the door before whirling around with a look of anger Cynthia had never seen. "I knew she was lying."

"Who?"

"Margo, who else?"

"Wait. To handle this I'm going to need more caffeine." Cynthia walked over and sat behind her desk. She noted a wound-up Ivy paced from

the door to the window and back before finally
sitting in one of the two chairs facing Cynthia's
desk.

Cynthia reached for the extra packets of sugar
she'd gotten from the shop. She removed the lid
from the coffee cup, added them, then opened
her drawer to retrieve two single container coffee
shots and added them, too. Only after stirring
the concoction of liquid caffeine and enjoying a
couple healthy sips did she nod at Ivy. "Okay,
what happened?"

"When I got here, around eight-thirty, the
phone was ringing. I didn't pay it much attention;
figured whoever would either leave a message or
call back. Then five minutes, it rang again. It was
Margo asking for you. I told her you would be
here at ten your normal time. Then she says,
'She's *still* not here?' as though she'd not heard
me. That was weird, but I thought it was Margo
being messy and went back to work.

"Five minutes before you came in, both Margo
and Tracy came over asking if you'd arrived yet.
By now I'm sure Margo is up to something. So I
said, 'As Tracy knows, Cynthia arrives at ten and
leaves around six.'"

"What did Tracy say?"

"She looked at Margo. Margo shrugged, and
said, 'I'm positive I sent the e-mail, and marked
it urgent.'"

"Sent what e-mail?"

"As soon as they left the area, that's exactly
what I checked out. She sent the e-mail, only she
sent it to the company department e-mail address,

not your personal one, and she sent it at around seven o'clock, Friday night."

Cynthia nodded slowly, as all became clear. "All right. Thank you, Ivy. I appreciate that information and will definitely take care of it."

Ivy stood. "If you need anything from me to back up your schedule or to prove you come in on Saturdays or, I don't know, maybe sneak into her office and rearrange some files or open up her database before my finger accidentally falls on the Delete button . . ."

"Ooh, remind me not to get on your bad side," Cynthia said, with a chuckle.

"People like her are so annoying." She reached the door. "Want me to leave it open?"

"Sure." Cynthia opened her laptop and turned it on. She opened her e-mail portal and quickly found the memo announcing a special, eight o'clock catered breakfast meeting with the board president and one other board member, one of the directors from H.E.L.P.'s umbrella company, and representatives from four similar agencies and organizations who all worked with clients from LA's judicial system.

She was angry, beyond livid, yet Cynthia calmly stood, picked up her coffee, and walked to the window. It wouldn't do to give in to emotions right now. She planned to not only keep a level head, but to not stoop to the depths that Margo had gone to get the director position.

This didn't mean that she'd go down without swinging. After several more minutes she walked back to her desk and sat down with purpose. Soon her fingers were flying over the keyboard as she put her plan into motion. Margo may have won that round by being underhanded, but she was getting ready to learn that there was more than one way to fight.

36

Byron looked at his youngest brother in amazement. Sometimes he swore that the near-decade age difference between them was akin to their being born on different planets. On the other hand, something to take his mind off Cynthia was almost worth the frustration.

"You're kidding me, right?"

"Naw, man." Barry stretched his long legs in front of him and clasped his fingers behind his head. "Your brother's got it like that."

"This woman is buying you clothes, phone, shoes, food, paying when y'all go out, basically taking care of everything but your living space—because your mama and daddy are handling that expense—and that's a good thing?"

"Of course." Barry chuckled, slowly shaking his head. "And don't look at me like there's something wrong with what I'm doing, like you're not mad at how I handle my ladies."

"So there's several? You've got the girl doing all of this for you and she's not even the only one?"

"Really, dog? You think one woman can handle all this?" Barry swept his hands over six feet and three inches of chiseled perfection.

"I think a woman's crazy to share her man."

"You think she knows? I need to hip you to the new school, son."

"Stop it, please!" Byron put his hands over his face. "You're killing me!"

"That's how a man does it in the twenty-first."

Byron muted the television and turned to face Barry.

"Hey, man! I'm watching that!"

"That might be how some men do it, but not the Carters."

"Man, don't come at me like you're my daddy. I know who I am. Turn the TV back up."

Byron aimed the remote and turned it off. His look dared the youngest member of this testosterone-heavy clan to protest. Older brother got the respect he demanded.

"I know you don't want to hear this, and it's probably going to take a few years and a couple heartbreaks before you come back and thank me. You may not ever appreciate what I'm about to tell you. That's cool, too. But a real man doesn't take from a woman, man. It's the other way around. A real man has too much pride to let a woman give him everything while he gives nothing back, not even exclusive access to his dick. He definitely wouldn't brag about it. That's not a man, Barry. That's an asshole.

"Instead of listening to what society, rappers, and your boys are saying about manhood, you should listen to the man whose roof you sleep under. When it comes to men, and how to be one? Willie Carter is one of the best."

Barry slowly nodded his head. "I feel you, bro. You're right."

Byron reached for the remote to turn on the TV but stopped when Barry stood up. "Real talk running you off?"

"Whatever, man. It's all good." He headed to the door. "You coming over for dinner this Sunday?"

Byron joined him at the door. "What's happening this Sunday?"

Barry shrugged. "Whatever it is has Mama cooking a roast and baking pies."

"You know I'm coming over for that!" Byron's phone buzzed. "All right, Barry. Take it easy. And Carter up, okay?"

"Carter up, huh? Man, you're crazy."

"Hello?" There was a smile in Byron's voice as he gave a last wave to his brother and closed the door.

"I apologize for calling."

"Why would you do that? I've been waiting all weekend to hear from you. After we talked, I couldn't imagine how you'd confront your parents."

"I didn't."

"Hold on, okay?" Byron walked from the living room to Tyra's closed door. He knocked.

"Yes, Daddy?"

"What are you doing?"

"Talking to Brittney. Is Uncle Barry still here?"

"No, he's gone."

"And he didn't say bye?"

"Ten more minutes and you need to go to bed. You've got school tomorrow."

"I can't wait till school is over!"

"Then it's good you've only got three more days. Ten more minutes."

"Okay!"

"Good night, Tyra Lily."

"Good night, Daddy."

"Okay, I'm back."

"So Tyra's in a single-track system?"

"Yes, both of us prefer it to the four-track schedule." He closed his door and walked over to the closet. "But we can talk about that some other time. I want to know what happened in Minnesota." He heard a sigh as he placed the phone on a shelf and stripped down to his boxers. Picking up the phone, he crossed to the bed. "Cynthia?"

"I'm here. So much happened, and is happening . . . I don't know where to start."

"Why didn't you ask your parents about what you heard Friday night?"

"Several reasons, but the main one is that it was Daddy's birthday. I didn't want to spoil it. Another is because I need time to digest that whole impossible situation and decide how I want to deal with it."

"That makes sense. What about Jayden's father? Did you see him again?"

"No."

Byron waited for her to continue. She didn't. "Why do I feel there's a 'but' after that?"

"Probably because of what I didn't tell you Friday night. Stewart wants to make up for the time he's lost with his son. He suggested we move to where he lives and work on becoming a family."

"Becoming a family. What does that mean exactly?"

"He wants to see if it's possible to get back what we once had, and . . ."

"Let me guess, get married."

"Yes."

"What do you want?"

"I don't know."

"What you probably don't want is a man who's unfaithful, and you know his track record in that department."

"People can change."

"All can. Few do."

"Why this reaction when you so strongly advocated how important it was for Jayden to know his dad?"

"Yes, Jayden knowing his father better, not you. I guess I shouldn't be surprised, though. Any man would be a fool to have an opportunity to make you his wife and not take it." He waited for her response. None came. "Looks like you're giving his offer some consideration."

"Shouldn't I? For the past eight years, I harbored

a huge resentment for what I felt Stewart had done. When Jayden inquired about him, I'd say as little as possible, as fast as I could, and then change the subject."

"Did you bash his father?"

"No, but I most certainly didn't praise him either. Besides, when a boy goes a lifetime without seeing his father, he forms a pretty negative opinion on his own. Knowing what I do now, that is something I truly regret, that and the time together they've lost that can't be gotten back."

"Let me ask you something, Cynthia, and I want you to be honest. Do you still have feelings for this guy?"

There was a moment of silence before she answered. "Before Friday, I thought the only feeling I had for him was anger and disgust. That's what he saw when we ran into each other at the club. But later, after learning what my mom did and hearing how he felt, how he says he still feels, I don't know."

"You talk about what your mom did, but he was a part of it, too. He didn't have to take their money and lose his son. But that's what he did. No amount of money in the world could come between . . ."

"Byron? Byron, are you there?"

"Yes, I'm here."

"What's wrong?"

There was a long pause before he answered. "I've been dealing with a situation that would make me the biggest hypocrite by finishing that line."

"I don't understand."

"Awhile back, during a disagreement, Tanya hinted that I wasn't only Tyra's father, but her son's as well." This time it was Byron who thought the call had dropped. "Cynthia, you there?"

"What kind of disagreement would make her say that?"

"She asked for a loan. I said no, which led to her saying she could get more than she'd asked for through the courts, if it were determined that Ricky was mine."

"Do you believe her?"

"No."

"Why not?"

"One, because she told me she'd thrown her boyfriend out when I found out the opposite was true. He left her and supposedly has another girl pregnant. Two, this isn't the first time she's sworn I was the boy's father and then backtracked and said she was lying."

"Then what would make you a hypocrite? I don't get it."

"If she lied once, she could lie twice. I can't take Tanya's word for whether or not little Ricky's my son. I have to know for myself."

"If he is, then what?"

"Then we go to court, and I prepare for battle. Because Tanya would be sure to make my life a living hell. We don't need that in our lives."

"Please don't say 'we,' Byron. I feel bad enough about contacting you as it is, but felt you were owed tonight's phone call."

"I won't disagree with that. If you hadn't called

me, you can best believe I would have definitely made sure we had another conversation."

"Why's that?"

"Because there's something you need to know. I'm not Ava's blood brother. We treat her and Leah like family, but we're actually not related."

37

The following morning, Cynthia's mood was sullen as she dressed for work. What Byron shared last night had taken her appetite and she still wasn't hungry this morning. All the way to work she tried to come to terms with how she was feeling and why. By the time she arrived downtown, she was able to admit the truth. Somewhere along the way Byron had gone from being a means to an orgasm to friend, from friend to confidante, and from that to someone she'd imagined in her life for a while, maybe even forever. But for that life to include someone like Tanya? That type of baby mama drama was a little more urban than Cynthia wanted to get. She'd added this reason on top of his familial tie with Leah to the reasons not to see him. But to find out he and Ava aren't related? And that he is working to put the madness with Tanya behind him? It all meant that there existed a chance for them to be together. The possibility without the probability was almost more than she could handle.

She arrived at work and found a response to one of the actions she'd taken to counter Margo's attempt at sabotage. *Excellent.* After speaking with Byron last night, and hearing how he'd decided on a proactive approach in dealing with Tanya, Cynthia had had a long talk with herself and had vowed to take back charge of her life. Here, at the agency, was where she would start. Tonight, she'd deal with Stewart.

"Cynthia, your nine-thirty is here."

She pushed the intercom. "Thanks, Ivy. Find out if she wants something to drink. I need about ten minutes."

"No problem."

Cynthia finished the e-mail she was typing and after pressing Send, scrolled through a few others that had been marked important. She responded to a couple that could be handled quickly, categorized the rest based on urgency, and made an appointment for a one o'clock massage. After the meeting scheduled for noon, she felt she'd need it.

Something was wrong. Cynthia knew as soon as the door opened and Leah walked through. She'd never been up for the prize of client congeniality, but over the past several weeks there had been progress. The week of Lance's birthday, when Cynthia had actually expected what was being shown right now, Leah had surprised her by opening up and sharing more about her brother than had ever happened in previous sessions.

What could have happened that has her so upset?

Cynthia closed her office door. "I would say

good morning, but it seems for you that might not be accurate."

"Where do you want me to sit?" No greeting, no eye contact.

"Why don't we sit on the couch?" Cynthia noted Leah's empty hands. "You didn't want anything to drink? Coffee, tea, juice?"

"I don't want nothing except to get this over with."

"For that to happen it would help for you to open up about why you're so unhappy right now."

"Why do I have to tell you what's going on in my life? Who are you to want to get all up in my shit, when I don't know your business? Huh?"

Cynthia prided herself on the calm demeanor she maintained while her insides were screaming. *Does she know that I slept with the uncle who isn't really her uncle but plays the part? Who told her? I do not need this to blow up in my face right now!*

In the time it took for her to gather her iPad and coffee from her desk and walk to the sitting area on the room's other side, Cynthia had gathered herself and decided on a simple strategy with Leah: professional, courteous, unperturbed. Starting with the expletive and insolent attitude she'd not address. She'd handle Leah with kid gloves at least until she learned what this client knew and act accordingly. This moment sealed the certainty of last night's decision. There was a reason for the just-incorporated rule regarding clients, families, and relationships.

And this was it.

Cynthia looked at Leah, who was still standing by the desk. "Would you like to join me?" Leah took a long, soft breath and looked from the floor to the window. Cynthia looked closely and thought her client's eyes were a little bright. *Is this a delayed reaction to the birthday?*

She continued to wait. Leah continued to stand.

"If you'd like, you can sit and I can work during your hour. Not only can I not make you talk, I wouldn't want to hear anything that was forced from you. Keeping you out of the judicial system is what brought you here. However, that isn't my only goal.

"I didn't grow up the way you did. And the way of life for teenagers has changed drastically in just ten, fifteen years—social media, texting, all kinds of pressure to look fabulous and have it all together. But one thing we have in common that doesn't change much no matter where you live or what you do or how you grew up . . . is making that transition from girl to woman. One of the ways we know we've reached a level of maturity is how we treat each other and the respect we have for other women."

Leah continued to stare out the window. But her body was less rigid and her face had softened. She was listening.

"When it comes to being female there are only three, four, five things top that we deal with: men, money, menstruation, men, family, career, and men. That's about it."

"Why'd you mention men so many times?"

"Because most of the problems not mentioned in what I call the top five are the result of a man. When I was around your age, it was a very difficult time. I'd just had Jayden and was navigating life as a single parent, something I never expected to do. Two friends I met in college and a third woman who joined the circle a few years later kept me from losing hope altogether. Being able to talk to someone, whether a counselor like myself or just a good friend who means you well, can make a huge difference in how you feel.

"I'm not here to snoop around your personal life. I'm here so that if there is something that's bothering you or making you sad or something you don't understand, you have a safe, confidential place to share it."

After a long moment, when it seemed clear that Leah did not want to talk, Cynthia returned to her desk and activated her laptop. After the session with Leah she had a phone conference scheduled with the mother and parole officer of a teen who'd failed a drug test. Now was a good time to take one last look at the information she'd compiled last night, along with the association and agency verbiage. This was the first of several steps in Cynthia's offensive strategy to become the agency's director, and to ensure that whatever unscrupulous actions used to undermine her work could be countered with the truth.

"It's about a man."

Cynthia looked over to see that Leah had moved to the window. She stood there, her face partially hid as she gazed at the scene below. Ten minutes had passed and so caught up had Cynthia been in mental preparation, she hadn't heard her move. "I'm sorry, Leah. What did you say?"

"You can't tell anybody what I tell you, right?"

"That is correct, as long as there is no potential harm to you or others. If it has to do with safety, well-being, or in some cases, the legal system, then that confidentially is waived."

She waited. Leah shifted her weight from one leg to the other but said nothing. Cynthia turned back to her notes. She felt good about the upcoming meetings, so she clicked on a priority folder and began checking mail. Another five minutes went by.

She heard Leah moving but didn't look up.

Leah slumped into the nearest chair. "Okay, here's what happened."

Cynthia closed the laptop. "I'm listening."

"I've been seeing this dude, Red. He's one of my friend's older brothers and we'd kick it when I went to her house. He's twenty-five."

Leah looked at Cynthia as though she expected a reprimand. Cynthia had a definite response to the comment but wisely remained silent. "Been there, done that, got the son to prove it," would not have been appropriate.

"I've known him for a long time, used to see him with his girlfriends and everything. He used to treat me like a little sister. But he knew I liked him."

That answered my next question.

"He asked me over and over to let him be with me. But I always said no because of all his other girlfriends. He promised that if I got with him,

he'd leave all of them alone. I knew he was lying."
Her voice dropped. "But finally I didn't care."

"Sometimes love is like that." Cynthia's voice
was soft, as Leah's had been.

"I knew he was lying."

Cynthia watched Leah struggle to fight back
the tears. She lost. In that moment, it was difficult
for her to maintain the professional distance that
was recommended. The past weekend's events
had brought up memories buried long ago, of a
young girl much like Leah: hurt, angry, confused.

Please God, don't let her be pregnant. "What did he
lie about?"

"Saying he wouldn't be with other girls."

"He cheated on you?" She nodded. "Are you
on a contraceptive?" Another nod from Leah.
From Cynthia, a silent sigh of relief. "How long
have you been sexually active?"

"Since I was sixteen."

Probably her first sexual encounter.

"Last night I was over at his house. He got a text,
then told me he had some business to handle
and that his sister would take me. So I'm, like,
cool, no problem. Me and his sister are driving
down the street when I see this girl go past us that
I recognize, headed toward their house. It's
this other girl who I know likes him. So I asked
his sister to stop and she wouldn't. We get to the
light and I jump out, and go back to the house."

Cynthia leaned forward, her elbows on the
desk and chin resting on her hands. Casual.
Comfortable. The way she wanted Leah to feel.
"Was the girl there?"

"Sitting in the very same spot I'd just left, the blanket was probably still warm from my ass laying on it. Guess that little trick was the business he had to handle.

"He came at me for two years, swore that I was the only one he wanted." She shook her head, angrily swiped at new tears following the trail old ones had traveled. "But he told me to leave, and let her stay."

"I'm sorry he did that. What would you like to have happen now?"

"Nothing, because I don't care about him anymore. She can have him."

"Are you sure about that? He's your very first love."

"Once a cheater, always a cheater."

"Without trust, it's impossible to have a successful relationship." She didn't answer, but she was listening. "Leah, perhaps this is a chance to focus on your needs and desires. You want to fulfill your brother's dream of going to college. It's not too late to do that. You need only a few more credits to get your diploma. We can still get you into a community college, and with a respectable GPA you can easily transfer to a four-year university. You're smart. You're beautiful. You deserve a man who can appreciate the amazing young woman that you are."

38

"Ava, what's up, sis?"

"My blood pressure." Byron smiled at this Liz-inspired answer.

"What's up with you?"

"Not much."

"Are you sure?"

"Cynthia called this weekend."

"I thought she ended things with you and cut off contact."

"She did."

"Not if you talked this weekend. I don't like that, her playing with your emotions."

"It wasn't that way. She was dealing with a difficult situation."

"Whatever. I—Leah, are you going to just walk by me without speaking?" Byron could feel the weariness through Ava's exasperated breath. "Ooh, I can't stand her sometimes."

"You know you love Leah. That's your baby."

"I love her with my whole heart. I don't like her much right now. Last week is when I thought she'd fall apart, and she didn't. I saw smiles on Lance's birthday and felt the sessions with Cynthia were paying off. Then last night she came in late, way after I'd gone to bed, with no real explanation. And just now she walked by without speaking, with a frown on her face. I don't know what else to do with her."

"I'll call her."

"You can if you want, but I'm not sure it'll help. Mama said she called twice and left messages. Leah still hasn't called her back. I think it has something to do with Aaron. Besides thoughts of her brother, he's about the only one who can get her this upset."

"She still messing with that punk Red? He's the last person she needs to be around right now."

"Tell me about it."

"Do you think she's—"

"Of course."

"But she's only—"

"Seventeen. You think she just started?"

"Okay, this is too much information for an uncle. In my eyes, I still see bubble gum and pigtails."

"Well, that's the only place you'll see them."

"Wow."

"The world's a whole other place for kids these days. To be honest, I was thankful she lasted that long. Our neighbor was pregnant at fourteen and they used to be best friends."

"I remember."

"Yes, and last I heard she's had two more kids."

"Speaking of kids, I hired a lawyer who's served Tanya with papers forcing a paternity test."

"Good. It will be good to get a confirmation one way or the other."

"I also told Cynthia we're not related."

"And?"

"I guess we'll see if this revelation makes a difference."

39

That she'd made it through the week without calling Byron was a miracle, possible only through the help of her brother. If Jeff hadn't called last night, giving her a place to vent about Margo, she surely would have broken her own rule again. She could have called the girls but figured they were as tired of hearing about the drama at H.E.L.P. as she was of dealing with it. Thank goodness for the director on her very first counseling job who'd stressed the importance of documentation. She had a record of every occurrence since Ivy's first warning.

After her Tuesday meeting with Tracy, she'd skillfully used a "chance" social meeting with Byron (okay, a little creative license never hurt anyone) to ask the director for clarification on the agency's interpretation of "family" mentioned in association guidelines as it related to these potential interactions. The jury was still out on how much Tracy may have thought she knew based on whatever Margo had told her. She didn't show her hand. Cynthia wasn't worried. She hadn't shown all of hers either, namely, that Byron and Ava weren't blood-related. If Margo continued to try and use this as leverage for the promotion, Cynthia knew a better time would come for this card to be played.

It was a quiet Friday. In what had become a Friday night ritual, Jayden was spending the night at Bobby's house. With Bobby's sister being so much older, his parents welcomed the company for their son. Cynthia, on the other hand, had the nerve to feel a bit hurt that he preferred doing this to spending time with her. At least that's what she told herself. She knew the real hurt came from missing Byron, not from missing the company of an only child.

Except . . . not really. This thought increased Cynthia's restlessness. She walked from one room to another, her mind as cluttered as her house was clean. That Stewart had two other children was yet another bit of information that had trouble going down. During their tell-all dinner, Cynthia learned that her eight-year-old son had more than the older brother she'd known about. He also had two half sisters, aged six and four.

"Stewart, why did you have to be married when I got pregnant with Jayden," she whispered, opening the patio door and stepping out into the warm June air. *Why did you have to stay married and father more children?* The most important question came last. *Why did you have to say you still love me, want to marry me, and complicate my life?*

She needed answers to so many questions. For Jayden's sake alone, she should have already called him. Byron was one of the main reasons she hadn't.

Tired of thinking, Cynthia went back inside to grab her purse. If she was lucky, there'd be a halfway decent movie playing at the local theater. She exchanged her mini housedress for jeans and a simple shell, and pulled out a light jacket in case the theater was cold. Purse on shoulder, keys in hand, she headed for the door and had just closed and locked it when her cell phone rang. *Byron!*

Not quite. She didn't answer. The phone stopped ringing. Not ten seconds later, it rang again.

Her heart clenching at the thought that something could be wrong, she answered. "Hello, Mom."

"How dare you!"

Something was wrong, but not in the way she'd thought. She unlocked her door and went back inside, tossing her purse beside her as she sat on the couch and braced herself for the latest incident that had Anna Marie in a tizzy.

"Cynthia? Hello?"

"Mom, it's been a tough week, so whatever you've called to discuss, can we do so calmly?"

"Calm? You, the very reason for this evening's disgrace, want me to consider your feelings and be calm?"

"This must be about Stewart."

"This is about me being blindsided at a charity event and hearing for the first time—and from that social-climbing Jenny Whitman no less—about my daughter's very public meeting with a still-married Stewart Monihan whom she's somehow learned is the father of your child. Because of your shamelessness, Cynthia, your mistake is now public. Have you no decency at all, or at the very least, shame? You may have chosen to move to the other side of the country, but your father and I live here!"

"How did my having dinner with Stewart reveal his connection to Jayden?"

"The news got back to his wife, who refused to keep quiet. She told Jenny that Jayden was his son."

Cynthia was surprised that this news didn't faze her. She guessed it was because of the distance between her and her mother's super judgmental clique, and that her "mistake" was almost nine years old. Then again, it could be that her cold-hearted mother who'd paid off and separated her grandson from his father had the nerve to highlight her error.

"Cynthia, did you hear what I just said? Everyone knows!"

"I'm sorry that this has upset you, Mother." The sincerity didn't show in her voice, but she meant what she'd said. "But this news becoming public is not my fault and, as far as I'm concerned, is no longer a problem."

"My grandson being labeled a bastard is not a problem? I cannot believe this news leaves you unperturbed."

"Quite frankly, I'm surprised that Stewart's identity wasn't revealed before now. And if anyone ever utters such a word about my son and I find out about it? They're going to be a sorry muh-fuh."

"A what?"

"Never mind."

"The scandal that's almost a decade old has come back to ruin me. The memories alone have almost sent me to bed. His wife having just lost a baby when his mistress becomes pregnant. For shame!"

The only thing missing from Anna Marie's emoting was someone to catch her should she swoon.

"I was never his mistress, not even his girlfriend. I was a young, naïve woman who got caught up with a very experienced man. I was frightened, and alone, and received very little comfort or understanding."

This snapped Anna Marie back into snippy character. "Are you trying to make me feel guilty?"

"I'm sharing this experience from my perspective, something you've never asked about and something I've never shared. Those were the loneliest nine plus months of my life, and by far the hardest. Compared to that time, bearing the brunt of people's opinion is a cake walk."

"Carlton said you and Stewart met by accident. Is that true?"

Cynthia didn't miss her mother's abrupt change of subject. Her veering from any hint of wrongdoing on her part was nothing new. The anger that was simmering now began to boil. She took a breath. "Yes, I went to the club to see Father. It was a spontaneous decision that at the time felt horrendous, but that I now don't regret."

"I don't see why not. It has only led to disastrous complications."

"Really, Mother? What on earth about the supposedly sullied reputation of your grown daughter who moved away years ago is causing you such problems?"

"Have you forgotten life in society? Did you not hear what I said occurred tonight? No doubt at this very moment they're discussing my adulterous daughter and her illegitimate son. I can't even think of facing the women tomorrow at the fashion show that I helped organize. I'm trying to decide whether I'll come down with a migraine, or a fever."

"Why don't you come down with a case of the truth?"

"I beg your pardon, young lady! How dare you show such disrespect."

"How dare you pay off the man who disrespected me and deprive your grandson of a father!" The only sound heard was the sound of Cynthia's breathing, sounding a bit like steam from a boiling kettle. "It is enough that you've labeled me all these years, as if your entire life has been flawless. But, lady, when you describe my child as something wrong and improper, you have crossed the final line."

She gripped the phone so hard her hand shook, and she was close to tears. But she'd stood her ground against the indomitable Anna Marie Hall. In thirty years, this was a first.

"Very well, Cynthia." Her mother's tone held a perfect blend of hurt and resignation. "Since you insist on a level of insolence I would not have imagined . . . I will bid you good night."

The click was soft, almost imperceptible, yet in spite of how angry she'd been with her mother, it pierced Cynthia's heart. All her life she'd tried to be the good little girl who would make Anna proud, and all her life she'd failed. With the skill honed over more than thirty years of practice, her mother had managed to unearth the child laden with such an impossible task. She sat there, her mind recalling years of blame and shame and guilt at not being as good as the daughter whom her mother had envisioned. Next would be either a call or text from her father, who her mother would have goaded until he'd do anything to shut her up, which usually meant siding with Anna. His text came within thirty minutes. **Dear, please apologize to your mother. She is completely distraught.**

Cynthia wasn't aware of when the tears started and didn't remember curling up on the couch. All she knew was that for one amazing moment, she'd felt proud and right for stating her truth. Now, all she felt was sad.

The next morning, Cynthia woke up to the sound of her phone and a crick in her neck. It was the call she'd expected. "Good morning, Mother. I was expecting your call."

"Good morning, Cynthia."

Her mother was waiting for the apology she knew would come. Cynthia knew because this manipulation had been used to reign in those around her for as long as Cynthia could remember. She wouldn't be surprised to learn her mother had begun honing them in childhood.

"I apologize for last night's behavior."

"You don't sound sorry."

She wasn't. "I am."

"I'm glad to hear that, Cynthia, because I've been up all night and working half the morning for a way to rectify this situation and to repair the Hall standing in this town."

Cynthia sat straight up. The pseudo-silky quality of her mother's voice so alarmed her, she forgot her neck was hurting. The last time her mother sounded like this she'd gotten shipped off to up-state New York to spend the last month of her pregnancy with an aunt she barely knew.

"I'll need your help, of course."

This was exactly why Cynthia was afraid.

"As harshly as they were delivered, I thought long and hard on your comments regarding Jayden. I have a tremendous amount of love for that little boy and would never wish him harm. Nor will I apologize for actions taken with only the best of intentions. Everything I've ever done has been to secure the best future possible for Jayden . . . and for you."

"I'm sure you believe that."

"Because it's true!"

That her mother probably believed those words was enough to make Cynthia throw the phone. Instead, she chose to get off of it as soon as possible.

"Okay, Mother. Since as you say, the whole town knows that Stewart is Jayden's father, what in the world can I do to change that situation?"

"There's nothing we can do to change that, dear, but we can make it legal."

"How, by putting Stewart's name on the birth certificate?"

"By putting your name on a marriage certificate."

"What?"

"I've talked to Stewart and found out that his divorce is in progress. He wants to marry you and help take care of Jayden. I'm sure you'll agree this is the perfect solution, a quaint garden ceremony done as quietly and quickly as possible. If all goes well, this could happen as early as the fall. While not my first choice, some of the colors of this season are quite lovely. I'm thinking burgundy, deep lavender, and a tangerine orange would make a lovely tableau. Doesn't that sound stunning? Cynthia . . . hello?"

"Mother, I didn't agree to marry Stewart when he asked me. I am still not agreeing to marry him."

"That will change when you hear what he's agreed to."

"What? Receiving more money from you as incentive, maybe a million this time? I've got to go."

And she did. She basically hung up on Anna Marie Hall, and didn't feel bad about it. Getting her meddling mother out of her personal affairs was long overdue. But she planned to do just that.

40

It hadn't even been a week, but for Byron it felt like forever since he'd talked to Cynthia. He didn't think it was possible to know someone for such a short time and miss them so much. Good thing he was a secure man; otherwise, this sentimentality would leave him embarrassed. As it was, he felt like Jerry Maguire. Cynthia completed him.

It was Tyra's weekend with Tanya, but Byron had found enough to stay busy for most of the day: breakfast at his favorite spot, car wash, haircut, a visit to the folks. Douglas was there and they ended up riding together to their brother Marvin's house, shot the breeze for a couple hours. But as afternoon turned to evening, Marvin had plans and Douglas had a date, leaving Byron all by his lonesome. Unable to think of anything interesting to do, because all he wanted to do was see her.

Without further thought, he picked up the phone and tapped the message app. He cleared his throat—an unnecessary move since the message would be read, not heard—and tapped the microphone.

> Cynthia: Why haven't you called since I told you the news? Ava is not my blood sister. Even though Leah views me as her real uncle, and that's probably why you're still being silent, this noncommunication isn't working for me. And it's not like I don't care about Leah, because I do. But the thing is, I care about you, too, and believe you feel our connection the same as I do. I understand you've got a job to do and rules to follow. But how does that work when it messes with your life like it's messing with mine? We've got to do something about this. I miss you.

Byron, why'd you do that? She's going to think you're a lovesick puppy. He was a lovesick puppy. *If the fellas had any idea I am sitting here with a schoolboy crush.*

I've got to get out of here. Just as he was about to jump up from the couch and make a mad dash away from his thoughts, his message indicator chirped.

The high-school crush kid was replaced by the brothah with swagger who knew she'd text back. He tapped on the icon with a megawatt braggadocios smile.

> **Always the confident one. How are you so sure my life is messed up?**

He walked over and sat down on the couch, pulled off his shoes, and propped his feet on the table. Someone felt this was going to take a while.

Because I haven't been able to massage that spot that makes you hit high notes, and that's a note few if any other man can make you hit.

At the very thought of massaging and hitting, his instrument hardened in preparation for action. Byron shifted on the couch and repositioned the unruly member, even as he forced other thoughts so that they both could calm down.

Byron Carter, you are nothing if not confident.

He laughed out loud, sounding like a man who'd just won a bet.

Am I wrong? You told me yourself that you'd never had multiple orgasms until I happened to you. Are you going to tell me that the man who left you hanging after one quick nut made you sing?

The response was longer in coming this time. *Have I gone too far?* He refused to even worry about that. As far as anything he could say on this phone wasn't as far as he wanted to go. Culver City is as far as he wanted to go. Cynthia's bedroom and into her softness is the distance that was on his mind.

I've thought about what you shared about you and Ava. A great deal, actually. This technicality does not change the fact that Leah views you as her very real uncle, which is why our being together continues to feel like a line of impropriety that you're trying to make me cross.

What's improper about what we're doing now? Uh-huh, thought I didn't know that word? See why I need you around me. So I can become all edu-ma-cated. LOL.

You're. Silly.

But I made you smile. I've got a friend over here who wants to make something else smile.

Please don't talk like that. There's nothing I can do about the way you're making me feel.

Don't act like you don't have a box of toys. A big Rambo-styled dildo. Very poor substitute.

No, I tried that once. I just couldn't get into it.

I wish I could get into it.

Byron!

Baby. I'm hurting. If I go blind, it will be your fault!

LOL!!! Shut up!

:)

**I should not have called you from
Minnesota. That was selfish and unfair.**

You were drunk.

I was a tad tipsy.

As a skunk.

Perhaps I'd had one too many.

You know what they say about drunk folk.

What?

That a drunk tongue speaks a sober mind.

Meaning ...

When you got upset, I was the first one you
called.

**Sorry to burst the bubble you're blowing,
but outside of my family, you are the only
person who knows about ... everything.**

See? Even your girls don't know, and y'all
talk about everything. See how special I am?
Shoot ... I'm going to keep on blowing. And

you should come over and help me. Nobody
from your company lives over here. Tyra's
with her mother. I can't even meet your son.
Who's going to know? I'm not talking and I
know you won't tell.

Seconds after he'd sent this one, another followed.

Never mind. I know what you're going to say.
Disregard what I just sent.

And then another.

Hell, no. Don't disregard that. Get your soft,
sexy, smell-good behind here so I can . . . you
know . . . lick the tootsie roll.

When she didn't respond immediately, Byron
got up and walked into the kitchen. He opened
the fridge, stood in front of it and studied its lean
contents, and finally settled on fixings for a
turkey sandwich and a beer. He'd slathered on
mayo and was painting the other piece of bread
yellow when his phone dinged. A smudge of mustard marked the spot where he'd tapped the
screen to read her message.

**Yes, I do. BTW, during a meeting this
week with my director, I asked what
constituted family re our agency's
interpretation. It's a bit vague in the
national guidelines. She advised that if in**

**question, to air on the side of caution.
If I weren't in line for the director
position, and if I didn't have a pseudo-
detective as a coworker who wants the
position as much as I, perhaps I would be
less cautious. And there's something else.**

What?

He successfully juggled his phone, a plate, bag
of chips, and bottle of beer from the kitchen to
the living room.

**The night of the art show in Santa Monica,
someone saw us.**

Who?

**Unfortunately, the woman I'm up against
for the new job.**

She told you?

**If you knew Margo you'd know how unlikely
something that straightforward would be.
She quizzed Leah about you and then
insinuated to me that she knew I was out
socially with a client's family member.**

WTH? When did she talk to Leah?

**When she arrived early and was waiting in
the reception area. I came in to them**

chatting. That's when I knew for sure we could no longer communicate.

Like we're doing now. :)

Byron placed his head back and stared at the ceiling. This was an impossible situation. Here was a woman willing to put a client's needs above her own desires, a client whom he happened to be quite fond of, and what was he doing? Everything possible to try and get her to change her mind. He heaved a sigh and tapped the microphone icon.

All right, then. I guess I'll let you go.

What do you have planned for the evening?

I don't know, but I'm going to get out of the house and find something to occupy my mind.

Something, or someone?

What, you can't see me and I can't see anybody else?

The pause was lengthy enough for him to eat half his sandwich and make a respectable dent in the bag of chips.

Enjoy your evening, Byron.

Wait, you're mad now. Let's not leave on a sour note.

I am not angry.

Yes, you are. But that's cool, though. That's how you're supposed to feel about your man.

Didn't we just discuss how we are so not seeing each other?

If I find out somebody else is making you sing like Mariah, I'll be mad.

I probably shouldn't say what I've been thinking but ...

What??? Don't leave me hanging like that.

Leah has one more month of court-mandated weekly sessions. After that, I'd planned to continue the meetings, pro bono, at least twice a month. Once I have been given a case, I like to stick with the client. The stability aids and often expedites their path to rehabilitation. But perhaps this one time I could assign her to another manager and eliminate even the appearance of a conflict of interest.

Byron's heart soared for all of five seconds, until he remembered Ava's comments about how much Leah had improved under Cynthia's care, current Redman situation aside. His inner Jekyll said Leah would be fine, that they were all qualified to do the same job so what difference would it make?

Inner Hyde got an attitude. *Don't be a jerk. Do not jeopardize your niece's well-being so you can be satisfied.*

That is so tempting, but I couldn't ask you to do that. Leah has had enough interruptions in her life. But if you're still single when the sessions are over, all bets are off! I'm going to come for you gun blazing. And you know when I fire, I hit my mark.

He waited for her to say something. *She's probably mad because I've got that kitty humming again.*

Take care of yourself, sexy. Let me know when you get that promotion.

Ah, finally a place where that air of certainty is advantageous! Thank you for the vote of confidence.

You're welcome.

Good-bye, Byron.

His thumb hovered over the mic. Thinking it might be easier to type than to say, he tapped the screen. The keyboard appeared. It wasn't easier. *Just tell her good-bye, dude.*

No. Instead, he tossed his phone on the sofa cushion and picked up his beer. He wasn't going to speak something that he knew straight out was a lie. Unless he woke up six feet under, this was definitely not his last conversation with Cynthia.

He had to say something. It would be rude not to respond. So he finished his beer and picked up the phone.

See you later, baby. Be good.

41

"Wow, girl. I thought my mama was a piece of work, but what your mom did was gangster! I'm not talking Crips and Bloods. I'm talking Bugsy Siegel and Al Capone!"

"If the situation involved her social status or reputation, even Al wouldn't stand a chance against Anna Marie Hall."

It was sistah-girl chat time on a Sunday afternoon. Cynthia had just revealed to her BFFs what until now only family and Byron knew, not only that Jayden's father was married at the time he was conceived, but that her parents paid him off to stay that way.

"My mom would do something like that," Gayle said. "No, on second thought, she'd have made me have an abortion, the less expensive solution. A quarter million dollars could buy her too many designer fashions."

"I'm sorry you've spent all of these years with no one to talk to about this." Dynah's voice was soft, and sincere, perhaps hearing the residual pain that the other girls missed. "I can't imagine having to navigate school, relocation, and being a new, single mom at what, twenty-two?"

"Yes, I was twenty-one when I dated Stewart, twenty-two when Jay was born."

"But we're your girls, Cyn. I remember asking you about Jayden's dad and wondering why you were so evasive, almost like you didn't know. Remember, Gayle, I even mentioned how strange that seemed. And you had no more information than I did. I thought we talked about everything. Why'd you feel the need to keep it from us?"

"I can answer that in one word, Lisa . . . Mother. In her opinion, sleeping with a married man was dreadful enough—"

"But you didn't know. He lied!"

"A fact that was moot, given we found out after the horse had already left the proverbial stall. Her words were the A on my forehead, my prison the home of a great-aunt who lives in upstate New York. By the time I moved here, her words had taken root and I believed myself to be that scandalized woman guarding this . . . shame . . . even though Jayden is the brightest spot of my life."

"We haven't touched the big question."

"I know where you're going, Gayle, and I don't have an answer for that."

"For what?" Lisa asked.

"For whether or not she's going to show up at the wedding it seems her mother has already planned."

Cynthia's chuckle held no humor. Dynah

conveyed the incredulity Cynthia had felt for these plans.

"Do you want some advice?"

"Sure, Gayle. What should I do?"

"Marry him, of course. And before you begin firing your objections, I'll explain why. One, he is your son's father. Two, he's wealthy, successful, established, and obviously loves you to want to do right after all these years."

"But he took my mom's money when the decent thing would have been to tell her where to take that money and demand a relationship with his son."

"No, the decent thing would have been for him to keep his married dick inside his married pants."

"Ha!" No one could speak truth like Lisa. That's what Cynthia most loved about her.

"Since that did not happen," Gayle continued, "Stewart had to make decisions based on the big picture, and the entire picture, which involved more people than just you and your family. As despicable as it was for him to lie to you, the fact is he was married and had a young child. He was in the early stages of a career that is difficult at best, the success of which is driven by relationships and status, where decisions are made on the golf course and in country clubs. His road was probably not as hard as yours, Cynthia, but I doubt that it was easy."

"What do you think, Dynah?"

"Marriage is not something to be entered into lightly and when it is, I think that decision should

be based on love. Is that what you feel for your
son's father? Because not long ago you were into
the other guy. What's his name?"

"Don't help her remember," Gayle interjected. "A blue collar versus a bona-fide DHOP
is something not worth wasting time in being
compared."

"What about you, Lisa? Should I marry for
love, or because of the lifestyle Stewart can offer?"

"Look, life is not a romance novel. I'd go for
the money; then I could buy me some love."

When the girls ended their call thirty minutes
later, Cynthia was more confused than ever.

Byron wasn't confused. He was hot, angry, and
tired of sitting in front of the house he and Douglas had watched for the last hour.

"What do you say, Byron? Should we maybe try
a few of the hangouts again, see if anybody has
heard or seen anything?"

"That's what we did for the last four hours."
His attempt to stretch out his back turned into a
bear of a yawn. "I say we wait here for another
fifteen minutes or so. He has to come home
sometime, and my bet is she'll be with him."

"He" was none other than Aaron Smith, otherwise known as Redman.

"I still can't believe Leah didn't come home.
The last time she pulled that stunt, me, Mom,
and Dad spoke to her about it. I even promised
that if she hung with this program and got into
college, I'd help her buy a car." Byron reached

for his phone. Still no response from the calls
and texts he'd sent her. "She's never gone this
long without calling me back. It's total disrespect."

"She didn't call her mother back," Douglas
said, his speech smooth and unhurried, just like
his dad. "So I don't know why you think she'd
call you."

"It's worked before. Leah knows how much
Ava worries ever since Lance got shot. That's
what makes me so angry about this, what she's
putting her mother through."

"Yes, but for all intents and purposes she is
grown, doing what grown women do."

"Then I say don't half step. Own that status. If
she's grown enough to lay up with some dude still
living with his mama, then she's grown enough to
get out of Ava's house, get a job, get a car, and
everything else that a grown woman needs to
handle her business."

Douglas turned his head to view the side
mirror. "I think I see Gavin's car."

Byron checked through the rearview mirror.
"Yep, that's him. He probably knows where we
can find Aaron." Byron snatched the keys out of
the ignition. "Let's go do this."

"By." Douglas stopped his brother with a hand
on his arm. "Let's keep this cool. You know Gavin
carries heat."

"Well, I tell you what. If he doesn't get his
brother to bring our sister's daughter home?
He's going to be carrying the teeth he picks up
after my fist leaves his mouth."

Whatever Douglas said was cut off by Byron's slamming door. A shred of common sense allowed him to slow his pace, lose the frown, and walk up to Gavin Smith's car door more civilly.

The Smith brother who'd gone to school with Nelson stepped out of his car. "What's up, Byron?"

He held out his hand. Byron tapped it and got straight to the point. "We're trying to find Red. Do you know where he is?"

"Why are you looking for him?"

"Because he's with my niece, man. She's only seventeen."

Gavin locked his car and began walking toward the house where all of the Smith children still lived along with their mother, her boyfriend, his siblings, and several children. Douglas joined them. "Haven't seen you in a while, Gavin? How are you doing?"

"Fine until I got accosted by your hotheaded brother at six in the morning. He's messing up my high."

Douglas slipped between Byron and Gavin. Byron cut him a look, but remained quiet.

"Ava's really worried, dog, and we've been out all night. You know how mean the streets can be. Having already lost a child, she's just that much more protective of the one she has left."

"I understand, man. It's not like Aaron kidnapped her."

Byron placed a firm hand on Gavin's shoulder. "Do you know where they are?"

Gavin shook him off, his expression one of

somebody clearly annoyed. "No, you need to watch your hands, partner."

Byron took a step toward Gavin. "You need to watch your mouth."

Douglas stepped between them. "Gavin, if you hear from your brother, can you let me know? Because the next step is to get the police involved and with Leah only seventeen and Aaron twenty-five . . ."

"How are y'all so sure she's with him?"

"Because that's who she was seen with last night."

Gavin pulled out his phone. "What's your number?" Douglas told him. Gavin called Douglas's phone. "All right, I'll save your number. If I find out anything, I'll give you a call."

Byron held out his hand. "I was a little rough earlier. Sorry about that."

"No worries, man. I'll let y'all know if I hear anything."

As soon as the brothers were inside the SUV, Byron let out a string of expletives.

Douglas's calm demeanor did not shift. "Man, everybody's concerned. You have got to calm down."

"Leah is only one of the reasons I wanted to coldcock his ass. The other is for the weapons and other illegal activities he's into; that makes the neighborhoods unsafe for our kids. From what I hear, Aaron is trying to follow right in his footsteps. He can follow him to hell if he wants to, as long as he leaves Leah with us."

Byron started his car and couldn't get off the

block fast enough. An hour later, when they returned to Ava's house, no one had heard from Leah and she still had not come home.

After giving his teary sister a hug, Byron called the police.

42

The alarm sounded, but Cynthia didn't need it to wake up. Her roiling thoughts and vacillating emotions had kept sleep at bay for most of the night. Before their standing Sunday chat, she hadn't given serious consideration to her mother's suggestion of accepting Stewart's round-the-way proposal. For a moment, sure, simply because he was Jayden's father and living under the same roof would give them time to bond. But for her, that's where the benefits ended. Yes, he was handsome. But that was an attribute that had dropped increasingly lower as she matured. She didn't want to marry someone whose face would scare away babies and puppies, but she didn't have to marry someone with model-perfect features either. He was wealthy, and successful. For her, money wasn't a motivator and success was relative. With smart, safe investments and a stable economy, Cynthia could live comfortably for the rest of her life and not have to work. That part of Stewart's success could be connected to Jayden's lack of a father tarnished what other women would find most impressive. And finally, there was Lisa's comment when she told the girls how well that Stewart was endowed. Byron Carter had forever closed the book on the argument "size matters." A trumpet could outdo a tuba if the right person was blowing.

Her cell phone rang, startling her out of her thoughts. She glanced at the clock. Only 7:15. There were only a couple people who'd call at this hour, neither of whom speaking to before coffee was a good idea. She reached for her phone and looked at the caller ID. The number was one she didn't recognize.

"Hello?" She cleared the frog from her throat as she placed the call on speakerphone. She leaned against her cushioned headboard and went to her e-mail screen.

"Good morning, Cynthia. This is Officer DeWitt calling. I'm sorry to bother you at this hour, but there's been a development in the case of one of your clients, one that may revoke the diversion program put in place to keep her from lockup. I thought you'd want to know."

Hearing revoked had gotten her attention. Lockup pulled her out of bed. "Which client?" She asked the question but felt she already knew.

"Leah Thompson. She apparently left home on Saturday morning and while her mother and others have contacted her with instructions to call, she hasn't been heard from since that time."

"How did you find out about this?"

"A missing persons report was filed. I was flagged as soon as her name entered the system."

Cynthia was in her closet, reaching for apparel she could don quickly. The thought to go to Ava's home and meet in person was instinctual, not required. Having heard of Lance's murder following a night he'd not come home, Cynthia could only imagine how Ava felt right now. And Byron? He was probably worried out of his mind as well.

"What's the next step in the procedure?"

"Normally, we'd issue a warrant for her arrest."

"I'm hoping you can hold off on doing that," Cynthia quickly responded. "Her brother's birthday happened not long ago, which reopened emotional wounds."

"In that case, she should have called one of us for additional assistance. It's what's stated in the information she received and no doubt reiterated by you as well." Cynthia sent a text to the babysitter, to see how early she could arrive. "Some think she's with a boyfriend, quite likely someone with a criminal record. This, of course, is another violation of the program conditions."

This wasn't news to Cynthia. It's what she expected. As soon as the officer had said she was missing, she thought about Leah and her lashing out at Aaron. Cynthia had seen straight through the flimsy veil of anger to the truth. This young man was Leah's first love. His betrayal had not only hurt her but left her feeling bereft and alone. She felt it wouldn't take much of an apology to get back in Leah's good graces.

"Is there any way I can have a day or so to speak with her mother and also check the files for information that might be useful in finding her?"

"Seeing your genuine interest in the clients

you serve is one of the reasons I called you. You want them to succeed, and so do I. So, yes, I'll hold off, but about the best I can give you is twenty-four hours. We all believe this is a voluntary disappearance, but should it turn out that foul play is involved, then the time that we're idle will prove significant."

"Thanks for calling me, Officer DeWitt. I'll keep you updated on anything I find out. And will you do the same?"

"Absolutely."

Cynthia took a quick shower. By the time she finished, her summer sitter had texted back. She was on her way over.

"Good." Cynthia brushed her hair into a simple ponytail, ran a mascara brush through her lashes, and dabbed on lip gloss and perfume. Before heading into Jayden's room, she scrolled her priority file for Ava's number and called.

"Good morning, Ava. This is Cynthia Hall."

A moment of hesitation and then Cynthia heard Ava's greeting. "I understand that it's early and this call is unexpected. The reason is because earlier this morning I was contacted by Leah's parole officer. I assume she's spoken to you as well?"

"Yes."

"And you've still not heard from Leah?"

"No, not a word."

"Officer DeWitt has agreed to give us a little more time to locate your daughter before a warrant is issued. I'd like us to meet as soon as possible and can either come to your house or meet down at my office."

"Coming here would be best. I'm trying to stay close just in case she comes home."

"That's my hope as well. I'll be leaving my house shortly and should be there in twenty minutes or so. Try to stay positive. There are a lot of us pulling for your daughter to be okay."

Her sitter took longer than expected and traffic was a mess, so it was nearly forty minutes later when Cynthia arrived at Ava's house. It wasn't until she didn't see Byron's silver SUV that she acknowledged the part of her that had wanted him there. He'd been on her mind all weekend while she grappled with what decision would be in Jayden's best interest and had lost count of how many times she'd wanted to call. Byron's easy manner, straightforward approach to life, and lack of judgment made him easy to talk to. Unlike a lot of men she'd known, who quickly became bored with a conversation not centered on them, he was also an attentive listener who'd ask clarifying questions and repeat portions of what was said back to make sure he'd understood correctly. True, she missed his totally magical pocket trumpet but even more, she missed him.

Concerned eyes met weary ones as Ava opened the door. "Morning, Ava."

"Hi, Cynthia. Come on in."

One look and Cynthia knew that Ava had had an even worse night than she. Dark circles surrounded bloodshot eyes. A headband held back hair that had seen neither comb, brush, nor wrap. "No need to ask how you're holding up," she said, following her into the living room. "Difficult is probably too light a word to describe this."

"I have no words left." Ava walked past the living room into the dining room. "Have a seat," she threw over her shoulder. "You want some coffee?"

"Yes, please." Cynthia started to rise.

Ava waved her down. "Don't worry, I'll get it. Cream and sugar?"

"Yes, thank you. Lots of both."

As she waited, Cynthia looked around the simply decorated home. Family pictures in a variety of frames covered almost every surface. One wall held an obvious tribute to Lance. The photos gave a pictorial of his life: newborn baby, toddler, T-ball, kindergarten, football, high-school graduation, and several of him smiling with family and friends. She walked over to the wall for a closer look at one with Leah. He looked to have been twelve or thirteen in the picture, which would have made Leah seven or eight. He's standing with one foot in front of the other, arms crossed, and head tilted, with a confident smile to the camera. Leah has eyes only for her brother. One foot is turned inward and her hands are clasped in front of her as she looks at him with rapt admiration, as though he hung the moon and as if the sun was shining because he'd told it to. She felt when Ava walked up beside her, but continued reading the story that this picture told.

"That's one of my favorites." Ava's voice was low as she held the mug of steaming coffee for Cynthia to take. "It was Lance's birthday. He'd turned twelve. Byron had purchased six tickets to Magic Mountain, for me, Lance, Leah, and three of our friends."

"What a thoughtful gift!" Cynthia took a sip of coffee. "This is perfect, thanks."

Ava returned to the couch. "Byron has always been that way, very concerned for others with a heart of gold."

"He's very worried about Leah, as am I."

"Why are you so worried about her?" Ava set her cup on a cork-styled coaster. The question was asked in a mildly curious tone, but there was a hardened look in her eyes.

Cynthia was taken aback by the question, and gathered her thoughts behind a sip of coffee before she too sat down her mug. "Because she's my client, of course, one who I believe could have a bright future and one I'd like very much to keep out of jail."

"I appreciate everything you've done for her. Until a week or so ago, I was sure the counseling sessions were working to turn her around. Then all of a sudden, bam. She's right back to being the girl I barely know, the one Lance's death created. After getting your call this morning, I thought, wasn't that around the same time that she cut communication with Byron"—her eyes slid to Cynthia and back to the wall—"again?"

"Whenever something either did or didn't happen between Byron and I has absolutely nothing to do with Leah's behavior."

"What about yours?"

"Mine? Are you suggesting that I changed the way that I act professionally based on a personal matter, and this somehow led to your daughter's running away?"

"Leah left here to run behind someone she

has no business being with. Let's get that straight. But I can't help but wonder about the coincidence in timing, just like I can't help but try and figure out the real reason you're with Byron. I love my brother, but let's face it. Women like you don't usually go for the blue-collar types."

"I can assure you that every interaction with your daughter, whether within a counseling session, by phone, or casual chitchat afterward, has been professional and genuine. I became a counselor to make a difference in the lives of young people who didn't grow up with the types of advantages that were the norm in my circles, benefits that were often taken for granted. People often judge based on the wrapping, but no human package contains a perfect gift. When young, some make mistakes that affect the rest of their lives. I know how hopeless one can feel when that happens. I care, Ms. Thompson. That's why I'm showing such concern for your daughter, and that is why I'm here."

Cynthia looked directly at Ava without batting an eye, as she worked to slow her escalated heartbeat. The woman was beside herself with worry and fear for her daughter, a fact Cynthia had used to excuse Ava's less-than-pleasant mood. But there was no excusing a thinly veiled putdown or the implied accusation that Cynthia's involvement with Byron gave her less influence with Leah.

"I do believe you care about Leah," Ava said. "And I want you to know I appreciate all you've done. The way I feel about my child comes very close to the way I feel about my brother, and my entire family. The way you were acting, interested one minute, gone the next, I felt you were just toying with Byron. He doesn't need that. And he doesn't need to be used to satisfy a curiosity."

"Just what type of curiosity do you think he'd be satisfying?"

Ava's countenance softened. "Can we just be girls for a minute? I've often wondered what it would be like to be with a rich man, someone who grew up with all kinds of advantages, like you did. Maybe you just wanted to try out somebody from the hood, a brother who grew up like the clients you counsel."

Cynthia's first thought was not to answer. After all, her personal life was none of Ava's business. But considering the unusual set of circumstances that brought about this topic in the first place, she decided to be truthful, and hoped that doing so would stop the questions and suspicions, and get the focus back to why she was here.

"I initially went out with Byron because he was cocky and annoying, and much like you've done just now assumed quite a bit about me. I thought I'd meet him for coffee and be on my way. Surprisingly, I met a man who I found to be very comfortable in his skin, genuinely interested in me as a person, and easy to talk to. We had things in common, which I didn't expect. The more I was around him the more I came to care for him. I didn't expect that either.

"I would never play anyone's heartstrings. I know what it's like to be hurt. It was in the interest of this case and my client that I have limited contact with your brother, so there would be no question as to my professional commitment. That is the only reason I backed away from your brother, Ava. He's still cocky and quite annoying at times." Ava laughed. "But he is also an amazing man."

"Well, well, well." Both women jumped at the sound of the male voice coming through the front-door screen. "I am happy that you now admit what I've told you all along."

43

"Oh, Lord. Talk about bad timing." Ava walked over and unlocked the screen. "I hope you also heard her say you were annoying as hell."

"No, I didn't hear that part. Hey, sis." He gave Ava a hug.

Cynthia started talking before his back foot hit the living-room floor. "How long were you out there?"

"Long enough to know that we need to talk. Later, though, not now."

"Any news?"

Ava stood next to Byron, wringing her hands. Cynthia almost regretted getting angry at the earlier comments. Interest in her and Byron's relationship had kept Ava's mind off of her missing daughter, at least for a while.

"Actually, yes. Gavin called Douglas and told him that Aaron is in Las Vegas."

"Vegas!" Cynthia and Ava exclaimed in stereo.

Ava followed Byron, who walked over to sit on the couch. "Leah's in Vegas?"

"Douglas said Gavin thinks so. That's where Aaron is, and he's with a girl, but Gavin said he wouldn't give a name. Don't worry. Nelson is working on getting me and Daddy buddy passes."

Ava sat back. "Daddy's going with you?"

"You know Leah's his heart. He doesn't say much, especially around Mama, but he's been really worried about her. He said coming along if for nothing but the ride will make him feel better than sitting home wondering what's going on."

Cynthia walked past the sofa and sat on a matching love seat. "Did Aaron's brother say where they were staying?"

"If he knows, he didn't tell Douglas."

"I wonder why not?" Cynthia speculated.

"Because he knows my brothers," Ava responded. "They're all respectable now, with good jobs and even better reputations, but there was a time when if one of them had a beef with you, you stayed off the block."

"I was pretty riled when I saw him Sunday morning," Byron admitted. "And truthfully, I don't need to see Aaron's behind even now. I just want to see Leah. And get her home before she jacks up all of the progress she's made."

"I almost wish I could go with you," Ava mumbled.

"No, you need to stay here."

"Ava, I agree with Byron. You'd want to be able to contact her probation officer as soon as she arrived. However, I think my going to Vegas might be a good idea."

Byron's head whipped around. "You? Why?"

"A couple of reasons. As the counselor assigned

to her through the system, I'd have access to certain information that would otherwise be confidential and not released to just anyone who asks, including relatives. Hotel records, for instance, and other documents that might help us find her. Secondly, if she is located, I'd be a less threatening, more neutral person for her to speak with. Byron, you've just admitted being upset to the point of threatening violence against her alleged travel partner, a move that would heighten an already tense situation and potentially cause Leah to revert further into a shell of silence. I believe she'll talk to me. She knows that whatever is discussed between us will remain confidential and that assurance, I believe, has helped gain her trust."

"What about your job?" Ava asked. "I mean, will it be a problem for you to do this?"

"Going to Vegas is doing my job. Before arriving here I spoke with my assistant, and left word for my boss. It is in the best interest of the agency for this case to be resolved in a positive manner. My being successful in keeping Leah out of jail means that everyone wins."

Byron looked at her, one brow arched and twinkling eyes. "Everybody?"

Cynthia returned his gaze but didn't answer his question.

Ava was ready for the search to begin. "How long ago did you talk to Nelson?"

"Texted him as soon as Douglas heard from Gavin, I think around two, three o'clock this morning. He told me the girl he gets them from arrives around nine and he'd text me then."

Cynthia reached for her bag and stood. "Why wait on his text to go to the airport? If you know the airline, then I suggest we go to the airport now. That way, when your passes come in we can catch the next flight."

Ava nodded. "By, I think that's a good idea."

After deciding that Cynthia would park her car at the airport and Byron would pick up Mr. Carter and meet her there, the two left Ava's house and walked to separate vehicles. Cynthia quickly set her GPS for the fastest route to the airport and then made calls to the sitter and work.

"Hey, Ivy, it's me. I just spoke with Tracy and let her know that I won't be in today. I'm handling a sensitive client situation, but for the most part will be available by phone."

"Oh, my goodness. I hope everything turns out okay."

"Me too. In the meantime, could you please cancel the afternoon appointment I had with the Morgan Foundation? If they suggest a reschedule, make it sometime next week."

"Got it."

"Also, I need you to check into flights to Las Vegas leaving today, any time after, say, ten o'clock."

"You're going to—"

"Careful! The cubicles have ears and if anyone there other than you or Tracy mentions this trip, I'll know someone talked."

"Totally understand. Can I use your office to make a call? I may need to speak to someone personally to gather the info you've requested."

"Of course." Cynthia's caller ID flashed. "I need to take this call but aside from the time in flight, I should be available." She activated the incoming call. "Good morning. This is Cynthia Hall."

"I know who it is, beautiful. I'm the one who called."

"Hello, Byron."

"I appreciate what you're doing for Leah. I know I'm not the reason, but it makes me feel good to know you care."

"You are correct. Leah Thompson is the reason for my actions. Given a similar situation, I would do the same for any of my clients."

"Dang, girl. You could have at least acted like your trip to Vegas was just to be able to spend time with yours truly."

"And take away your chance to assume? Never that."

He laughed. "It was good seeing you. And I don't mind saying that aside from finding Leah and getting her back home, being able to hang with you is the best part of this trip. Matter of fact, Daddy snores. I think if we have to spend the night, I should stay with you."

"That's not going to happen."

"Why not?"

"Because for one thing I—hold on, Byron. Let me see who this is." She tapped her steering wheel. "Good morning. This is Cynthia Hall."

"Good morning, Ms. Hall. This is Stewart Monihan. It is a pleasure to hear your lovely voice."

"I can't say that I feel the same. How did you get my number?"

"Please don't be upset with me."

"You don't have to worry about my being upset,

I'm way past upset. I'm past livid and headed toward crazed. How dare you get in cahoots with my mother to plan a future to which I haven't even considered, let alone agreed to do!"

"I have only the best intentions, Cynthia. Your mother called me, understandably distraught that word had leaked regarding Jayden's parentage and equally angry that I'd gone back on my word and revealed the financial exchange. I don't regret telling you the truth, Cynthia. But I deeply regret my decision, even though my accepting the bribe isn't for the reasons you think. Yes, I was ambitious and protective of my reputation. But I was equally protective of yours. My wife had threatened to expose you had I not agreed to your mother's deal to leave you alone."

"And now it seems you've once again teamed up with my mother, this time to keep me forever. Look how we've come full circle." Sarcasm oozed through the phone line.

"Our meeting wasn't planned. We ran into each other at an event. She called me the next day, totally heartbroken that the town would find out what happened years ago. I know the two of you rarely see eye-to-eye, but she loves you, Cynthia, and has your best interest at heart."

"I believe she loves me, in her own way. But I've come to know a different level of love that allows me to see everything and everyone more clearly, including you and my mother. If her heart is breaking it is because of her interests, and the repercussions this news might have on her life. I'm still trying to figure out the angle by which a marriage between us would best your business interests, but I'm sure your desire to make things right between us, as you say, is not just about love or simply about getting to know Jayden. It's about business, it's about money, and it's about your career."

"In our world, love and business are often bedfellows. I won't deny that and neither would your parents, my parents, nor anyone in our circles. So when your mother questioned my plans for the future, I was truthful. I told her about my impending divorce, the desire to marry you, and the plan to become a father to the son I don't know. It's already been eight years too long."

"Stewart, I've waited that long to hear you say you want to be in Jayden's life and will do everything possible to make that happen. But your being in my life is a different matter, and something that with everything else that's going on I can't even deal with right now. We can talk later."

"Promise?"

"Yes, later tonight, I'll call you."

"Thank you, my love. I'll be waiting."

Cynthia ended the call and saw that Byron had hung up. It was just as well. He wouldn't have liked knowing who'd interrupted their conversation, especially since Stewart's ultimate goal was to insinuate himself in her and Jayden's lives . . . on a permanent basis.

44

By noon the three-person search party—Byron, Cynthia, Mr. Carter—had all landed in Las Vegas. Byron rented a car and then immediately headed to the hotel where Douglas was informed Aaron was staying. On the way, they discussed the best way to approach the sullen young man who'd not returned Douglas's calls and as of ten o'clock this morning had stopped answering his brother's calls as well.

"I definitely shouldn't be the one who calls him," Byron said, clutching the wheel the way he wanted to Aaron's throat as he navigated the crowded streets of Sin City. "Maybe you should call him, Daddy. That you're Leah's grandfather isn't a guarantee that he'll be more respectful, but he might at least listen to what you have to say."

Cynthia, who sat in the front passenger seat, nodded. "I think that's a good idea."

Mr. Carter took in the passing scenery as he rubbed his chin. "I don't know about that. Leah didn't call me back and that's rare. It hurt my feelings that she'd treat me that way."

"Please try and not take it personally, Mr. Carter." Cynthia offered a sympathetic smile. "Leah's actions are all because of conflicting emotions and those she's still grappling with regarding her brother's death."

"I know. It's just hard to see a child . . ." The man, who in the moment looked older than his fifty-five years, ran a weary hand over his face. He then sat up and clapped his hands together, as if the gesture could chase away his melancholy mood. "Never mind all that. We're here to get my granddaughter and bring her back home. I'm here to do whatever I can to make that happen. Cynthia . . . tell me the game plan one more time."

Twenty minutes later, the trio pulled into the parking lot of the Downtown Grand hotel, located ten minutes from the strip and less than a mile away from the city's famed Fremont Experience. However, none of them was focused on entertainment possibilities. And truth be told, Leah wasn't all of their singular focus either.

Byron dropped back to let his dad enter the hotel first, and remained behind to walk beside Cynthia. "What's going on with you?"

"What do you mean?"

"When we met at LAX, I could tell you were upset about something. Don't tell me Leah either. Because I know it's more than that."

"I could say the same about you," Cynthia whispered, before placing a smile on her face as Mr. Carter turned back to them.

"Everything all right?" he inquired, looking from Byron to Cynthia.

"Everything's fine, Dad."

"As long as whatever you two are conspiring about is legal, I won't press."

Cynthia stopped several feet from the front desk. "All right, guys. Just hang tight while I go to the front desk and see what information I can ascertain. I'll be right back."

The two men watched Cynthia walk away. Mr. Carter turned to Bryon. "That's a real nice lady right there." Byron nodded. "By that look in your eye, though, I guess you already know."

Byron cut his eyes at his father before his lips twitched and a grin escaped.

"Y'all got something going on?"

"We're friends."

"Uh-huh. I watched you at the block party, saw how you got a little perturbed when your brother pulled her away to introduce her to the neighbors. Can't say I blame you, time for you to settle down. I'd fathered all five of y'all by the time I was your age, and basically adopted Ava."

"Yeah, well, thank God I've only got one so far."

"Yes, indeed, son. Thank God for that."

His father's relief reminded Byron that he hadn't heard from Tanya or his lawyer in about a week. As soon as this situation with Leah was over, he'd have to deal with a woman of whom his father had never approved about a potential child Mr. Carter knew nothing about.

* * *

On the other side of the lobby, Cynthia's credentials and position as an intermediary of sorts between her and the legal system had given her the access she needed. The hotel manager had confirmed that an Aaron Smith had indeed checked in and had been accompanied by a young woman who looked like the picture that Cynthia had showed her. While not providing their room number, she had connected her to the room via a house phone. Cynthia nervously tapped her nails on the table by the phone, praying someone would answer.

The phone rang to the point where Cynthia was sure no one was in the room. Just as she was placing down the receiver, she heard a voice.

"Yeah."

"Hello, Aaron?"

Pause. "Who's this?"

"My name is Cynthia Hall. I'm Leah's counselor. How's she doing?"

"How'd you get my room number?"

Cynthia ignored the young man's brash manners and stayed focused on the end goal. "I didn't," she said as pleasantly as if Aaron, also known as Redman, wasn't totally out of line. "Once I explained the seriousness of the situation, and the very real possibility that Leah leaving the state might send her to jail, the desk clerk connected me to your room via the lobby house phone. May I speak to her, please?"

"The lobby? You're in Vegas?"

"Yes, I'm in the lobby of the Downtown Grand."

Cynthia waited as the sound of muffled voices came through the phone. While not able to make out the words, she could tell from the tone that neither Aaron nor Leah was too happy about her surprise visit. They'd be even less thrilled to know that she was not alone.

"Hey, look, uh . . ."

"Cynthia."

"Yeah, Cynthia. I wish you'd called before you drove all the way down here because I could have told you that, uh, Leah wasn't with me."

"Really? Then who is?"

"I don't mean to be rude, but that's none of your business."

"And I don't mean to be rude, but I think you're a liar."

"Look, I don't even know you. So this conversation is a wrap—"

"I have news for you as well, Aaron." This sentence came out as one long word, so quickly did she speak before he hung up the phone. "I did come for Leah, but I also needed to talk to you."

"What do you need to talk to me about?"

"About the laws and statutes in the state of California, where at the age of seventeen Leah is still a minor, and under the guardianship of her mother. Now, I have managed to get Leah's mother, Ms. Thompson, to hold off on filing charges, but if Leah is not returned to her residence within twenty-four hours, you'll be looking at some very serious offenses."

"What the hell are you talking about? Leah is here because she wants to be here!"

Amazing how certain words could make people

invisible seconds before magically appear. "She may be here of her free will, but not with the permission of her legal guardian. Which is why if Ms. Thompson doesn't see Leah by this time tomorrow, you'll be facing charges of sexual assault. Because you're more than three years older than Leah, this will more than likely be handled as a felony, punishable by up to four years in state prison. Now, is Leah still not available or is there any way she can come to the phone?"

After an hour of negotiations—where Cynthia convinced Leah to return to Los Angeles, Aaron to lose a bit of attitude and give Leah's uncle and grandfather deserved respect and Byron not to turn the hotel lobby into a boxing ring—the two agreed to come down.

Forty-five minutes after that, Leah got off the elevator. She was alone.

Cynthia noted the tightness in Byron's jaw, and the way his eyes drifted past Leah to the elevator. "Where is he?"

She placed a calming hand on his arm. "Hello, Leah." She forewent the more formal handshake greeting and enveloped the clearly confused, vulnerable, and frightened child in a warm hug. "Thank you so much for agreeing to come back with us. Your mother has been worried out of her mind."

"You knew she'd be worried. How many times have we told you to return calls, no matter what!"

"Sorry, Uncle Byron." She dropped her head as if contrite, but Cynthia didn't think she was sorry at all.

"It's going to be all right, Granddaughter." Mr.

Carter walked over and placed an arm around Leah's shoulders. She turned into his chest, and cried. "Now, now, you just get it all out. You're safe and that's all that matters."

During this exchange, Cynthia shot Byron a warning look. The look he returned didn't give her much comfort. Still, she saw him try to relax before he spoke again. "Leah, where is Aaron?"

"He's not coming down." Given his reaction, Cynthia was truly glad he didn't respond to this comment. Her chin began quivering. "He said we can't be together anymore until I turn eighteen."

The disgust with which she made this statement assured Cynthia that her assumption was right. Her client was angry, not sorry. Either way, she was in the lobby and going back home.

"Everything works out for the best," Cynthia offered. "Part of the conditions for your probation is that you finish school. Time apart from Aaron will allow you to focus on your summer courses and receive your diploma. Graduating high school and beginning college courses is the most important thing right now for you to do."

Leah was obviously not convinced.

Cynthia gently steered Leah away from the hotel entrance and led them a short distance toward the bank of elevators. Once out of the hearing range of Mr. Carter and Byron, she placed her hands on Leah's shoulders. "I know how you feel about Aaron. Every woman breathing, who's past the age of . . . twelve, knows what it's like with that first special crush, or kiss, or love. It took courage for you to leave the hotel room and come with me."

"He didn't want me to. But he didn't want me to go to jail and I didn't want him to go to jail either."

"Leah, even though you've agreed to come back with us, you still violated the terms of your agreement and are not out of the woods. I'll do everything I can to keep you in counseling rather than in jail. But from here on out, I need you to do something."

Cynthia paused, waiting for Leah to look at her. Finally, Leah did. "What?"

"I need you to do everything you can to get through these ninety days, your summer classes, and to graduate high school. Before I go to bat for you . . . do we have a deal?"

After a pause, she nodded.

"Good." Cynthia looked up to see the two Carter men watching them intently. "I think we've kept your grandfather and uncle waiting long enough. Let's rejoin them."

"Can I ask you something first?"

"You may."

"Can you and I sit together on the plane, away from Grandpa and Uncle Byron? They're both so mad at me that I know I'm going to get it from them later. But I can't do it right now."

"There's something I'd like to discuss with you, so I have an even better idea."

They walked over to where the two men stood. "If it's all right with you two, I'd like to take Leah out for a bite to eat, take care of some official matters, and bring her with me on a later flight. I promise to deliver her personally at Ava's door."

Mr. Carter deferred to Byron, who gave Leah a long look before turning to Cynthia. "I guess that's all right." He looked back at Leah, who averted her eyes. "Stop looking at me like you're three years old and scared of a spanking. Unfortunately, you're too old for that. And even though I'm angry enough to get back to LA on my own steam, I still love you, Leah. Very much. Now come give your uncle a hug."

Leah gratefully walked into his arms. Byron looked over her head and winked at Cynthia.

She winked back, and smiled.

45

Cynthia gave Ava one last wave before getting into her car and driving away. It had been a long, exhausting day, but a fulfilling one. It was moments like this and clients like Leah that was her sole reason for getting into what for people in her circle was a very unlikely career. When she'd opted for a degree in sociology it was because while she hadn't decided on a career choice, this degree offered many paths: law, government, politics, advertising, business, etc. Upon graduation, she was leaning more toward advertising and marketing, which is why her choice for a master's degree was business administration. It was during those lonely days and heartbreaking nights at her great-aunt's house, when she felt completely abandoned and cried herself to sleep, that those thoughts changed. In those dark moments, she vowed to do everything she could to help other young women who'd dared to be human and make a mistake not endure a similar experience.

Driving away from Ava's home and reflecting on the day's experience, more life-altering decisions were forming. Ones that would take her farther away from a life of privileged society but closer to her heart's desire. Making these decisions would have consequences and benefits. But given all that had happened in just two short months, Cynthia was ready to face the ramifications and receive the rewards.

Her phone rang. She looked at her dash and remembered the missed call she'd seen once taking her phone off airplane mode. Sooner rather than later, this situation would have to be dealt with. It was one of the life-changing decisions looming in her future.

"Hello, Stewart."

"Hello, Cynthia. You sound . . . strained."

"It's been a very long day, one that's just now ending. I see I missed your call."

"Yes, you did. But I'm glad to hear your voice now." Said in a way that at one time would have wet her panties. Cynthia refused to be sidetracked. She was thirty-one not twenty-two, and no longer a fool.

"I assume you're calling concerning Jayden. I agree that steps need to be taken to establish a relationship with him. It's a busy time on my job, a lot going on, so why don't we talk this weekend, say, Friday evening?"

There was a beat of silence before he responded. "Sure, what time?"

"Jayden and a few of his friends have a standing overnight play date on Friday. It usually begins with dinner, so he'll either get dropped off or picked up around six-thirty. I know that's a bit late on the east coast, but—"

"It's okay. Call me at six-thirty. Until then my sweet C—"

Cynthia ended the call in a way that was not sweet at all.

As soon as Tanya walked through the door, Byron knew that agreeing to meet her had been a mistake. It was seven o'clock on a Wednesday evening at a brightly lit, highly trafficked, kid-friendly good old Micky D's. Tanya was known for dressing sexy, but the loud red tank top showing more breast than it covered up was totally inappropriate for . . . well . . . any place public.

Tanya was oblivious. Swinging ample hips that framed a butt round enough to give the moon competition, she sat down with a saucy smile. "Hey, baby."

Byron settled against his seat. "Why'd you come here dressed like that?"

"What? Everything's covered and that's all that matters. I can't help it because I've got so much sexy it's spilling out of my clothes. You used to not have a problem with it."

"I wouldn't now, except you're my daughter's mother, and therefore an example. What would you do if you saw her in something like that?"

"I'd tell her she'd better appreciate what her mama bought her."

Byron shook his head. "Look, you asked to speak in person. I'm hoping it's about the paternity case, so here I am. Have you set a date to get tested?"

Tanya looked around. "Why'd you pick this of all places? All bright and loud and stuff. Let's go somewhere quiet and have a drink."

"That's what got me Tyra—someplace quiet, and drinking."

"I'm good, huh."

"I'm on the route early tomorrow, Tanya. What's this about?"

"Dang, where's the fire? You suggested the cheapest place on Crenshaw and still haven't offered to buy my food. You're slipping, dude."

"Would you like something to eat?"

"Yeah," she drawled. "But it's not on the menu."

Byron reached for his keys. "Something told me not to come here. I don't have time for games."

"Sit down and slow your roll."

He did, begrudgingly. She heaved a sigh. Had he been a betting man, he would have put twenty on the chance of patrons seeing a nipple. He would have lost. Her large melons rolled and swayed with her breath, but settled back inside the two fingers of cloth hiding them before exposing herself to the young boy sitting near them and messing him up for life.

"I have a confession."

"Okay."

"I lied."

"About?"

"About little Ricky. He's not yours."

Byron stared at her. "See, that's the problem with liars. It's hard to believe them, even when they act like they are telling the truth."

"Whatever. I'm being truthful, okay?"

"Really? Like you were being truthful about you kicking Rick to the curb when the truth is he's set up house with another woman?"

"He did that to piss me off because of how I acted after the block party. He saw how finding out you were seeing somebody made me feel."

"Oh, and decided to go make a baby to get back at you? That makes sense." He shook his head.

"Because of that and because he heard me tell someone that you were little Ricky's daddy. He knew I'd drop him in a heartbeat if I could get you back." She raised her eyes, gave him a sexy gaze through long, thick individual lashes that looked freshly applied. "You still seeing that girl you brought to the block? Because I heard she's one of them Benjamin stitches, the ones who you can't even step to unless he's got a big presence in your wallet."

Byron took in her flawless makeup, perfectly manicured hands, meticulous weave, and waxed, arched brows. For a woman who claimed to never have money, and except for the bazookas threatening escape, her look was on point.

"Who I'm seeing is none of your concern. The only business between us is Tyra and the paternity test that I still want taken."

"Why? I said I was lying and that makes me feel bad enough. Why pay all that money to have a test done? Heck, I could use that money."

"Tanya, what is this, the third or fourth time you've done this? First, when you were pregnant. Then, when you and Rick broke up right after little Ricky was born. Y'all got back together. I didn't hear from you. Two years ago, you were at it again, and now we're back for another round. I don't want to take your word on something this important. I want an official answer so we can settle this once and for all."

"So, you're not going to call your attorney and get him to pull the case on this, or have it dismissed, or whatever they do?"

"No, I am not."

"I know why you're trippin', but whether or not you're little Ricky's father is not going to help your situation. A high-maintenance chick like the one I heard you were with ain't gonna settle for your sorry bus-driving ass."

That comment was a sayonara note if ever Byron had heard one. He finished his soda and reached for the keys. "Answer the court order, Tanya. The testing center already has my DNA. All they need are yours and your son's to test. I'm not going to let this go, so you might as well go on down there. That way you'll have one less reason to deal with this sorry-ass bus driver."

Upon leaving the fast-food establishment, he pulled out his phone, barely waiting until he'd cleared the window through which he was sure Tanya sat watching. There was no thought that he shouldn't call her. The only thing that would be improper is if Cynthia didn't answer the phone. Tapping her soothing, smiling face, he clutched the phone like a lifeline, as though hearing the voice on the other end would pull him back into reality from the twilight zone.

"She lied. Again."

Three words formed by a mind only now acknowledging the impact similar words had on him moments before, how a few letters organized into a word and those words into a sentence structure could change, transform, impact a life—raise or ruin—based on the slightest change in a letter's position, or the adding or subtracting of same. *You are the father. You are* not *the father.* Three letters, the lack thereof had changed many lives, including his. The paternity test would confirm her words, but in his heart he knew they were true.

"Byron?"

"Yeah." He started the car and was soon in the thick of Crenshaw traffic. "She lied."

Silence as Byron imagined Cynthia trying to figure out the riddle, even as he tried to piece more coherent sentences together while remembering to breathe.

"Are you talking about Tanya? You're not her son's father?"

"No!" There it was, relief masquerading as air, rushing through his lungs and expanding his rib cage. "Woohoo!" His shout was loud enough to get the attention of the woman in the car next to his at the light. He didn't care if he could be heard in Arizona. Finding out that one didn't owe a huge amount of child support, almost ten years future and eight years past if a judgment was retroactive, was like winning the lottery. When people hit the jackpot, they screamed.

"Woohoo!" He laughed and clapped his hands, so much so that the woman in the car next to him smiled and gave a thumbs-up as the light turned green.

Cynthia laughed as well, his joy infectious. "I guess congratulations are in order."

"You'd better believe it! I'm going through with the court order to make it official, but I believe she's telling the truth this time. And come Friday night, we're going out to celebrate."

"I'd love to, but I can't. The promotion announcement will be made any day now. Unfortunately, I can't be seen with you . . . in public."

"I'm going to give you a pass for what you said because it now sounds like you're not opposed to meeting behind closed doors. But before we get together, there's something I want to know. Is this change of heart an acknowledgment that what we have is a connection worth pursuing and a relationship that could last? I don't want to get with you only for you to tell me later there's another conflict of interest that has you on the run. I'm handling one situation that's been a constant battle for almost ten years and I don't want to start another one. Nor do I plan to keep getting bounced back and forth like a ping-pong ball, or have my love for you taken for granted."

A million thoughts drifted through the silence before she responded. "I'm sorry for the way I've handled us. There are many reasons, but I offer no excuses. I have been on the run, and gone back and forth based on my waffling feelings. Again, I am sorry for the anguish that dealing with my pain caused you. Believe me when I say that given my life's experiences, I was doing the best I could at the time.

"Since meeting you, I've been shown another life, for me a better life. Nothing has been the same since the day my car broke down and I got on your bus. Everything about my being attracted to you was impossible, and I worked hard to get you out of my system. That's hard to do with a man who loves his family immensely, treats a girl who isn't even his real niece like a daughter, is raising his daughter, faces down a gun to save my honor, plays my music box like a Julliard-trained pianist, and cherishes me in a way that I'd never experienced. Have I left anything out?"

"Probably, but I like how what you're saying so far is sounding, so don't stop now, baby girl."

"I have had a change of heart. I believe ours is a connection worth pursuing. I admit we are in a relationship, one I want to see continue. I don't know how this will affect my bid for agency director but will have to take my chances and hope all works out. Finally, when I think of you and balls, it's not ping-pong."

"Ha! Is that it?"

"No, there's one more thing."

"What's that?"

"I love you, Byron Carter."

"I love you, too, Cynthia Hall."

46

Friday came and with it the opportunity to relieve the crick in her neck from dodging the knives Margo aimed at her back. Now, however, they were a little less sharp. Her rival had chosen the day after Cynthia went to Vegas, retrieved Leah, settled down the parole officer, thus helping her client avoid jail, and get commendations on the way she'd handled the situation to do a tell-all with Tracy about her "dating" the client's relative. That the only date Margo knew of was the time she'd spotted her and Byron at the art show in Santa Monica, an outing that in no way seemed inappropriate or even necessarily romantic, did not help her cause. Nor did the "blood relation" card Cynthia finally played. The bottom line? Deciding to voice a claim to have "very damaging" information on Cynthia that could prove "traumatic" for the agency on the day after Cynthia had returned from an agency success story made Margo come off looking petty and sounding ill-informed.

Not that her accusation hadn't presented a problem. While Cynthia had admitted her evening with Byron, she'd stopped short of admitting the relationship status she'd only recently admitted to herself. This decision may come back to haunt her, but she'd had to take her chances. By the time she broke this news to Tracy, she hoped Leah would be well on her way to receiving her diploma and becoming not only a successful case in the files of Cynthia Hall, but a closed one.

Having promised Byron a night of "celebration," she placed a call to Stewart through her car's Bluetooth. She was relieved when the call went to voice mail. "Stewart, this is Cynthia. I'm sorry to have to cancel tonight's discussion, but something came up that cannot be helped or avoided. Please accept my apologies and give me a call tomorrow. I should be free any time after nine."

Mission accomplished, she turned up the radio and sang out of key, hurrying home to spend time with Jayden before he went on his play date, and she invited hers over.

By seven-thirty Jayden had been safely delivered to Bobby's house for a night at the skating rink, and Cynthia had showered and changed for a casual evening that at Byron's insistence included dinner at a restaurant. She would have been fine with one pizza and two climaxes and not necessarily in that order. Byron assured her that he'd not leave her hungry. Cynthia assured him that he'd have his work cut out. A month had passed since their last encounter. She was starved.

She'd just sprayed on cologne and reached for her purse when the doorbell rang. She almost skipped down the steps with the glee of a child meeting Santa. Had anyone asked, Cynthia would have had to tell the truth—Byron's candy cane was quite a present.

"Hello, there—ah!"

Before she could finish the greeting, Byron had swept her off her feet, closed the door with his heel, deposited her on the couch, and begun undoing all the work she'd done in the previous hour: hair mussed, makeup smudged, clothes . . . coming . . . off. This rough and tumble taking without so much as a hello turned her all the way on and within minutes she was singing.

"I thought . . . you were . . . after we ate."

Byron answered her to the beat of his thrusts. "I. Changed. My. Mind."

An hour later, two freshly showered, hungry lovers left Cynthia's condo in search of food. They were giddy from the aftereffects of a good sexing, so much so that they didn't notice they were being watched, and recorded.

Early the next morning, Byron received a call from his attorney requesting a meeting. Cynthia joined him in the shower. She planned to pick up Jayden, take him to breakfast, and then spend the day doing whatever he liked. She also wanted to talk to him about his father, so she'd have a clear direction of where to take the conversation when Stewart called. Five minutes after Byron had kissed her good-bye, the doorbell rang.

She walked over to let him back in, unlocked and opened the door.

It wasn't Byron.

"Stewart?" She looked beyond him, wondering if his and Byron's paths had crossed.

"Oh, he's gone. And a good thing, too."

"Stewart, what are you doing in Los Angeles?"

"Will I be forced to explain while standing at your front door?"

"No, of course not." Cynthia moved aside. "Come in."

Stewart quickly scanned his surroundings. "Came to surprise you, and to meet my son. And from the looks of what I saw leaving your condo, I got here just in time. What street corner did you pull him from?"

"Excuse me?"

"You know, holding a sign, will work for food."

"Your snide remark is closer to the truth than you realize. Except I was on the street corner when he picked me up." She had more to say but was frozen silent at the words "bet I beat you," followed by the sound of tennis shoes pounding up the stairs.

She raced toward the door but stopped midway. Did she open it? Try and hide Stewart? Somehow prevent Jayden from entering his own home. Her attention went from the door to Stewart and back again. Her body followed. A step toward the door to, what, tell her son just a minute while she try and hide a grown man. Then toward Stewart. And back at the door as

Jayden ringing the doorbell was followed by a knock. "Mom! It's me. Let me in!"

"Don't say anything," she warned Stewart. "Hang on, Jay!" She opened the door. Jayden scurried past her and stopped short.

The look on her face must have telegraphed horror. Bobby's mother picked up on it at once. She prevented her son from following Jayden inside. "No, Bobby, we've got to keep moving. Good morning, Cynthia." The woman looked at Stewart, then at Jayden, and again, and once more before she said in a tone that was full of apology, "You didn't get my message? My sister went into premature labor and just gave Bobby a cousin. We're headed to the hospital now."

"It's okay," Cynthia said as brightly as possible. She hoped that Jayden wouldn't suspect anything wrong, even though at this moment everything totally was.

Cynthia took a moment to gather herself before turning around, a little self pep talk to regain control. *You can do this, Cynthia. Just act normal, introduce Stewart as an old friend who popped by for a visit, and then politely thank Stewart for his visit as she saw him out the door.*

That was the plan. But everything changed with a comment and a question.

"Hi, I'm Jayden. Are you my dad?"

47

Cynthia had her girls' attention. From her mother's presumptive wedding preparations, to Byron spending the night, to Stewart arriving the next day, to Jayden showing up totally unannounced, barging into the living room and coming face to face with his father, a better script could not have been written. For a blockbuster catastrophe, that is. It had been the worst possible scenario for how Jayden would meet him, yet she had to give it to Stewart. He'd handled the question with a calm assurance, followed up by a sincere, age-appropriate conversation with Jayden that reminded Cynthia of the good qualities that Stewart possessed.

"Girl, I can't believe all this happened in one single weekend. The only thing missing was a fight with Byron and this would have been a movie worthy of taking first place at the box office."

Dynah chimed in. "Lisa, you probably shouldn't say that with so much relish."

"Honey, the only thing I'm missing is the popcorn and chocolate-covered raisins. I just want to know about the sequel, because you know it's coming."

"Seriously, Cynthia," Gayle said, very seriously, "I can understand your being upset, but I'd like to offer another perspective. Since most of what occurred had to happen eventually, at least it all happened at once. Jayden met his father. Great! They hit it off. Even better! Your mother is planning the wedding. Takes the pressure off of you. For everything else your mother might be, she's an excellent planner of social events. Your wedding will be stunning.

"It's time to end the fling with Byron and accept the offer to try and rekindle passion with the type of man of whom most women can only dream. And I'm not just saying this because Byron's a bus driver and Stewart is a business mogul, although that in itself is a fairly significant detail. I'm saying it because Stewart is Jayden's father and the type of man you should marry."

"How can you sound so sure?" Cynthia asked this not because she'd planned to change her mind, but because Gayle seemed so sure of how her life should be lived.

"You're a Hall who grew up a certain way, are used to a certain lifestyle, and quite frankly have an obligation to allow your son the same privileges your upbringing afforded. We all know that's more than money. It's connections, and the right schools, and the right clubs, and attending the right parties to not only smooth your son's path but to ensure you're a shining star in society. I did a little research on Stewart and I must tell you he has a stunning portfolio. Quite the catch."

The old Cynthia would have agreed with anything Gayle said. The new Cynthia knew otherwise.

Dynah spoke up. "Cynthia, you know I've always advocated that you err on the side of love but at this point, I must agree with Gayle. Not so much because of materialism and status, although some of what Gayle said, particularly about connections and schools, is important, but because Jayden has a right to a healthy, ongoing relationship with his father."

"I agree, Dynah. But I don't have to be married to Stewart for that to happen."

"Jayden's relationship with Stewart will be much different if you're married and living in the same household and traveling in the same circles than if you live on opposite sides of the country with Stewart getting every other holiday and a month during the summer."

"No matter what we think it's Cynthia who'll be living with whoever she chooses, which is why it should be her choice."

"Thanks, Lisa."

"You're a smart woman, Cynthia," Gayle concluded. "Which is why I'm not going to contemplate anything other than purchasing monogrammed linen emblazoned with the letter *M*."

Cynthia actually laughed at this comment. "Be sure and keep the receipt."

Shortly after ending the call with Lisa, Dynah, and Gayle, her phone rang.

"Hey, sexy."

"Hi, Byron."

"How's my pretty lady doing today?"

"That's a good question."

"What's going on?"

"A saga of epic proportions, but in short, Jayden met Stewart. The two of them are together right now."

"Whoa, how'd this happen?" She told him. "I think that's great, babe. I've always been for Jayden meeting his dad. As long as he stays out of the way of what's happening between us, Stewart and I will get along just fine."

48

"Wow! You've got a swimming pool, Dad? Mom!" Jayden turned to Cynthia, eyes shining. "Dad's got a pool! I'm going to love it here!"

"Champ, why don't you go check it out and afterward see if you can figure out which of the upstairs rooms belong to you?"

"Thanks, Dad." Jayden walked over and gave his father a fist bump.

Two weeks had passed since Stewart showed up in LA unannounced. He'd returned to the east coast after returning with Jayden from their trip to the mall, but father and son had talked almost every day. There was no way Cynthia could deny it. Jayden had blossomed as a result of meeting and getting to know his father. He was a lot like Stewart in ways she hadn't noticed until seeing them together. To say he idolized him would be accurate, even the word *worship* wouldn't be much of a stretch. It helped that Stewart had purchased two of the games Cynthia had planned to hold until Christmas or some other special occasion.

It also didn't hurt that in their years apart Stewart had secured a pilot's license and took Jayden up in a snazzy Cessna and for a few seconds let him pilot the plane. Hard to beat that with a baseball game.

In watching Jayden investigate the beautifully landscaped backyard, she hadn't noticed Stewart walk to her side. His cologne crossed her nostrils just before he hugged her from behind, placing tiny kisses on her earlobe and pressing her against him.

"Um, it feels good to have you in my arms again. You don't know how many times I dreamed of this moment."

"At one time, so did I." Jayden was watching, so slapping Stewart's face was out of the question. Instead, she calmly stepped out of the embrace, smile in place, and put distance between them. "But time goes on and things change."

"Yes, fortunately for us they've changed for the better. We can finally be together, the way I've always wanted."

"You and your wife are finally moving forward with a divorce you say you've wanted for ten years. Good for you. But you keep forgetting that there is someone in my life now whom I care about."

Stewart tsked as though preparing to scold a naughty child. "Seriously, Cynthia. This nonsense about carrying a torch for this Bryan guy, a bus driver you've hardly known six months, for Pete's sake, is getting old. It's time to end it." He pulled out his phone. "Why don't you do it now?"

She crossed her arms. "You don't get it, do

you? You can't believe that I, Cynthia Eileen Hall, would turn down the great and powerful Stewart Monihan. How could any woman ever resist your charms, and how could any man compete with all you have to offer?"

"Exactly." Stewart beamed with a satisfied smile.

"I'll tell you who, and I'll tell you how. The woman who can say no to you is one who values herself before her possessions, who understands what true character looks like, and who has experienced what it feels like to be number one in a man's life. That isn't the woman you met all those years ago, but it's the one in this room right now.

"I'm the one who now knows how another man can compete with you. It's by displaying the character I just mentioned, valuing me for me, and not my social standing. A man can compete with you by having too much integrity to turn his back on a child whose DNA runs through his veins, even though the thought is one he doesn't want to entertain.

"The man who can compete with you is the man I'd love to marry, if ever I was fortunate enough for him to ask me. Considering that fact along with what I hope to be your continued presence in our son's life even though I've turned you down, you might want to keep his name straight. It's Byron, not Bryan. Byron Carter. And, yes, he is a bus driver, line 53 in case you're wondering. A savior if your car stops and you can't get a cab. And one of the best movers of human cargo in Metro LA."

This declaration was the end of Stewart's beaming arrogance and the beginning of Cynthia making yet another decision.

By evening, she'd removed her belongings from Stewart's home and into a hotel. She'd stopped by her parents' home to ask her father to take Jayden for his visits with Stewart, to tell her mother there would be no marriage to Stewart, and to tell them both about her bus-driving beau. As expected, her dad had been quiet and tight-lipped while Anna Marie had acted as though her decision to date a working class man would affect global warming.

"I will never accept him!" she declared, after wasting a half-hour worth of breath attempting to get Cynthia to change her mind. "He will never be welcome in our home!"

"That's unfortunate," Cynthia had calmly replied before gathering her purse and preparing to leave. "Because should he and I marry and you maintain that attitude, you'll never be welcome in mine."

49

On Sunday, the day after returning from Minneapolis, the babysitter had invited Jayden to her nephew's day-long birthday party at Legoland California, giving Cynthia and Byron some alone time that was as appreciated as it was unexpected.

"I don't know about taking our relationship public," Byron said, following Cynthia's sharing her plans for next week. "I kinda like these secret meetings, where we have to hole up in your bedroom, order in food and movies, and coordinate my home visits with your son's play dates."

"Are you saying you'd rather be kept a secret?"

"Hey, it works both ways. Considering how your constant presence would forever ruin my player reputation, I might want to keep you on the low as well."

"Player, huh? I've got something for you to play with all right." Cynthia threw back the covers and brazenly spread her legs.

"My baby's turned into a freak! I'm a lucky man."

He still felt this way an hour later, after being called a mistake by two women he didn't even know.

Cynthia didn't waste time in correcting the misconception of the two Chicago friends who'd surprisingly showed up on her doorstep. In fact, with only a few sentences, she cleared up several errors, beginning with making an introduction that was long overdue.

"I see why the phone chat was postponed. Y'all should have brought Lisa and we could have powwowed in person. Gayle, Dynah, this is Byron Carter, who, unlike you right now, is an invited guest in my home. Byron, these two women are like sisters to me. They owe you an apology, and now that we're clear on your place in my life, I'm sure one will be forthcoming. Which one of you two would like to go first?"

Cynthia looked from Gayle to Dynah. Both women remained silent. "My, my, isn't this interesting. A ride to O'Hare, four and a half hours on a plane, and a taxi to Culver City . . . and all of a sudden you two have nothing to say?"

Gayle was the first to regain her composure. "We have plenty to say, Cynthia," she said in a voice that was coated with forced civility. "But we'd rather have this conversation in private. We're here at the request of your mother and what needs to be said could best occur with him not around." The dismissive way she'd cocked her head let Cynthia know that her friend had regained her composure but not her common sense.

"My mother contacted you? Seriously? That woman is special, but I'll tell you this. There's nothing you share on her behalf that she hasn't told me already, and nothing you have to say to me about Byron that he can't hear."

Dynah had been more observant, and tried a different tact. "I can understand you being upset, Cynthia, but imagine getting a phone call from a woman you've never met who just happens to be the mother of one of your best friends. She first reached out to Gayle through an e-mail, remembering her name from one of your conversations after seeing the name online. Gayle called me and then the number she provided through the e-mail. Your mother is worried sick about you, Cynthia. I've never heard a woman so distraught."

She looked at Byron as she held out her hand. "Hello, I'm Dynah. I'm sorry for the way we're meeting, but it is good to finally meet the man we've heard about."

He shook her hand. "Nice to meet you, too."

Three pairs of eyes forced Gayle to show the manners she'd been taught. "Gayle Steele," she said with hand outstretched, her face resembling her surname.

"I've heard a lot about you ladies. All good things." Byron smiled with his usual camaraderie and ease, as if he hadn't just been called an error moments before. Sensing Cynthia's continued frustration, he took over the conversation. "Would you like to sit down? You're probably worn out from all that traveling. I was just getting ready to make breakfast. Nothing fancy, just an omelet, toast, and orange juice."

"You're going to cook?" Dynah asked.

"Yes, it's a skill your friend has yet to master."

Cynthia play-punched him. Dynah chuckled. "I can't argue with that statement." She walked over to the couch. "I'd love to join you for a bite."

Gayle gave Dynah a hard look. Other than the dismissive nod, and curt greeting, she'd not acknowledged Byron. "Cynthia, may I speak to you in private?"

"What part of my earlier comment did you not understand? I've missed a couple of Sunday sessions so much has happened of which you're not aware. I'll happily fill both of you in over breakfast. So what that means, Gayle, is not only will we not speak privately, but if you don't shape up and quit disrespecting a man who's not only been cordial in the face of your ill manners but who's offered you breakfast, you're going to find yourself on the other side of my front door."

"My concern for your future and that of your son is worth the risk of being tossed out on my backside. If I didn't speak my heart, Cynthia, I wouldn't be your friend. How can you turn your back on what Stewart can offer both you and Jayden?" She turned and addressed Byron directly. "I know this feels personal, but it really isn't. And I'm sure you're a nice guy. But I've known Cynthia a lot longer than you, and trust me when I say that you're not the right guy for my friend. Jayden's father can introduce and guide his son through a society where status matters, one that will prepare Jayden for a lifetime of success. The kind of privileged life he'll provide for Cynthia is one you can't imagine. If you care about her as much as she thinks you do, you'll encourage her to do what's in her best interest and that of her son."

Cynthia prepared to pounce, but Byron stilled her with a slight squeeze of her shoulder.

"You might have known her longer, but I don't think you know her well. If you did, you'd have no doubt that her being with me is in her best interest and her being happy is what's best for her son. If you'd taken the time to climb down off that high horse and get to know me, you'd know that I don't give a good got damn about you, your opinion, her mother's meddling, Stewart's status, or society period whether high or low. What Cynthia wants is the only thing I care about. Like you say, nothing personal, it's just the way I roll."

Gayle looked at Cynthia, her anger evident in the subtle shade of red spreading from her throat to her chin and cheeks. "Are you going to let him talk to me this way? I've been your friend for ten years!"

"And I hope you'll be here for ten more, Gayle, but that can only happen if you stop trying to change my decision and run my life."

Gayle took a deep breath. "I love you, Cynthia. When you come to your senses, I'm not sure Stewart will still be available. But I will, and I'll help you pick up the pieces, rebuild your status, and return to the life you deserve." She turned to Dynah. "Are you coming with me or would you prefer to find your own way back to the hotel?"

"If we can turn that orange juice into a mimosa, I think I'll accept Byron's offer for breakfast."

Byron smiled. "I don't know about mini whatever, but if you want alcohol I have some Hennessy."

The three of them watched Gayle walk toward the front door.

Byron turned to Cynthia. "Baby, does this mean she's not staying for breakfast?"

"Gayle, you're being stubborn, but you're welcome to stay."

Gayle answered by softly closing the door behind her as she left.

50

By Friday of the following week, Cynthia had implemented most of the decisions that would change her life. She'd written long letters to both Gayle and her mother, spoken with her resigned yet slightly disappointed father, introduced an excited and accepting Lisa to Byron over the phone, hired an attorney to handle custody arrangements with Stewart, and finalized plans with Byron for their children to meet. Now, it was time to tackle the one that could affect her chances for becoming the agency's director and potentially impact the trajectory of her career. She hoped for the best, but the single sheet of paper on company stationery, folded within the envelope she held in her hand, was proof that she was moving full speed ahead toward a life with Byron. There would be no turning back, or changing her mind.

After a deep breath and squaring of shoulders, Cynthia knocked on Tracy's door.

"Come in, Cynthia."

She did, and once Tracy returned to her seat took one across from her. "Thanks for agreeing to speak with me on such short notice."

"I'd planned to request a meeting this afternoon. You simply beat me to it."

"Yes, well, considering everything that's happened, I'm not surprised."

"By 'everything happening,' what exactly do you mean?" Tracy sat back, prepared to listen to what Cynthia had come to say.

"I'm speaking of the Thompson case, not only the positive outcome my going to Vegas helped ensure, but the potentially negative impact that what I'm about to share may have on my continued counseling of Leah and indeed my very employment at H.E.L.P.

"When Margo recently accused me of professional improprieties, she did so without having some of the information I later shared with you, that Byron Carter, the relative she accused me of dating, is in fact not related to my client at all, but is a play uncle. He and his family view Leah Thompson's mother, Ava, as a sister. It is this view that complicated matters. Blood relation or no, Byron Carter is Leah's uncle in every sense of the word. Which leads to my second revelation. I am indeed seeing Byron Carter on a social and even romantic basis. While this isn't a direct breaking of organization rules, it is an interpretation that bends them, even though in a previous meeting you agreed that direct family as it pertains to no fraternizing isn't clearly spelled out."

"This very well could present problems, Cynthia. Why didn't you share this information earlier, or begin a liaison with a client's family member in the first place?"

"When he and I met, I was not aware of the connection." She gave the short version of her and Byron's destinies colliding. "When I offered to meet for coffee I had every intention of it being a business meeting of sorts, for information on my client's extended family and nothing more. I didn't expect to see him again and most certainly didn't plan to fall in love with him."

Tracy's brow raised. "Love? How long has this relationship gone on?"

"Not as long as that word may imply. We've known each other for such a short while and because of the potential conflict, only recently labeled our being together a relationship, one that for a variety of reasons could not have been more unexpected.

"When I accepted the managerial position two years ago I immediately set another career goal, to learn as much as I could from you and others while in that position and use this knowledge to eventually secure a director position. At that time I had no idea you were planning to retire, and thought to head up my department for about five years.

"For almost two and a half years now, I've worked tirelessly to transform the young adult division of this agency into something the H.E.L.P. board members could be proud of. I've charted the progress of each client I've counseled and am happy to say that I have a one hundred percent success rate when it comes to reducing recidivism within this segment of society. Part of that was skill, but it was an equal amount of hard work, work that most in this agency don't know about. On several occasions, Margo has been quick to point out my nine-to-five schedule. What isn't known is that most of my Saturdays are spent in this office, and that many of the days I leave early it is to attend a school event or social activity of one of my cases. My hands-on experience didn't start with Leah Thompson. And it most certainly didn't occur because of her uncle, Byron. It happened because I cared about her the same as I cared about forty-two other young adults between the ages of thirteen and twenty-one.

"Again, I never meant for anything to develop with a client's family member. There were no plans to fall in love with Byron Carter. But that's what happened."

Tracy asked a few more questions. The last one came as she eyed the envelope Cynthia held. "Is that for me?"

"Only if my seeing Byron ruins my chances of continuing as Leah's counselor or becoming director. Given the friction between us, I'm sure you understand why if Margo is promoted I can't remain at the agency with her as my boss. Rumors that a decision has been made have been swirling all week and if she in fact has been selected, I'm prepared to resign."

"Well, sounds like you've thought of everything, covered all the bases."

"Yes, Tracy, I have. Becoming this agency's director is a position I not only desire but in which I believe I'll excel. Therefore, this decision was made only after due diligence and careful consideration of everything and everyone involved."

"Thanks for your honesty. A decision has been made on the director position and will be announced this afternoon. If still desired, I'll accept your resignation at that time."

Four hours later, the announcement was made. Cynthia walked into her office, picked up the envelope containing her resignation letter, and slowly walked across her office . . . to the shredder. Cynthia Hall, the newly appointed Director of the H.E.L.P. Agency, wasn't going anywhere.

That night, she and Byron celebrated by returning to the Luxe Hotel where the first sparks of love were felt. The next afternoon, she and Jayden met Byron and Tyra at the pier at Redondo Beach. Byron and Tyra were already at the restaurant and had secured an outside table to enjoy junk food and the ocean waves before going to the white shark exhibit nearby.

Byron stood as they approached. They hugged in greeting, brief and casual, but enough to elicit a frown from Jayden, a subtle side eye from Tyra, and curiosity from each. Both Byron and Cynthia caught these reactions. Both also chose to ignore them.

Once they sat down, Byron spoke first. "Tyra, this is my friend, Cynthia. Cynthia, this is my amazing daughter, the most beautiful girl in the world."

"It's a pleasure to meet you, Tyra," Cynthia said, reaching across the table for a handshake.

"Pleasure to meet you," Tyra dutifully responded.

"And this is my son, Jayden."

"Hi," Jayden said, seemingly flustered by the pretty girl who Cynthia noted at once looked a lot like her father.

"Hi," Tyra said, not as impressed.

"Jayden, Byron is a good friend of mine."

"It's good to meet you." Byron opted for a fist bump with the young man.

"Mom, can I go see the shark?" Jayden responded.

"After we've eaten, and after you've responded to Byron's comment."

"Nice to meet you," Jayden said, in a way that suggested it wasn't nice at all.

"I don't want to go see no stupid shark," Tyra said, with a pout that for ten-year-old girls seemed pretty much a requirement. "Daddy, can I go to one of those shops and get my name done on the wooden board like I saw online?"

"Sure, Tyra. You can do that after we've eaten and gone to the shark exhibit. Jayden might want to get his name done, too."

"No, I don't. That sounds like something for girls."

"So! Getting something to hang in my room is better than paying to see a fish who'll probably jump out of the water and eat you alive."

"They can't do that," Jayden said, as if trying to

convince himself. He turned to Cynthia. "Can they, Mom?"

"Ha! Look at him, Daddy. He's scared."

"I am not!"

"Yes, you are!"

"No, I'm not!"

"I told you, Cynthia," Byron said to her over the din of their children arguing. "Our kids were going to love each other. Everything is going to be fine."

Epilogue

Thanksgiving

Byron, Cynthia, and Jayden entered the Carter household to the sound of raucous laughter. Her heart warmed when her son was greeted by Douglas's daughter and two cousins, and promptly whisked away to parts unknown inside the Carter home. Once the kids stopped arguing, they each realized the other wasn't so bad and could even be liked at times. Cynthia was thrilled. Jayden loved Bobby and his schoolmates, but this was the closest he'd come to experiencing family who were near his age. Moments inside the door and she, too, was enveloped in the love.

"How the hell you walking in here empty-handed?" Liz boomed before rocking Cynthia in a massive bear hug. "You must think you over to Cynthia's folks' house. You can do that when you visit rich people. But for those living in the Wood"—she leveled her gaze at Cynthia—"you've got to pay to play."

"Actually, Mrs. Carter, I do have two bottles of wine in the—"

"Two? Did you say two? Okay, me and the mister are set for the day, what are y'all going to drink."

Byron, who'd walked farther into the house greeting people now came to Cynthia's rescue. "Mama, when are you going to stop teasing this girl? She still doesn't know that you're playing."

"I'm not!"

He put his arm around Cynthia. "That's all right, baby. Hang with me and you'll be going toe to toe with one Mrs. Elizabeth Carter in no time."

"Uh-huh, just for that I'm going to take the sweet potato pie I made just for you and give it to the neighbors."

Liz winked at Cynthia and walked off, with Byron on her heels. "Wait a minute, Mama . . ."

Cynthia walked into the living room. "Hello, everyone. Happy Thanksgiving."

"Douglas, Nelson, and various cousins and neighbors replied. Both brothers had invited female guests to dinner and introduced her to them. Ava walked in just then and gave her a hug. With her was a guy she'd met online. She'd joined the site on a twenty-dollar dare. Not only had she taken Byron's money, but within a month of being on the site she'd met her first steady partner since before her son's death. Cynthia didn't have to ask Ava if Phil made her happy. It showed on her face.

Not long after she'd sat down to the sound of multiple conversations happening at once accompanied by a football game playing in the background, Leah arrived in her snazzy white pre-owned Honda Accord. With her was a nice-looking young man, well-mannered, and wearing slacks that fit him around the waist. Cynthia took note immediately.

"She met him at *college*," Ava later explained, her pursed lips suggesting that she, too, was pleasantly surprised at her daughter's choice. "It's a shame, but I could almost kiss that girl for getting pregnant with Aaron's child and causing the breakup between him and Leah. She moped for a while, but Tashan seems to be helping her forget her first love. He's nineteen, studying to be an engineer."

The two women high-fived.

"You had a lot to do with that, Cynthia. You'll never know how much I appreciate everything you did for her."

"I think I have some idea."

While sitting on the couch, she engaged in a group text with her BFFs. Lisa and Dynah had remained in Chicago for the holiday, getting ready to enjoy dinner with their families. Gayle, who'd finally accepted Byron in a kinda sorta way, was in Virginia, meeting the prominent family of Mr. Metrosexual, her fiancé of three months. During a conversation between the two of them, Cynthia had asked Gayle if she was happy. Gayle had responded with a reminder of how many carats were in her ring, and how the band had belonged to her fiancé's great-grandmother, one of the country's Talented Tenth. Cynthia chose to let the moment pass, hoped for the best, and wished her friend well.

I've got to go, ladies. Byron's mom might need
my help in the kitchen. And just so you know,
I'm turning off my phone now and will miss
your snarky responses!

She put away her phone and joined Liz in the
kitchen, Mrs. Carter's favorite spot, and after admitting that she didn't really "cook" cook, asked
Liz if she wanted any help.

"How are you going to tell me you can't cook,
then ask if you can help me do it?" She turned to
the others in the large, airy room. "Did y'all hear
that?"

Barry grabbed a soda out of the fridge. "I
heard it, Mama. Damn shame, too." He winked at
Cynthia, who tried to swat him as he walked by.

Liz shook her head. "You're going to have to
learn to cook, Cynthia. What you have beneath
your navel isn't the only thing Carter men love to
eat."

Cynthia promptly turned as red as the velvet
cake sat perched on a cake stand and ran from
the kitchen with the peals of Liz's raucous laughter chasing her.

Two hours later, eighteen adults and children
stood in a circle in the Carters' backyard. Mr.
Carter had just said his once-a-year prayer.

"Amen!" the group said in unison, ready to
attack two tables of food, assembled and ready on
the patio.

"Wait! Hold it." Byron released Leah's hand,
who was to his right, and instead of letting go of
Cynthia's hand pulled her into the middle of the
circle. Her face showed her obvious surprise. "I

know everyone is ready to eat, so I'll make this quick." He looked at Cynthia, his expression a mixture of conflicting emotions. The dominant one, love, made the others disappear.

His siblings started to murmur.

"What are you doing, bro?"

"Is this getting ready to be what I think?"

"Uh-oh. Somebody's pregnant."

This brought on chuckles and a stern look and clearing of throat from Mr. Carter.

"Thanks, Dad." The lightness was just enough for Byron to regain his nerve. He turned to Cynthia. "When I first saw you standing at the bus stop, I thought, what the hell is a woman like that doing standing at a bus stop like mine?"

Everyone laughed.

"Hey, that's what I thought." He became serious again. "But right after that thought came another, that you were the most beautiful woman I'd ever seen. By the time you got off the bus, I knew that there was no way anything would come of the encounter. Even though I knew I'd never see you again, you stayed on my mind.

"Then fate stepped in and made my wish come true. Not only did I see you again, but something crazy happened. You were feeling the same thing I was feeling and even though there were obstacles, our being together was never a doubt in my mind. I want to put to rest how long we're going to be together right now. I only have one more wish, and you can make it come true." He pulled out a box and went down on one knee. "Cynthia Hall, will you make me the happiest man in the world by becoming my wife?"

Tears streamed down Cynthia's face as she looked into the eyes of love that came when she least expected. She began nodding, as she held out her hand and watched a beautiful solitaire ring being slid on her finger. "Yes," she whispered.

"What?" Liz placed a hand behind her ear. "We didn't hear you."

"Yes!" Cynthia yelled, acting more like Liz than Anna Marie. "I'll marry your son, Mrs. Carter. Because y'all know what? I love this man like a muh fuh."

*Stay tuned for the next book
in The Blue-Collar Lover series.*

ALSO AVAILABLE

Zuri Day turns up the heat with three sexy page-turning tales of unexpected love and introduces the Morgan men, three fine brothers who have it all, except what their mama wants most for them—wives. . . .

Meet Michael Morgan

In the world of sports management, Michael Morgan is a superstar. But his newest client, Shayna Washington, may be his most lucrative catch yet. The record-breaking sprinter with the tight chocolate body has a talent and inner light Michael knows he can get the world to sit up and notice. He's certainly paying attention—and suddenly the sworn bachelor finds his focus changing from love of the game to true love. . . .

**Pick up *Love on the Run*
wherever books and ebooks are sold.**

Meet Gregory Morgan

When artist Anise Cartier leaves Nebraska for LA, she's finally ready to put the past and its losses behind her. She's even taken a new name to match her new future. And she soon finds a welcoming committee in the form of one very handsome doctor, Gregory Morgan. Their attraction is instant. So is their animosity. . . .

**Pick up *A Good Dose of Pleasure*
wherever books and ebooks are sold.**

Meet Troy Morgan

Gabriella is a triple threat—singing, acting, and dancing—and has always lived the life of a princess. Now, her father is determined to marry her to someone who can help expand her brand and the Stone empire, not some ordinary Joe. Of course, Troy Morgan is anything but ordinary. But can bad boy Troy take a backseat to someone with more money, more fame, and more of just about everything than him?

**Pick up *Bad Boy Seduction*
wherever books and ebooks are sold.**

Grab These Novels by
Zuri Day

__Bad Boy Seduction	978-0-7582-7513-4	$6.99US/$7.99CAN
__Body By Night	978-0-7582-2882-6	$6.99US/$8.49CAN
__A Good Dose of Pleasure	978-0-7582-7512-7	$6.99US/$7.99CAN
__Heat Wave (with Donna Hill & Niobia Bryant)	978-0-7582-6543-2	$6.99US/$7.99CAN
__Lessons from a Younger Lover	978-0-7582-3871-9	$6.99US/$8.99CAN
__Lies Lovers Tell	978-0-7582-2881-9	$6.99US/$8.49CAN
__Love in Play	978-0-7582-6000-0	$6.99US/$7.99CAN
__Love on the Run	978-0-7582-7511-0	$6.99US/$7.99CAN
__Lovin' Blue	978-0-7582-5999-8	$6.99US/$8.99CAN
__The One that I Want (with Donna Hill and Cheris Hodges)	978-0-7582-7514-1	$6.99US/$7.99CAN
__What Love Tastes Like	978-0-7582-3872-6	$6.99US/$8.99CAN

Available Wherever Books Are Sold!

All available as e-books, too!

Visit our website at **www.kensingtonbooks.com**